MURDER

Lauren
Elliott

KENSINGTON BOOKS
www.kensingtonbooks.com

KENSINGTON BOOKS are published by

Kensington Publishing Corp.
119 West 40th Street
New York, NY 10018

All Kensington titles, imprints, and distributed lines are available at special quantity discounts for bulk purchases for sales promotion, premiums, fund-raising, and educational or institutional use. Special book excerpts or customized printings can also be created to fit specific needs. For details, write or phone the office of the Kensington Sales Manager: Kensington Publishing Corp., 119 West 40th Street, New York, NY 10018. Attn. Sales Department. Phone: 1-800-221-2647.

Kensington and the K logo Reg. U.S. Pat. & TM Off.
First Kensington Books Mass Market Paperback Printing: May 2020

ISBN-13: 978-1-4967-2709-1
ISBN-10: 1-4967-2709-6

ISBN-13: 978-1-4967-2710-7 (ebook)
ISBN-10: 1-4967-2710-X (ebook)

10 9 8 7 6 5 4 3 2

Printed in the United States of America

Chapter 1

Addison Greyborne stepped into the warm, New England morning, closing the front door of Beyond the Page, her book and curio shop, behind her. Her heart skipped a beat when the scent of the briny tang of the sea niggled at her nose. She licked her lips, savoring the taste of the tiny salt crystals on the tip of her tongue. The added aroma of fresh-baked bread from the bakery next door made—in her mind—the perfect start to a day.

In spite of the elation this moment brought her, she couldn't escape the twang of guilt that tugged at her chest. She had left her shop assistant, Paige Stringer, to sort through and catalogue a large bin of books a customer brought in to be sold on consignment, while she herself went out on this beautiful summer morning for a little adventure. However, one look at Paige's face through the bay window alleviated Addie's guilt. It wasn't often she met another person who matched her own love of books, especially unearthed treasures.

At last, someone else she knew who giggled with glee on every new find.

Leaving Paige to dive into the books with Christmas-morning gusto, Addie pressed the papers in her hand close to her chest and critiqued her window displays. The new summer dioramas were starting to come together, but she needed to make certain nothing was overlooked. Since the town council first announced that Greyborne Harbor was going to become a regular port of call for one of the small East Coast cruise ship lines, the whole town was abuzz. Addie's displays had always been eye-catching but now, with this new onslaught of summer tourism, she needed to step up her game.

The additions of a *Barbie* beach blanket, umbrella, bicycle, and picnic basket that Paige had borrowed from her daughter Emma's doll collection were perfect. Now Addie only needed an assortment of classic romance and mystery novels to showcase around the sand-and-water display to complete the scene. Her brief glance into the bin Paige was sorting confirmed she'd have plenty of quick summer beach reads that tourists flocked to, but the stockpile in her aunt's attic was running low on the classics. She needed to shore up her supply. Crossing her fingers, she hoped her recent run with Lady Luck hadn't run dry. The yard sale and auction flyer clutched in her hand gave her confidence. *That's it, girl. Stay positive. You're going to find some wonderful treasures today.* She approached the curb and headed toward her red-and-white Mini Cooper parked across the narrow street.

"Stop! Wait right there!"

With her foot hovering over the curb edge, Addie winced and slowly turned toward the one woman she knew was capable of unleashing that ear-splitting screech. "Serena, good morning. I see you're out and about early today. It's only nine thirty. Is your morning rush over already?"

"Why?" Serena Chandler, her best friend and local tea merchant, stood on the sidewalk, hands on hips, her big brown, not-so-innocent eyes locked with Addie's. "Were you hoping to make the great escape without me finding out?"

"Don't tell me you've been standing by your window waiting to pounce on me for the last half hour?"

"No, of course not," Serena shot back. "But I know you, Missy." She wagged a finger in Addie's direction. "So I got my eye on you."

"I was just . . . never mind." Addie tossed her long-ponytailed head back and gave her best imitation of a heartfelt laugh, which, judging by the look on Serena's face, was completely unconvincing.

"Is that why you have that girl-gone-crazy look in your eyes right now?" Serena tapped her fingers on her crossed arms.

Sensing Serena's impatience, Addie confessed, "Yes. I'll admit it." She ignored the self-satisfied smile creeping across Serena's face. "I'm heading out to the same place you warned me not to go to last night."

"And . . . that's because you—what? Can't stay away from a murder scene?"

"Give me a break, Serena. It's not like those murders at Hill Road House happened yesterday."

Serena's mouth dropped. "Did you not hear anything else I said last night?"

"Yeah, yeah, yeah. But you're forgetting one thing, my friend." Addie waved off the look of concern written across Serena's face and started across the road for her car. "I don't believe in ghosts," she called back over her shoulder.

A gasp escaped Serena's lips. "Just don't call me in the middle of the night when you have nightmares," she shouted over the engine roar of a passing car.

"Don't worry about me. It's you I have concerns about. You seem to be taking this tall tale a little too seriously." Addie turned and mischievously grinned at a now blotchy, freckle-faced Serena. "Besides, if it's so haunted, why wasn't it included in the annual Ghost Walk tour that was held in the spring?" She chuckled softly as she fit her key in the lock and flung her car door open. "While I'm there," she called over her shoulder, "I'll be sure to pick up a copy of *The Haunting of Hill House.* After all, if the estate is as riddled with ghosts as you say it is, I'm confident I'll find a copy of it there somewhere."

"Nice try, but I'm a classic film nut, remember." Serena's voice rose in pitch to a warbled quiver. "So I know that's a movie not a book."

"Yes . . . *and* it was based on the *book* by Shirley Jackson." Addie grinned over her shoulder at her friend whose face now matched her flaming red hair. Serena's freckles popped out as they did any time her emotions ran high. Addie wondered if she should tell Serena that it was happening again but had second thoughts about that when Serena snorted and flared her nostrils. It was probably best not to poke the bear anymore this morning, so she bit her tongue, tossed the flyer and her bag—a straw satchel—on the passenger seat of her car, and slid into her seat to the thwack of SerenaTEA's door banging shut.

Addie shook her head at her theatrical friend and inched out of her parking space—and slammed down hard on the brake as a white Lexus LS passed mere inches from her side panel. Her purse flew off the seat and smacked against the console, the contents tumbling haphazardly to the floor. Her hands still tight around the steering wheel, she glared at the car, then took a calming breath and did a double shoulder check. She was certain she'd done that on her first attempt to pull out, but maybe she hadn't. Sucking in a breath, she tried again.

At the corner of Main Street, she turned right and headed toward Hill Road. When she reached the top, Addie couldn't miss the large ESTATE SALE and AUCTION sign on the corner of the lot. The red banner placed diagonally across it promised FOUR DAYS ONLY! As she continued driving, she grumbled at the lack of parking. Bentleys, Hondas, and the occasional moped took up every nook and cranny on the street. It wasn't even 10 a.m. yet, the advertised start of the broker's preview. She'd had no idea that an auction in little old Greyborne Harbor would be this well attended. Spying a gap in the parking spaces in front of the main gate to the estate that was just the right size for her Mini, she turned on her blinker to claim the spot.

The same white Lexus that had nearly side-swiped her earlier flew past her and maneuvered into the spot she'd already claimed with her blinker! Addie gritted her teeth and growled, sending a dagger glare to the driver as she passed. It was unfortunate that the car's tinted windows shielded her ability to garner any sense of self-satisfaction from the act.

Addie drove to the end of the street, slipped into a space, and made her way back on foot to number 555 Hill Road. She fleetingly glowered at the Lexus as she walked past and then paused at the imposing front wrought-iron gate. When she forced the rusted gate to open, the air around her seemed to crackle and moan in defiance. She halted briefly at the bottom of the path and scanned the house, which was very much in the style of her own Queen Anne Victorian. She shivered at the faded paint peeling in swaths, the shutters hanging by one hinge, and the overgrown shrubbery clutching at the rotting porch. Dark storm clouds were beginning to move in and the dilapidated three-story, set against the backdrop of the turbulent sky, caused quivers to race up and down her bare arms. She hugged herself tightly as an unexpected icy windblast sucked at her lungs—the wind's cold hands twisted at her chest, ensnaring her. This certainly hadn't turned into a day when no jacket was required. Blowing out a sharp breath, she trotted toward the porch steps.

She tried to clear her mind of the tale Serena had shared with her last night of the infamous house. After all, Serena's creative imagination made for embellished tall tales. Even so, with every step Addie took to the front door, her heart thudded harder and the tale replayed over and over in her mind. Three people had suffered untimely deaths behind the very walls of this house. The same house she was about to enter. Maybe she shouldn't have been so flippant in dismissing Serena's concerns.

Addie bit her quivering bottom lip . . . her right foot alighted on the first porch stair . . . then her left. With each groan of the wooden boards under her feet, another shiver surged through her. The crows cawing at her from the treetops did nothing to ease her mounting fears. Every ghost story she'd read and every horror movie she'd seen flashed like lightning strikes through her mind. She wondered if this was how Lila Crane felt when she was about to enter the Bates house in Alfred Hitchcock's movie *Psycho*. Perhaps she was letting her imagination get the best of her. She swallowed. *But what if the rumors are actually true?*

Chapter 2

Addie faced the neglected mahogany door, grasped the weathered handle, heaved out a pent-up breath, and stepped into the foyer. She blinked in the gloominess. The major light sources came from a flickering overhead chandelier and the intermittent beams of sunlight streaming through the open front door. Dust particles shimmered around her, floating in the sporadic sunrays of the growing storm clouds outside. The fine hairs on the back of her neck prickled as the musty air closed in around her.

"Good morning," a gravelly voice whispered from the shadows. "Have you registered?"

Goose bumps erupted on Addie's arms. She jerked and squinted at the robust woman sitting behind a long, French Provincial table. "Umm, no. I guess I'd better do that." Addie forced a smile, handing the woman her business card, and wrote her name on the registration sheet. She noted the sign on the desk and stopped. "This sale is being conducted by the Edwards Auction

House?" Addie looked up at the dimple-pitted, pudgy-cheeked woman from under her creased brow.

"Yes, it is." The woman tapped her pen on the registration line. "Have you attended one of the company auctions in the past?" She smiled with satisfaction as Addie took her cue and completed the registration procedure.

"Yes, I have. Blake and I are actually old friends." Addie's mood lifted at the prospect of seeing a friendly face from her past in Boston.

She took her nametag and registration number from the woman's outstretched hand and headed toward the double French doors into the front living room. Not a living room in the sense of her own comfy retreat but a foreboding, formal parlor. There was nothing warm and inviting about this mausoleum of a room currently set up with a hodgepodge of antique tables to display the auction items on.

She eyed some of the other eager bidders as they made their way around the small room, ticking off inventory they found to be acceptable to bid on tomorrow, and smiled to herself. She recognized some from when she had worked at the Boston Library; a few she knew through her late father's and fiancé's antiquities retrieval work. She'd had no idea that a small-town auction would attract dealers from as far away as New York. This might prove to be an interesting crowd to bid against.

Addie crossed the foyer, zigzagging around a group of brokers she knew. She made small talk before moving back through the crowd to snag a variety of pamphlets and the auction catalogue she'd missed on her arrival. Even though she'd viewed the catalogue online, she gave the print ones a quick once-over. They appeared to contain the same information as her flyer.

Wednesday, today, was the preview for the *Private Bidders Auction*, which was scheduled to be held the following day. Friday was the *Public Silent Auction*, and Saturday and Sunday were the *Public Outdoor Yard Sale—leftover inventory permitted.*

She tossed the material into her oversized straw satchel and headed for the study, across the foyer and opposite the parlor. Inside the small room two keen brokers were discussing the merits of a pedestal-based antique globe that they slowly spun in their hands while examining the etched surface with a magnifying glass. She glanced around the room, noting nothing of interest to her as most of the books on the shelves appeared to be reference journals and encyclopedias. Then her gaze landed on a green-shaded, antique banker's lamp displayed on a side table alongside a rare Georgian Irish decanter marked WATERLOO CO. CORK, circa 1815.

She blinked. Twice. This was tempting. Even though she knew they would be pricey, she hesitated, but then . . . Nope, she was on a quest and couldn't allow herself to be sidetracked by all the bright, shiny objects around her. She had another goal on her mind. Addie excused her way through a logjam of people to the library. For her that was where the real treasures would be found.

She stood openmouthed in the double-wide doorway. Now *this* was a bibliophile's paradise. Her eyes widened as they took in the splendor of the room. It was everything her own library wasn't, and she could see now why the front study was half the size of hers. The missing square footage in the other room had been added to this one. This was exactly what she'd always dreamed a home library should be, starting with the large, ornately carved desk set in front of an inglenook fireplace that was flanked on either side by built-in bookshelves that extended floor to ceiling around the perimeter of the massive room. In front of each of the three, lead-pained windows were six leather armchairs placed in groups of twos, each pair snuggled up into cozy reading nooks created by their placement on Oriental throw rugs laid over the polished wooden-planked floor. This was her Disneyland, and her heart danced like that of a ten-year-old girl who had just entered the library in *Beauty and the Beast*.

She inhaled the stale, dusty, aged-leather scents hovering in the air and stepped inside. An icy chill wrapped around her. Glancing at the large closed windows, she rubbed her hands over her arms and took stock of the bookshelves. In the light of the room—growing muted by the increasing storm clouds outside—she spied a woman crouched down in front of a barrister's bookcase. The woman shook the unyielding door latch and stood up, her long, wavy, auburn hair swinging across her back. She straightened her embroidered suede bomber jacket and adjusted the sunglasses propped on top of her head, then tapped her bloodred manicured fingernails on the glass door.

Addie squinted. *It can't be.* "Kalea Hudson? Is that you?"

The woman swung around. Her face lit up with recognition. "Hi, cuz."

"What on earth are you doing here?" Addie dashed toward her and flung her arms around Kalea's neck, squeezing her in a tight hug.

"I was just in the neighborhood." Kalea squealed, returning her embrace.

"I'm not buying that." Addie eyed her. "Greyborne Harbor is hardly on a direct route to anywhere, and an auction preview is the last place I'd expect to find you lurking about."

"What? Can't a cousin drop into town unannounced?" She shifted her weight onto one beige, skinny-panted hip and fluttered her long false lashes. "And, I'll have you know"—she flicked a strand of hair out of her eyes— "that I'm not the same party-girl you once knew. I have expanded my horizons."

"I always did hold out hope that you'd come to your senses." Addie smiled and held her by the shoulders. "But it's been years. Since college, if I remember correctly. Why didn't you call and tell me you were coming to town?"

Kalea's cheeks rosied against her porcelain complexion. She draped an arm around Addie's shoulders and squeezed. "I was going to drop in on you after I finished here. You know, a surprise, but it looks like you've found me out. So, surprise!"

"Aw, I've missed you. Ten years is way too long."

"I totally agree." Kalea grinned at her cousin. "But I promise now to keep in better touch since I've settled down in Cape Cod—"

"What are you doing in here?" a voice shrieked from the doorway.

Addie spun around and looked at the enraged bird-like woman looming in the door.

"Didn't you see the door sign?" The woman's beaked mouth set firm-lipped. "This area is not prepared for viewing."

Addie glanced at the open door. A No ENTRY sign was taped on what would have been the exterior side. She could tell by the set of the woman's jaw that she expected an answer. "I'm terribly sorry. It was open when I came in and I didn't see—"

"Yes . . . me . . . me, too." Kalea's voice faltered.

The woman crossed her long, slender arms in front of her navy two-piece, pencil-skirted suit that cried

Saks Fifth Avenue, and flipped her brown, up-swept haired head, tapping her foot, glaring at them. Addie studied the hawkish woman, who peered back at her just as intently—except in the woman's case, she appeared to be ready to swoop in on her prey. This, and something in her mannerism struck a familiar chord with Addie. She flipped through her mental files but came up empty. Nothing in her recent memories could help her place this woman.

"Addie, I can't believe it!" A tall, middle-aged man with hair graying at the temples swept past the bird creature in the doorway. "I had no idea you were in Greyborne Harbor," he said as he rushed over to plant a light kiss on her cheek. "As soon as I saw your name on the registration sheet, I had to come and find you."

"Blake, it's great to see you." Still struggling to place the woman hovering in the door, Addie took one more glance at her before refocusing her attention on her old family friend. "I don't think it's been since my father's funeral, right?"

His lips tightened and he dropped his darkening gaze, nodding. "Well," he said, apparently shaking off his melancholy, "I see you've had the pleasure"—he cleared his throat—"of meeting Charlotte McAdams, co-owner of McAdams Insurance. Our appraisers on this contract."

A light switch flipped on in Addie's head, and a smile tickled the corners of her lips. "We never got as far as formal introductions." Now she knew who the woman was—at least by reputation and observation of her sometimes testy encounters with Addie's old supervisor at the Boston Library. Part of Charlotte's reputation was how disagreeable she could be to work with, but no one ever negated her abilities as a top-notch appraiser. Addie couldn't help but feel a little starstruck and awed in her presence.

"You know these two?" Charlotte glared at Blake.

"Yes, this is Addie Greyborne, the daughter of my dearest and oldest"—he crossed his heart—"friend. And, if I'm not mistaken"—he looked at a silent Kalea—"this is her cousin Kalea Hudson."

"I'm surprised you remember me, it's been years." Kalea blinked in surprise.

"It's the big hazel-green eyes—they're the same as Addie's. One of the many wonderful features she inherited from her beautiful mother, as I'm sure you did from her equally beautiful sister."

"Umm, thank you." Kalea hesitantly smiled, glancing from Blake's beaming face to the piercing birdlike eyes scrutinizing them from the doorway.

Charlotte's nostrils flared. She stomped her clickity-clack, gray high-heeled shoes across the wooden flooring to the leather chair behind the desk, and noisily began to shuffle a stack of papers. "Well," her voice sliced the air. "This reunion is touching. However, I have work to finish before the auction tomorrow, so if you don't mind . . ." She waved her hand. "Take this somewhere else and let me finish up here."

Blake's jaw tensed. "Charlotte," he said, his voice straining to remain level. "My company has used the services of McAdams for over thirty-five years. At no time under the direction of your father were either I or any of my clients ever subjected to such contemptuous treatment. Now apologize to these young women and don't ever let it happen again."

Charlotte rose to her feet to meet his narrowed glare as she leaned on the desk toward him. "You do realize, Blake, that we would not be in this mess if you had listened to me a month ago, when I informed you that there wasn't enough time to appraise and catalogue the contents of this entire property in time for the *premature* auction date *you* set."

"You've had well over four months to do a job that would have taken any other insurance team two months to complete. What am I paying you for? The wasted time you've spent driving back and forth to Boston to check up on your incompetent brother and so-called partner, Duane?"

"How dare you speak about incompetency, when just this week your crew discovered *that*"—she pointed to the barrister's bookcase—"in a storage space in the attic. Something they should have found months ago."

"And they would have," Blake's eyes flashed, "had it not been for all the distractions you and your brother created with the inconsistencies between your appraisals and inventory lists." The explosion of hatred in Charlotte's eyes matched Blake's as his voice dropped to a barely audible whisper. "Remember, my dear, your father is not dead. He's retired, and he's only one phone call away. How do you think he will react when I tell him what I suspect the two of you have been up to? Especially when it's not only his company's good name you've placed in jeopardy, but also mine. And I *won't* let you take it down!" He spat out his last words standing tall and formidable. "Since it appears you'll have a long night of work ahead of you appraising the books in the barrister's case, I'll leave you to get started. Just make certain that *all* of the inventory found in it is accounted for." He pushed past Addie, without even a glance in her direction, and strode out of the room.

Addie jumped as he slammed the doors behind him.

Chapter 3

The tension in the room was stifling. Addie tilted her head toward the red-faced Charlotte, who appeared on the verge of bursting into tears. Addie couldn't really blame her. Obviously, everyone's nerves here were on edge as the auction loomed closer but based on what Addie had just witnessed between Charlotte and Blake, she sensed their conflict ran deeper than pre-auction jitters. Her Curious George ears had perked up with a few things that had been said, but meddling in Blake's private business affairs wasn't something she could allow herself to get mixed up with. However, ensuring the success of the auction for her old family friend *was* something she could involve herself in.

She glanced over at the barrister's case. All her instincts told her that she should help Blake's auction house retain its sterling reputation, but something gnawed at her and she couldn't say the words she needed to. She looked back at Charlotte, who was known to be crusty on the outside. However, judging by the dampness on her cheeks now, Addie could see that inside she was really a soft dough ball.

Addie's gaze drifted around the room, drinking in the magnificence of her dream library—a place she never wanted to leave. Her mind raced. With her new life here in Greyborne Harbor, such as it was in her little bookstore, would she ever again have the opportunity to explore a room like this, or the chance to work with one of the East Coast's most highly acclaimed appraisers? *Oh, what the heck!*

Addie drew in a deep breath and mentally crossed her fingers, hoping that Charlotte's softer side would still prevail and that Addie's next words wouldn't come back and bite her. "Maybe I could help out. I mean, if this is the last room to audit before tomorrow."

"You?" Charlotte swatted at her dewy cheek as if to displace a fly. "What would you know about rare and vintage books?"

"Because that's what she handled for years at the Boston Library and the British Museum," squeaked Kalea from over Addie's shoulder.

Addie spun around and quirked an eyebrow at her cousin, who flashed a sheepish smile.

"I might not have kept in touch with you, but I did stay up-to-date with what you were doing and where you were," said Kalea.

A twang of guilt plucked at Addie's conscience. She hadn't kept up with her cousin's latest life events at all, now she felt horrible about it.

"You said the Boston Library and the British Museum?" Charlotte snapped, her bird eyes narrowing on Addie's. "Where did you study?"

Addie accepted the hawkish woman's challenge and braced herself. "My degrees in Literature and Ancient History were from Columbia. I also completed course work at the Smithsonian, and then I worked at the Boston Library and the British Museum, researching and cataloguing old and rare books."

"What did Blake say your name was again?"

"It's Addie . . . Addie Greyborne."

"Yes . . ." Charlotte stroked her chin, slowly nodding. "I've heard about you."

"You have?" Addie could barely contain her excitement over the fact that this woman, who was in the top of their field, actually knew about her.

"You might prove useful to me after all. What about you?" She pinned Kalea with a steely gaze.

"I'm a paralegal and just have Addie's interest in old stuff, but I don't know much about appraising it."

"Pfffft." Charlotte waved her hand. "Then, Miss Greyborne, you may start with that bookcase and its contents that Mr. Edwards so eagerly dumped on me this week with, as you no doubt heard, clear instructions to have it catalogued by tomorrow's ten a.m. auction start." She opened the top drawer to the desk, pulled out a box of cotton gloves, and shoved it and a key ring toward Addie. "But before you start appraising, you two can move all these boxes of other books out of the way and line them up in order according to the lot sale numbers I have marked on each crate."

Addie looked at the dozen or so boxes. Kalea groaned. "Why didn't you just leave them on the bookshelves? Wouldn't that have been more convenient?"

Charlotte puckered her lips. "For who? Certainly not for the auctioneer. He'll need easy access to the lot numbers, and that's impossible when the shelves they came off are way over there behind the desk and his podium will be over there beside the table."

Kalea's shoulders slumped. Addie knew the scolding she had just received was totally unnecessary. Even though Charlotte was correct in her reasoning her delivery was completely uncalled for. Addie's heart went out to her cousin because she had attended enough auctions in her day to know that the auctioneer would have an assistant who, prior to a lot number being called, would fetch the items and display them—in this case, on the table—in time for the bidding to commence.

She'd explain the procedure to Kalea later; right now she could only fume inside. Addie didn't care if Charlotte was in a bad mood because of frayed nerves or the altercation she'd just had with Blake, her rudeness was unacceptable. Addie opened her mouth to reprimand the hawk-woman on her crass behavior when she spun toward her on her spiked heel.

"Since this latest imposition by Mr. Edwards appears to be taken care of, if you'll excuse me, I have another pressing matter to deal with." Charlotte stalked out, banging the doors closed behind her.

"Whoa! The nerve of that woman. I was ready to pop her, right here and now."

"Me, too." Addie's brow creased. Well-respected appraiser or not, her behavior just now was inexcusable, especially since they were volunteering to help her out. In Addie's mind Charlotte McAdams had just slipped off the pedestal Addie had placed her on. "Are you okay?"

"Yeah, I'm fine. She's exactly like my old department supervisor at the law firm. I developed a thick skin because of her."

"That's too bad. I hope she was let go because of the way she treated you, as I imagine someone *that* nasty"— Addie glared at the closed doors—"treated everyone the same way."

"It was kind of my fault, though." Kalea traced the toe of her shoe over the carpet edge.

"Don't ever think that being verbally abused by anyone is your fault, it's—"

"Even if you're dating her husband, the senior law-firm partner?" she said, looking up sheepishly.

Addie's hand flew up in a stop motion. "I don't want to know."

"Let me explain. I know that sounds horrible, but I'm not a home wrecker."

Addie turned her attention to the boxes on the floor.

Kalea grabbed Addie's arm and spun her around. "They were in the middle of a nasty divorce, and Nolan and I just sort of clicked. But his soon-to-be ex had issues with that. I think she was afraid I was after his money, and then there'd be less for her to get her hands on."

"Were you?" Addie pinned her with a knowing look. "I remember how you behaved in college with every man you dated. You actually kept a ledger of what their net income earning potential was going to be as a way of measuring if you'd see them again or not."

"That was just my way of getting a dig in at you. College was supposed to be fun, and you were *soooo* serious about everything." Kalea flashed a hesitant grin.

"You called my course load stuffy and outdated. As I recall you actually said, 'Something only old spinsters would be interested in.' Which makes me wonder what happened to you, because the Kalea I knew wouldn't be caught dead within miles of an auction preview."

Kalea heaved out a breath. "It's because Nolan is a collector, and he's gotten me interested in all this." She waved her hand at the boxes of books and chuckled. "Well, sort of. I'm still learning, though."

"Is that why you're really here, for this auction, and not to see me?"

"No, I really came to see you. When I got into town, I saw the flyer for the auction preview and thought I'd just stop in here for a few minutes before I dropped in on you. Like I said, I'm just learning about all this stuff and I wanted to surprise Nolan with a special gift. That is, if I can find something here for him that's not too expensive."

Now it finally made sense to Addie. In spite of Kalea's profession to having expanded her horizons, Addie still knew her cousin well enough to be aware that she hated all things old—unless they were men who had money. And true to her cousin's MO, a man *was* involved.

"Come on, you can give me a hand. Maybe I can help you learn a little more about rare books, and you can impress your boss-slash-*whatever* he is with your newfound knowledge of his hobby."

"Perfect." Kalea rubbed her hands together. "Where do we start?"

"First, let's get these boxes moved so we can begin the interesting part of what might be a very long day."

"Did you understand what she meant with her lot-sale numbers and all that?"

"Yes, and I agree in theory with her, but she could have been nicer in her explanation, so I'll translate for you. It's important in an estate sale of this kind to have all the auction items sorted and divided into their separate sale packages beforehand. If they're marked clearly and made easily accessible, the sale moves faster because the auctioneer will have an assistant who will display the items in each lot sale on the table prior to the bidding. That way, attendees can actually see what they're bidding on."

Addie scanned the room. "It appears Charlotte has the shelves over there on the sidewall, closer to the center table and where the podium will be, broken into group or lot sales. Here . . . see how these shelves are tagged?" She pointed to a cardboard memo card hanging at one end of a shelf. "She's sorted them up into publishing dates and genres. These lot sales appear to be ones that are considered collectible but aren't actually rare books the same with the ones in these crates. Let's get them out of the way, and then we can get to that table and try to figure out what she's done with the individual books I see sitting on it."

Addie moaned as she pushed the last box into place.

"I know, my back is killing me, too," Kalea said, rubbing the small of her back.

"No, it's not that." Addie held out her hand. "Look, one of my brand-new acrylic nails broke off."

"Now, that *is* a catastrophe." Kalea examined her own fingers. "But good luck finding it in these boxes so your esthetician can reattach it."

"No, I've been thinking of having them all removed. It was a silly whim my friend Serena and I had last weekend. They really are impractical for my type of work."

"You're kidding, right?" Kalea looked wide-eyed at her. "I love my nails and can't ever imagine not having them."

"Obviously, you're not doing much typing these days, are you?" When her cousin's face turned a slight shade of crimson, Addie knew right then that when she began dating the senior partner, her duties as a typist and paralegal had also changed. "Forget about it. Let's see what Charlotte has planned for the books on the center table."

Addie picked up a reddish-brown cloth-bound book. "Look, it's a 1935 printing by The Limited Editions Club of New York of *Ulysses* by James Joyce." She scanned the other books on the table. "These books all appear to be ones that Charlotte thinks should be auctioned off individually tomorrow, as they'd be worth more money."

Addie placed the opened book back on the table and waved Kalea to her side. "Did you know that only fifteen hundred copies were printed of this one and this is number 1459? And see here, it's signed by the illustrator, Henri Matisse, on the Limitation Page." She tapped her finger on the page. "It's worth about seven thousand dollars in today's market."

"What about this one?" Kalea pointed to a pale green covered book stamped in red and green. "The *Wonderful Wizard of Oz* by L. Frank Baum?"

Addie picked up the book and turned to the title page. "It's a first edition, too, originally published by the George M. Hill Company in 1900. Given its worn condition, it's probably worth about twenty-eight thousand."

"Dollars?" Kalea snatched the book from Addie's hand. "Wow, I had no idea books could be worth that much."

"That's nothing compared to some that trade for millions."

Kalea traced her fingers over the cover illustration of the red-maned lion wearing green spectacles.

Addie slid the book from Kalea's hands. "I guess with books like this in the library, we'd better get those gloves on. We don't want to leave oily finger residue on any of them."

"I'll grab them." Kalea dashed over to the desk, pulled out four cotton gloves, grabbed the key ring Charlotte had left, and returned to the glass case.

"I think this lock up here at the top, acts like the master. One key should unlock all six of the double doors. It's a small keyhole, so try that one." Addie pointed to a small brass key.

The locks clicked. "Smarty-pants." Kalea grinned when the doors opened.

Addie crinkled up her nose and chuckled. "By the look of all the books in there, I'd better text Paige—she's my shop assistant—and tell her I might be longer than I thought."

When she finished sending the text, she crouched down beside Kalea and pulled on her gloves, nudging her cousin to do the same. "Well, well, what do we have here?" Addie slipped a worn novel from the bottom shelf and whistled. "It's an 1888 first edition of *A Study in Scarlet* by Arthur Conan Doyle. Did you know that this was the first Sherlock Holmes book he wrote?"

Kalea peered over her shoulder. "What's it worth?"

"This copy is about twenty-three thousand, but if this is what I think it is . . ." She pulled a plastic enclosed journal from its place beside where the book had sat on the shelf, carefully removed it from its protective covering, and gasped. "This . . . is the first *ever* published copy of the story that appeared in this 1887 edition of *Beeton's Christmas Annual.* It was like the original printed proof of the story that was published in book form the following year." She stroked the cover. "Out of all of Doyle's books, this was always my favorite. Because it was the reader's first introduction into how the genius of Sherlock Holmes's deductive mind worked. Basically, Doyle started a revolution with Holmes. His character raised the bar for every other author and all the detective novels that followed. I can't believe this is a copy of the proof."

"What's a proof?"

"It's a typeset edition of a book for proofreading and correction before publication. Although this wasn't intended as an actual proof, it served as one because a few minor changes were made to the book edition a year later." Addie traced her gloved finger over the words *A Study in Scarlet* on the front page of the magazine. "A copy of this sold a few years ago for over one hundred and fifty-six thousand."

"Say what?" Kalea stole the journal from Addie. "Wow, no wonder Nolan wanted me to stop by here on my way to meet him."

"What do you mean he wanted you to stop by here?" Addie fixed her gaze on her cousin. "Didn't you say you came to visit *me* and then just stopped in here *after* you saw the flyer?"

"I meant"—Kalea's cheeks burned with a fiery glow—"he'll be so glad I stopped at the auction after I saw the flyer." She added, dropping her voice, "before I went to meet up with you and then him next week."

Addie was taken aback. Had Kalea simply misspoken now or were her earlier words about visiting her only an effort to save face when Addie spotted her in the library? It made Addie wonder if her cousin even knew she lived in Greyborne Harbor in the first place or whether her arrival here on the same day as the auction preview was—as she let on—purely a coincidence.

Addie eyed her cousin warily, rose to her feet and walked toward the desk. Her mind replayed what Kalea said now versus when they greeted each other. Maybe she'd better keep Kalea close, just so she could keep an eye on her. Something about this whole visit wasn't sitting right with Addie because obviously there was more going on with Kalea's newfound interest than she first let on. Addie glanced down at the rare magazine in her hand and then back at her cousin, in time to witness her finishing off a text message and tossing her phone into her handbag.

Chapter 4

The hairs on Addie's arms prickled. She squirmed on her chair with the uneasiness of being watched and glanced toward the doorway expecting to see Charlotte monitoring them. When she didn't, her eyes darted over to her cousin sitting cross-legged on the floor, scribbling furiously on a pad of paper, surrounded by books from the barrister's case. Her wedge sandals and suede jacket, discarded hours ago, lay in a heap at her side. The contents of her oversized handbag—granola-bar wrappers, tissues, and cell phone—were haphazardly scattered everywhere.

Addie puffed out a deep breath. This wasn't the first time today she'd had the feeling of being watched. She'd tried to put the sense that the walls were closing in on them down to the fact that they were hungry and tired. Still, she knew that if it hadn't been for the moments she and Kalea had shared of pure childlike silliness—an automatic reversion to their antics when they were little girls—to relieve the tension . . . well, she doubted she would be able to leave here not being a firm believer in Serena's tall tale.

She yawned, stretched out her stiff shoulders, and checked the time on her cell phone. It was almost three and there had been no word from Charlotte since she'd left this morning to check on *whatever* that other pressing issue was. "How many are left to go through?" Addie asked, tapping her pen on the inventory list she worked on at the desk.

"Last book." Kalea kicked at a granola-bar wrapper. "I don't know about you, but I'm starving. Do you want to get a bite to eat when we're done here?"

Addie's stomach picked that exact moment to agree.

"It sounds like you need it." A soft laugh escaped Kalea's throat. "I hear the restaurant at the Grey Gull Inn where I'm staying has great food. We could go there."

"Perfect. It'll give us time to catch up, too."

Kalea nodded in agreement and returned her attention to the book in her lap.

Addie sat back, watching her cousin. In spite of her initial misgivings about Kalea and her motives, Kalea had proven to be an adept assistant today, catching on quickly. However, it did make Addie wonder if she had more experience at appraisals than she'd let on. Kalea's innate ability was uncanny for a beginner. She even proved a fast learner in cross-referencing book titles and the book's condition on the various appraisal websites, such as the Library of Congress, The British Library, and the Bodleian Libraries at the University of Oxford, although working as a paralegal she would have a good understanding of research methods. Addie studied her young protégé—something about the situation didn't sit right. She couldn't put her finger on it, but a long chat over dinner might just provide her with some helpful insights into the cousin she hadn't seen for ten years.

The doors swung open and a short, bald man stared at her through his marble-sized eyes.

"I'm sorry, this room isn't available for preview yet." Addie smiled apologetically and met his unblinking, beady-eyed gaze. His fists tightened into balls at his sides as he walked toward her. She reached for a letter opener on the desk. Out of the corner of her eye, she glimpsed Kalea rising to her feet and grabbing one of her wedged sandals to brandish like a weapon.

The man noticed Kalea's reaction and stopped; a harsh laugh erupted from his chest. "Relax, Queen Charlotte ordered me in here." His eyes fixed on Kalea, a leering smile tugging at the corners of his thin, upper lip. He sniffed and held out a child-sized hand to Addie. "I'm Robert Peters, Charlotte's assistant and *slave*."

"I see." Addie ignored his outstretched hand and slid back into her chair, toying with the letter opener still in her hand.

"As the queen doth command, I am merely her servant to do her bidding." He swept his hand across his midsection and bowed low from the waist before slumping into a leather armchair beside the desk. His gaze refocused on Kalea, who stood unmoving from her position beside the barrister's case.

Addie swallowed the acidic taste in the back of her throat. From the challenging look in Kalea's eyes, though, Addie guessed she was no stranger to lewd attention. If this weasel of a man picked up on even one thing as he held her in his sights, it better be that Kalea would fend off any of his unwelcome advances. Violently.

Addie stroked her neck, studying his bulbous-nosed

profile. When he jumped to his feet and clapped his hands, her body jerked, betraying her feigned nonchalant attitude.

"Where are we at with this room?" He glanced at the stack of books Addie had arranged on the table for the live auction and then at the stack in front of the bookcase that she had arranged for lot sales. Each was marked in the same manner that Charlotte had catalogued the previous ones. "It looks like you've made quick work here—perhaps too quickly for her majesty's liking, though."

Addie shoved the letter opener aside and moved around the desk toward him. "It has been over five hours and there was only the one bookcase to appraise. I think that *two* experienced"—she glanced at Kalea—"appraisers can accomplish a lot in that time."

"We'll see if *she's* in agreement with you. Nevertheless, you're done here now." He waved his hand. "Go. I'm here to relieve you." Robert looked at Kalea. "You may stay if you like, though." His top lip curled up in a half smile. "I always do like a bit of company when I work."

Kalea grabbed her jacket and other shoe, slipped them on, scooped up her bag and its disarrayed contents, and dropped it all on the table of books they had catalogued. She dug through her bag, tossing out other odds and ends onto the table, fished out her phone, tucked it into her jacket pocket, straightened her collar, shoved everything back into her handbag, and shouldered it. Robert's tongue caressed his bottom lip as Kalea strode over to him. His chest puffed out as his face lit up in a wide, leering grin.

"You, sir . . . are a *pig*!" She flipped her head and stalked out.

Addie grabbed her purse and walked past Robert,

who stood openmouthed in the middle of the room. "She's not wrong, you know. I may have used a stronger description, but I guess *pig* covers it fairly well." Her lips formed a twisted smile as she followed her cousin to the door, sidestepping a head-on collision with Charlotte as she swung into the room.

"Miss Greyborne, how did you make out? Or will I be here till past midnight to finish this room?"

"No, I think the appraisals are complete. I'm certain"—she glanced back over her shoulder at Robert—"your competent assistant will have no problem finishing up any loose ends."

"Good." She rubbed her hands together. "Did you find anything of great value, or will I have to dig through it all to find out what to set as lot sale items and what can be—"

"It's all been catalogued as per your methods." Addie stuffed her used cotton gloves in Charlotte's hand. "I assure you that everything is in order. However, there is one collection I left on the table that I wasn't certain how you would want to proceed with the sale of, so I've marked it for your attention."

Charlotte glanced at the balled-up gloves and then to the table.

"It's the entire Sherlock Holmes first-edition series and a few other Sir Conan Doyle works. It's all there and marked."

"A complete set of Sherlock Holmes first editions?"

Addie stopped short of telling the dour-faced woman about her discovery of the first-ever publication of A *Study in Scarlet* in the 1887 *Beeton's Christmas Annual*. She'd already done more than her part for this unappreciative woman. Charlotte could discover that little treasure on the table later when she inspected Addie's work, as she no doubt would.

Addie glanced over her shoulder at Robert, who had edged toward the table and the pile of Holmes books. "From what I discovered in that barrister's case, the estate should do fairly well tomorrow," Addie side-stepped away from Charlotte and her equally unlikable assistant. "But I have to go now. I do have a business of my own to run so I hope you find everything in order. If you have any questions, call me." Addie tucked her business card under the gloves still housed in Charlotte's palm.

"Thank you," Charlotte mumbled, turning the card over in her hand. At least Addie thought she said thank you, because the sound she made was more like her regurgitating a mouth full of marbles.

Addie suppressed a snicker as she sauntered out the door. That was probably the first time Charlotte had ever even tried to utter those two little words to anyone, and she hoped that the garbled noise she heard wasn't her choking on them.

As the doors began to shut, Charlotte's voice cracked. "Robert, we need to talk now! There's been another theft—" The closed library doors snuffed out the rest of her words.

"Addie, my dear." Blake waved at her from the front door where he was chatting with Kalea and another man. "I was just thanking Kalea here for the two of you stepping up today and helping this old man keep his business afloat despite the dragon lady I have to deal with. Your father would be so proud of you."

"No problem. We're happy to help out. It's something he would have done, too."

"I know you've saved me a lot of stress this evening. I'm not sure about *her*, though." His head ticked toward the hallway in the library's direction. "But I do know that we might be finished setting up before midnight now."

Addie glanced questioningly at the other man, who had clearly caught the attention of her cousin as she fluttered her lashes and coiled strands of her long hair around a finger.

"Forgive me, Addie." Blake's voice broke the spell that engulfed the foyer. "This is my nephew, Garrett Edwards, my brother's youngest."

Garrett smiled fleetingly at Addie before returning his focus to Kalea, mirroring her teasing stance as he swept a shock of raven-black hair from his forehead. It was clear to Addie that these two were locked into a mutual-admiration ritual that left her with the discomfiture of intrusion.

"Addie," Kalea murmured, "Garrett was just telling me that he's recently graduated with his MBA from Harvard and is going to take over Blake's company when he retires. Isn't that wonderful?" She cooed, locking her eyes with Garrett's.

Addie did an inward eye roll. For all her cousin's protests and declarations, Kalea hadn't changed at all since college.

Blake leaned toward Addie and cupped his hand around his mouth. "My retirement won't be for a few years yet, my dear," he whispered. "It was a carrot his father and I had to dangle for him to come and work for me." A sly glint glimmered in his eyes.

Addie smiled apologetically at Blake. "Kalea, I hate to interrupt, but I'm starving, and I need a coffee. Besides, I think we've kept Blake and Garrett long enough. I'm sure they're busy."

Blake grinned and motioned to the door. "Thank you again, ladies. I'll see you tomorrow morning, Addie, bright and early."

Addie sensed he wasn't oblivious to the fact that his poor nephew was being reeled in by someone akin to a black widow and wasn't going to miss the opening Addie had left for their hasty departure.

As Kalea and Garrett exchanged a few whispered parting words, her fingers trickled along his forearm. She then flipped her amber waves behind her shoulder and topped it all off with a come-hither smile as she turned toward the front door. It swung open and a small crowd of people spilled into the foyer, forcing Addie's group backward for fear of being trampled.

Addie's hand shot to cover her mouth to suppress the hysterical laugh that the scene conjured in her mind: a gaggle of squawking geese. She really needed to eat. Something. Anything. *Would Kalea notice a missing granola bar from her purse?* No laugh escaped but the ungodly sound from smothering it did manage to slip past her lips. Thank heavens Blake picked that exact moment to approach the group of eight and hadn't heard the ghastly noise she'd made.

"Good afternoon, ladies and gentlemen. I'm Blake Edwards of Edwards Auction House. Are you here for the brokers preview?"

"Yes, we are," a sandy-haired man singsonged in an Irish lilt as he produced a card from the inside pocket of his navy blazer, presented it to Blake, and extended his hand. "Good afternoon, Mr. Edwards. I'm Philip Atkinson of Dublin . . ."

Addie's knees turned to Jell-O and her peripheral vision blurred. Disembodied voices drifted in and out of her head, but she couldn't make out any words. *Philip Atkinson?*

Addie had never met the man, but she'd had more than her share of unpleasant dealings with him on the phone and by e-mail when she worked at the British

Museum. He was a ruthless broker who would stop at nothing to acquire whatever book or relic his high-paying clients paid him to secure.

Addie struggled to refocus on the group just as they moved toward the registration table.

Blake touched Addie's elbow. "Addie, are you okay?"

"Yes, I'm fine. There have just been a few surprises today, and I guess with not eating, it all got the best of me."

"Would one of those surprises include seeing Mr. Atkinson again?"

"You know?"

"Only what your father told me."

Addie scanned the foyer on the lookout for prying ears. "Which was what?"

"Only that Atkinson tried to tarnish your reputation as an appraiser at the British Museum by accusing you of being a fraud."

"Did Dad tell you why that all happened?"

"No, but I could tell he was very upset. He even called and asked me to accompany him to London to help you out, but that was the last word I heard about it. So I assumed you managed to salvage your good name on your own. You did, didn't you?" Blake's eyes narrowed.

"Yeah, it took some time and a few lawyers running interference later, but Philip finally withdrew his charge—with an apology—and said he had made an error in assessing my appraisal skills, and it was all dropped."

"Good," Blake said, grinning. "Then it all worked out."

"Look, Blake, Philip would only be here for one rea-son, and that's because something was advertised in your catalogue that one of his clients wants desperately."

"That's what brokers do, isn't it? They track down and acquire pieces for their clients."

"Yes, but this particular broker has no scruples and will do anything to get his hands on what he's after."

"I can handle Philip Atkinson. Remember, I learned about how brokers operate from one of the best, your father." He patted the back of her hand. "Now you get home, little lady, and get some food into that belly of yours. Okay?"

Addie's heart resumed a healthy rhythm. "Okay."

"Promise?"

"I promise. If you promise me you'll keep a close eye on Philip. I don't trust him."

"You have my word." He kissed her cheek.

Addie followed Kalea, but as they started out onto the porch, frigid air swirled around Addie's bare legs like an icy fog. The fine hairs on the back of her neck tingled, and like earlier today in the library, she had the same overwhelming sensation of being watched. She glanced over her shoulder and down the corridor, half expecting to find Philip staring at her, but out of the corner of her eye she glimpsed a shadowy figure at the top of the staircase. Her mouth went desert dry. She gulped, trying to swallow the grit lodged in the back of her throat.

"Are you okay?" Blake waved his hand in Addie's face. "You look like you've just seen a ghost."

Addie glanced at the top of the stairs, now apparition free, and then back at her old family friend. "I'm fine, really. It's just been a long day, I guess." She refused to double-check for ghosts.

"Kalea," he called, "I think it's best you take Addie out for a strong coffee and get some food into her immediately. The day appears to have gotten the best of her. Working with Charlotte tends to do that." His laugh was short and humorless. "Now scoot. I'll see you tomorrow. And thank you both for saving my butt today." Blake waved as the door clicked shut behind them.

"Mind telling me what just happened to you?" Kalea leaned into Addie's ear and whispered. "I've never seen the color drain so fast from your face, not even that night you took me to the bar for tequila shots on my twenty-first birthday."

Addie paused on the pathway and glanced back at the house. The derelict hanging shutters, framing the windows, gave the impression the house had eyes, and they were mocking her. "It was nothing, just overtired, I guess." What else could have caused her ghostly sighting—hallucination, she corrected herself.

"You probably just need food and some rest."

"Yes, and I can't wait to tear into a steak at the Grey Gull Inn."

"Well . . . there's kind of been a change in plans."

"What do you mean?"

"I mean I'm going to have to reschedule our dinner. Something came up at the last minute."

"Would that something be Garrett Edwards?"

"Look, I'll call you first thing in the morning. We can come to the auction together. How's that?"

"I told Blake I'd come in early to help with the setup. I'm pretty sure you won't want to be here at eight a.m."

"Eight's fine. I'm happy to help out and it will give us more time to visit."

"Okay, then. Call me"—Addie pressed her business card into Kalea's hand—"and we can meet here, or you can stop by my house for a quick coffee first, and then we come over together, whatever you prefer."

"I'll meet you here," Kalea said, stuffing the card into her pocket, "but I'll let you know if I'm running late. Mornings aren't really my thing." She chuckled as she steered Addie through the front gate. "At least let me drive you·to your shop now. You're so pale. I'm guessing that you're in no condition to drive."

Addie's head jerked. "*That* white Lexus LS is your car?"

"Yes. Well, Nolan bought it for me as a birthday gift, but it's mine. Why, is there a problem?" She looked blankly at her cousin.

"Thanks, but I think I'll drive myself." Addie swung on her heel, now fueled by adrenaline, and marched up the street toward her Mini.

"I'll call you first thing in the morning," Kalea called after her.

"Yeah, yeah, yeah." Addie waved over her shoulder without looking back.

Chapter 5

Addie parked in her spot at the back of Beyond the Page and raced inside to the front counter. "Thank you so much, Paige. You're a lifesaver. I really didn't think my little outing would take all day." She dropped a pod into the coffeemaker and glanced around the shop. By the stacks of books sitting beside the leather reading chairs, and the number of empty paper cups in the trashcan, the store had been busy today. While Addie waited for her coffee to finish brewing, she caught Paige staring at her. "What?"

"Is it true?"

"Is what true?"

"Were you actually *inside* Hill Road House?"

"Yes, of course I was. That's where the auction is."

Paige rounded the carved-oak Victorian counter. "Did . . . did you see her?"

"See who?" Addie's head jerked up. "My crazy cousin? How did you know she was in town?"

"What? No, I didn't even know you had a cousin." Paige's eyes fixed wide on Addie's. "I was talking about *her*. Kathleen Gallagher, the young woman who mysteriously fell down the stairs and died in the house. Some say she was pushed, but they could never prove it."

"Pffft." Addie waved her hand, retrieving her coffee from the machine. "Surely you don't believe Serena's tall tale, too?"

"It's not a tall tale. They say Kathleen's ghost drove her in-laws insane, and Arthur and Maeve Gallagher leapt over the upstairs railing to their deaths. When their bodies were found, their faces were all twisted up, like they'd been scared to death."

"That's the silliest thing I've ever heard." Addie slid onto one of the three counter stools, took a sip of her coffee, and shivered. The vision she'd seen at the top of the staircase and the memory of the cold air wrapping around her legs replayed in her mind. "You've read too many mystery thrillers." She set her cup down. "Didn't you tell me once that Daphne du Maurier's *Rebecca* was your favorite novel of all time?" Her brow rose as she looked up at a pale-faced Paige.

"Well, yes, but—"

"Aha." Addie took a sip of her coffee. "You just proved my point. The power of suggestion."

"No, but—"

Addie's arched brow couldn't mask her involuntary eye roll.

Paige let out an exasperated breath and began retrieving books from the pile left on the floor by a chair, banging them noisily onto the shelves of the book trolley.

Addie chuckled to herself and took another sip from her steaming cup. "By the way, I found some great books that I'm going to bid on at the auction tomorrow. I'll probably be there most of the day. I'm also going in early to make sure Blake doesn't need any help finishing the setup." The only response was the creak of the trolley wheels. "How did you make out with that crate of consignment books? Were there many of those light, romance novels we need?" There was still no answer, and the trolley had gone silent.

Addie rose from the counter and made her way around the first row of bookshelves. No Paige. She skirted her way to the next shelving unit, and there was still no sign of her assistant. When she finally came to the last row along the wall shelves, there she was sitting on the floor, a book opened in her lap. "What are you doing?"

"Research." Paige blinked up at her.

"Anything I can help you with?"

Paige closed the book and struggled to her feet.

"That's a copy of June Winslow's *The Ghosts and Mysteries of Greyborne Harbor,* isn't it?"

Paige placed it back on an upper shelf.

"Why are you researching local pirate legends?"

"I wasn't. I was hoping it mentioned something about Hill Road House."

"You should have just asked me. I read that one for the book club, many times over, and know for a fact that there's no mention of Serena's tale in it."

"Well, there should be." Paige righted the books on the cart. "There has to be something in one of these books to prove to you what Serena and half the town say is true."

"You want actual proof of ghosts?" Addie shook her head. "Come on, Paige, you know as well as I that people write books all the time trying to *prove* the existence of ghosts, but no one can confirm it. I think it's highly unlikely you'll find what you're looking for in any of these." Addie gestured to the bookshelves. "It's just not scientific. It's all fiction."

"Just promise me you won't go back there again."

"Why are you and Serena making such a big deal

about this? I'm going to be attending an auction—that's all. It has the books we need. In fact, I saw a few outstanding copies of Jane Austen's *Sense and Sensibility* and her *Pride and Prejudice*, and an early edition of Emily Bronte's *Wuthering Heights* that's to die for."

"Let's hope you don't." Paige shoved the cart past Addie.

"Paige, what's going on with you and Serena? This is so out of character."

"We just know you, and we're worried." She sniffed. "If anything were to happen to you"—a tear trickled down her pale cheek—"I . . . I wouldn't be able to—" The tears turned into a full-out sob. "You're like family to me. More than any of my older sisters are and . . ."

"Oh, Paige." Addie's chest tightened with the same force that her arms did as they wrapped around the girl. "Nothing's going to happen to me. I'll be fine. No ghosts are going to hurt me, I promise."

"But what if they do? We both know you, and that it won't take long until you start investigating those old mysterious deaths just for fun. Because that's what you like to do. Then Kathleen Gallagher's ghost is going to get all riled up and . . . and . . . and who knows what. But there's going to be trouble. There always is."

"From the research I did last night after Serena told me the tale, I'm pretty certain the police did their due diligence when they investigated the three deaths back in 1949. I'm not about to start poking my nose into cases that were closed years ago."

"Hmm, we'll see," Paige said, shaking her head as she shoved the book trolley around the end of the row.

Later that evening at home, Addie was subjected to the same utter nonsense—at least it was in her mind—

of an extended version of the same warning courtesy of Serena, who dropped in for a routine evening chat. After an hour of sensing the same frustration that parents must have with trying to rationalize with a two-year-old, Addie feigned exhaustion brought on by her busy day and showed Serena out. Closing the door behind her, she leaned against its smooth mahogany finish and heaved out a deep breath.

It was times like this that Addie second-guessed her decision last year to offer the empty two-bedroom apartment above her garage to Serena and her fiancé, Zach Ludlow. Serena swore to her at the time there wouldn't be an issue with uninvited visits but . . . who was Serena kidding. It certainly wasn't Addie, and it had turned out just as she suspected it would. Especially since Zach worked most evenings at the Grey Gull Inn as a waiter while he finished his internship with Dr. Lee at the naturopathic clinic down on the boardwalk. Although Addie loved her friend dearly, there were times, like tonight, that the three-car-garage driveway just wasn't wide enough for her liking.

"Now, *that* was exhausting." Addie flipped her home security alarm to *armed* and headed to the kitchen to make a cup of tea and heat up some leftovers before she curled up on the sofa with her laptop for an evening of research. She wanted to find out the estimated current values of the Austen and Bronte books she'd seen today. If she didn't have her top bid already in mind when she attended the auction, she knew herself well enough that she could easily get carried away and end up paying too much, given how badly she wanted them.

At 8 a.m. the following morning, Addie parked her Mini behind a black SUV with vanity plates that read

ACSNER and laughed. Blake was already here. But
there was no sign of Kalea's Lexus, and Addie hadn't
heard anything from her yet this morning. She was
certain the plan had been to meet before the auction
and attend it together. On the other hand, it wouldn't
surprise her if her cousin was simply avoiding the possibility of chipping a manicured nail by actually partic-
ipating in manual labor and would show up just in
time for the auction to start.

Addie puddle-jumped to the front gate. The rain
shower they'd had last evening didn't last long, but by
the look of the lake-sized puddles she had to maneu-
ver around, the storm had carried a fair bit of moisture. When she reached the gate she winced as she
pushed it open. Silence. There was no cheeky objec-
tion to her entry today. She looked up at the towering
chimneys on Hill Road House, surrounded by the early-
morning crystal-blue skies. She smiled and marched up
the pathway that was now framed on either side by a
freshly mowed lawn.

Addie noted the addition of a sign pointing to the
rear of the house, announcing the direction of the
weekend yard sale. Blake's crew had been busy this
morning, and she half hoped the inside was equally as
prepared. Between the flashing images of whatever it
was she'd seen at the top of the stairway intertwined
with the unsettling words of warning from Serena and
Paige, she had slept little and fretfully. The last thing
she wanted to do was set up roomfuls of folding chairs,
but a promise was a promise, and she mustered her
inner depths for a smile she knew lurked somewhere
in there.

The entry hall spilled over with the delightful scents
of fresh-cut flowers. Two tall lamps, positioned on either end of a long, marble-topped table on the side-

wall, shed a comforting light that had been absent the day before. The whole atmosphere of the house had changed. It felt warm and alive. She glanced to the top stair landing, apparition free, and smiled at the recollection of her previous day's foolishness.

She spotted a man carrying folding chairs under both his arms, heading down the corridor toward the back of the house, and inwardly groaned. Then Blake's voice cracked from the study behind her, and a young woman darted out—her face as white as a sheet as she sprinted past Addie into the parlor across the hall.

"I don't care what you think you saw!" Blake cried out, close on the woman's heels. "You can't go around telling people. It'll scare off—" At the sight of Addie, he stopped, his face lighting up.

"Good morning, my dear." He lightly kissed her cheek.

"What was that all about?"

"Oh, it's nothing. A few of the staff have reported seeing things in the hallways and at the top of the stairs. I think it's just a combination of being overtired and letting their nerves get the best of them. You know they hear so many of the rumors about the house around town."

"Yes, the power of suggestion can be a strong one." Addie's gaze flicked toward the second floor, a shiver snaking across her shoulders.

"Are you ready to tackle some folding chairs?"

"That's what I'm here for. Any help you need, just point me in that direction."

"I was only teasing about the chairs. I think—" His forehead furrowed at the sound of crashing chairs, "I *hope* my staff has most of that under control now."

"I'm here. At least let me help you with something."

"Well." He stroked his chin and scanned the foyer. "There are always those little last-minute details to look after."

"Anything, just tell me what to do."

"Okay, if you're willing, why don't you do an inspection of the dining room and kitchen? I'll do the same in the study and living room, and then we can meet up at the library to see how Charlotte and Robert are making out in there. She insisted on setting that room up herself and said they had everything arranged *just so.* To quote her exact words—*I don't want your minions messing with my system.*"

"Sounds great." Addie shrugged. "And since I'm acquainted with how she has the books categorized, I can give them a hand if they're not quite done."

"There's no excuse if they're not. After all, you completed all the last-minute appraisals yesterday, and she and Robert stayed late finishing up the paperwork. Since we haven't seen either of them this morning and their cars are here, I expect they either came in very early or stayed the night to finish the setup and then fell asleep. Make sure you knock loudly. The room has to be ready to go in just over an hour."

"Okay, see you soon." Addie ambled to the dining room. She hoped that when the time came, she wouldn't have to wake Charlotte, who was sharp-tongued enough when awake. Addie couldn't imagine what she'd be like when roused from sleep.

Addie stepped through the double-wide pocket sliding doors. This room was one she had missed on her tour yesterday and was surprised to see the massiveness of it. This house was similar in style to hers but had all the square footage hers lacked. *On the other hand, how often have I used my formal dining room?* She could probably count on one hand the number of dinner parties she'd hosted these past two years, so this would be wasted space for her.

A dark cherry-finished dining table had been placed along the far wall to use as a display center for this room's auction items. There was, by a quick count, a complete twenty-plate dinner setting of Hutschenreuther cobalt-and-gold dinner plates. They looked to be in excellent condition. Addie knew that set alone would bring in some fairly high bids, as would the Victorian Bohemian crystal stemware. But she wasn't here to shop for more collectables. Her late aunt had left her more than enough porcelain and crystal, most of which was still stored in the attic and garage. She certainly didn't need any more. Refocusing on the room setup, she angled the folding chairs just right toward the auctioneer's podium. She moved on to the next room Blake had tasked her with.

Aside from a few vintage pottery mixing bowls and some copper cookware, there wasn't much to see in the kitchen. Blake obviously didn't expect much interest in this room from the brokers, as there were only half a dozen chairs set up. Most of what was here, he probably expected would go at the public auction or yard sale. Brokers weren't usually as interested in these finds unless the cooking containers or tools dated back to the 1700s or earlier.

Next stop on her to-do list was the library. She knocked on the closed door and waited. She knocked again. "Charlotte, it's me, Addie. I'm here to help with the setup." Still no reply.

Addie pressed her ear to the wood paneling and strained to hear any sign of movement behind the doors. The design of this room's entrance was different from the other rooms'. Although it was still in the Victorian double-wide fashion, they opened inward, contrary to the other rooms where the pocket doors slide out of the way between the walls on either side of the entry. She suspected this room was designed as such so that the occupant could lock these doors for privacy or security whereas the pocket doors had no locks.

"Is there a problem?"

"No." She met Blake's gaze. "But there doesn't seem to be anyone in there, and the doors are locked. Do you have the key?"

"Yeah, sure." He retrieved a set of keys from a trouser pocket.

"Perfect."

"This is the master. It opens all the rooms." Blake jiggled it in the lock.

When she heard a click, she turned the door handles and pushed. They didn't move. She pushed again.

"Let me try." Blake stepped in front of her. "Sometimes these old doors stick." He heaved against the doors. "That's odd."

"Maybe there's something blocking it?"

"No, it feels like it's catching at the top. It seems to be bolted from the inside." He pounded his fist against the door. "Charlotte? Robert? Open up. We need to get in there."

Addie pressed one ear to the door, sticking a finger in the other to block out background noise.

"Well?"

"Nothing." She met Blake's look of concern with one of her own. "Is there a key for the top latch?"

He shook his head. "No, it's a sliding bolt on the inside." Blake caught the attention of a young man carrying a folding chair under each arm. "Jeff."

"Yes, Mr. Edwards."

"Is that handyman still around?"

"Yeah, I saw him in the backyard fixing that bent tent pole we need for the yard sale."

"Could you go and get him? Tell him to bring his tools."

"No problem." Jeff dashed off.

"What are you thinking?"

"I'm thinking that the two of them have fallen asleep in there."

"Then they must be pretty sound sleepers."

A few moments later Brian, the town handyman, appeared with a toolkit in hand. Blake explained the issue, and Brian set to work. He drew a flashlight from his tool belt, clenched it between his teeth, and pointed the beam to the top of the doorframe. He shoved hard against the door, inserting a screwdriver between the door and the frame. "I'm afraid there's nothing I can do to jimmy the bolt, and if I take a pry bar to it, it's going to damage the entire frame."

"I don't care." Blake snorted. "The real-estate agent, what's his name that works for Maggie Hollingsworth, can worry about that. I just need the door opened now."

"Okay, if you say so. Addie, can you hand me the pry bar?"

"Exactly what am I looking for in here?" Addie rifled through the various tools.

"It's the one that looks like a small crowbar."

"Okay, got it." Addie grabbed it with both hands. "It's heavier than it looks."

"It should be. It's made of carbon steel. Another name for them is a wrecking bar so they have to be made strong," Brian said as he shoved the flat end into the crevice flanked by the door and frame and pried at it to the tune of cracking wood. "Got it!" He handed the bar back to Addie, who dropped it back in his tool bag as he swung the door open.

The crowd of staff that had gathered in the hallway breathed a collective sigh of relief.

"Back to work, everyone." Blake clapped his hands together. "We're live in less than an hour." The group scurried off, leaving the three of them alone. "Thank you, Brian. You can add this little mishap to my bill."

"Nah," Brian said, closing his toolkit. "It was nothing, and I'll come back later to see what I can do about that damage up there." He tapped on the splintered doorframe.

Addie stepped past him, stuck her head inside, and took a hasty glance around. "There's no one in here."

"There has to be." Blake came to her side. "The door was bolted from the inside."

"Take a look." She waved her hand. "Do you see anyone? Oh, wait. What's that?" She pointed to the desk chair turned away from them. "Is that Charlotte's hand on the arm?"

"See? I told you she was probably in here sleeping."

"Charlotte?" Addie called hesitantly as she moved toward the desk. With no reaction from the woman, Addie's gut tightened. She reached for the chair and swiveled it toward her. Bile rose to the back of her throat. The ghastly look on Charlotte's face shook her to the core, and she clasped a hand over her mouth to stifle a scream.

"What's wrong with her?"

Addie took a sharp breath and winced as she placed two fingers on Charlotte's neck to check for a pulse. "She's dead." Addie stood as upright as her quaking legs would allow. "Judging by how cold her skin is, I'd say she has been for a while."

"I'll call nine-one-one."

"Tell the operator what we found so they can dispatch the appropriate response teams."

Chapter 6

Hands on her knees, Addie gulped in deep breaths. No matter how many dead bodies she stumbled across, she'd never get used to it.

"What do you think it was, a stroke, a heart attack, or what?" Blake's voice resonated like cymbals in her ears.

Addie stood upright and tried to focus on his question. "I don't know. Probably. She was alone in here by the look of it, and the door was locked from the inside. I can't see any wounds or marks to make me think otherwise. But we'll have to see what the coroner says."

"You're right." Blake wavered when he stood up from the chair beside the desk. Addie could tell that in spite of the animosity that appeared to exist between him and Charlotte, this shook him. "I guess I'd better go let the staff know there's been an incident, and not to panic when the authorities show up."

Addie nodded. "I'd better stay here, though, until the police arrive. They might be upset if we left the body unattended."

"I hope for your sake it's not too long, but I'll try and come back to keep you company after I deliver the news." On unsteady legs, Blake made his way to the door. "Not sure what I'm going to say to them, though." His voice faltered as the door clicked softly closed behind him.

This was a first for Addie—not finding a dead body but being trapped in a room with one, especially one that had such a haunted look in its eyes.

For no other reason than to hold on to her last shred of sanity this house threatened to take away from her, she knew she'd need to avoid glimpsing the body in the chair at all costs. When she and Blake arrived, she'd turned the desk chair toward her from the fireplace direction it had been facing. Not wanting to leave more contaminating prints at the scene, she'd left it in the position it was at the moment, facing the window. By her mental calculations, in front of the fireplace and behind the chair, where Blake had been sitting, and directly in front of the desk or by the door, appeared to be the only areas in the room where Addie *could* escape that ghastly look in Charlotte's eyes, an image that would take her years to un-see—if she ever could.

Right now, she needed to focus on something else. *The room, look at the room. What do you see?* The fireplace, a beautifully carved marble mantel with matching pillars framing each side. Something like this could only have been created by a skilled stonemason. She wondered if it had been a local artisan or if the piece had been shipped over from Europe, a common practice of the more affluent in the early nineteenth century. She examined the deep-set inglenook firebox with wrought-iron log burner. If it were just a touch deeper, it would have made the perfect colonial cooking hearth.

She took a step back to admire the craftsmanship of the built-in bookcases on either side of the fireplace and heard a crunch under her foot. She glanced downward. It appeared she was tracking ash bits across the hearth as another wood charcoal piece crumbled under her step. She assumed they had been sparked embers from the fire that Charlotte must have ignited last night judging by the fresh, half-burned logs in the grate. Burned pits dotted the floor in front of the fireplace, and ash was now spread across the wooden floorboard onto the area carpet the desk sat on. It was a shame that Charlotte had been so careless as to burn a fire without the protection of a fire screen. The entire house could have caught on fire or at least the books on the floor.

Books on the floor. In the excitement of discovering the body, she'd completely missed seeing them earlier and reached to pick up the one closest to her foot. Then she stopped—*don't contaminate the crime scene.* The words of Marc Chandler, the chief of police, echoed in her mind. This was hardly a crime scene, but if she touched *anything* else, he would no doubt reprimand her. She was already going to have to explain her prints on the chair back. She pulled her hand away and left the books where they lay.

Then a thought struck her. If she hadn't turned the chair, the book would have been directly at Charlotte's feet, as would the other one poking out from under the desk. Addie squinted to try to see if there was actually a dark spot on the cover of the second book, or if it was just a trick of the lighting. Her gaze traveled upward, and she spotted something else she'd missed in the heat of the moment. A tipped-over teacup. The contents had obviously dripped down the side of the desk onto the book below it. *Charlotte must have been*

*working on these books when . . . when, what? She clutched at
her chest, knocked the cup over, allowing the books on her lap,
on the desk, in her hands, to slide to the floor?*

It was going to be impossible to inspect the cover
for damage without leaving a trail of fingerprints behind, and then she glanced back at the ash that had already been tracked onto the area rug. Too late, the
scene was already contaminated. Fingers crossed,
Marc wasn't back from his vacation and Sergeant Jerry
Fowley would go easy on her. She snatched up the
book and turned it over in her hand. The calfskin
cover suffered from the teacup mishap, and when she
opened the book to inspect it closer, she gasped. It was
Washington Irving's *The Sketch Book of Geoffrey Crayon,
Gent.*, his collection of thirty-four essays and short stories published in 1819. Irving's most famous stories included in it were "The Legend of Sleepy Hollow" and
"Rip Van Winkle."

She didn't remember seeing this one yesterday but
remembered marking up her version of an auctioneer's tip card. It was a plain index card on which was
noted the book's publisher, publication date, auction
house inventory number, and current market value.
Kalea had tucked the card, as instructed by Addie, inside the cover and title page. This particular book was
in good condition, not prime, but good. The last few
pages didn't open completely, and the paper was
lightly browned along some of the edges. Addie had
the same edition in her own collection, and she knew
hers was worth about nine thousand dollars. This one,
given its wear, would still have gotten Blake about
seven thousand at the auction. As it was now, with the
tea-stained cover and discoloration, he'd be lucky to
get eight hundred to a thousand.

Addie knew this book had been on the table with

the others she and Kalea appraised yesterday. Charlotte must have been checking their work last night when . . . *The poor woman.* Addie looked at the teacup and tried to paint a picture in her mind of what Charlotte was doing when the incident happened. But there was nothing else on the desk that would indicate what Charlotte was working on.

Keeping half an eye on where she stood in relation to the body and the chair, Addie stepped around the desk to her right and paused at the door. She strained to listen for sounds of the police having arrived. *They might not think this is an emergency, but they aren't trapped in the room with the body, either. And where is Blake?* He'd had plenty of time to inform the staff of an "incident," as he called it, and to return to keep her company through this. Because it was all getting a little bit too creepy for her liking, what with the dead body, the look on the face of said body, and the fact that no matter how hard Addie tried to stay out of the line of sight—so to speak—she still felt as though she were being watched. The same uneasy feelings she'd had yesterday resurfaced and she kept trying to tell herself it was simply the power of suggestion, the same thing she had mocked Paige for.

Well, enough was enough. She could only stay calm and levelheaded for so long in this room that seemed to be filled with gaping eyes. She'd call the police directly and tell them to get a move on it. She tugged her phone out of her front skinny-jeans pocket and saw a missed text from Serena.

Stay out of trouble!

Too late, my friend, Addie replied. **It's already found me!**

Out of habit, she punched in Marc's cell number but caught herself. Since he'd been away, Jerry was acting chief of police, but she didn't have Jerry's private cell number. If she did call Marc, for all she knew, since he hadn't contacted her recently, he might answer from a beach on the Riviera, and she wasn't sure she could handle that right now.

In an attempt to keep her mind occupied, and not think about Marc's possible whereabouts or the charge she had been delegated to watch over, she scrolled through her messages and recent calls and growled when there was still no word from Kalea. She tucked her phone back in her pocket, not certain if she should be relieved or concerned that her cousin had ditched her again. But it really wasn't out of character for the girl she knew back at college. Although, yesterday Addie had a glimmer of what an actual adult relationship with Kalea could be like. At least she *hoped* what one would be like, but obviously her cousin hadn't changed, and it wasn't meant to be.

Unless, of course, Kalea had arrived and was out there somewhere and couldn't get in because Blake had closed off the room until after the police came. Fingers crossed, that was it, and she didn't need to write off her cousin for another ten years. On the other hand, her cousin could have at least called. Addie cursed her lack of mental capacity the day before after she'd been rattled by whatever it was she'd seen on the stairs. She hadn't even thought to get Kalea's number from her. Now she had no way of reaching her to find out what was going on.

Frustrated with herself, Addie's eyes darted around the room, and her gaze landed on the table where the individual books set for auction were displayed. She hissed a swear word under her breath. *Why did I even bother?*

After all the time she'd spent organizing their placement, either Charlotte or Robert had gone ahead and added their own touch. *Robert! Where was he?* Blake had told her his car was here, but there had been no sign of him. *Was he the reason, not Garrett, that Kalea had a last-minute change of dinner plans?* Her stomach pitched at the thought of that one, but with her cousin, one could never tell what attracted her to most of the men she dated. Addie shivered. There was that feeling again. She glanced at the desk chair to make sure she hadn't wandered into its line of sight and crept to the table to see what havoc Robert or Charlotte had wreaked on her work.

It was pure chaos. Books were everywhere. The auction tip cards she'd printed and painstakingly tucked into the top of each book had all been removed. There was no system now. There was no way the auctioneer would be able to sort the lesser-valued ones from the higher-priced editions, like the four-book Holmes collection, not to mention the valuable copy of *Beeton's Christmas Annual.* Which were now mixed in with—*Where are they?*

Frantic, she flipped up books and scanned spine titles, sorted through the stacks, and stopped when she spotted the cover for *The Hound of the Baskervilles* on the far back corner of the table. Her heart thudded as she opened the cover to the title page. It was just as she feared when the aged but still glossy cover caught her eye. This was a book-club replica. A few years back a publisher had released a series of classic novels reprinted to look like the originals. She had this same set in her store and knew they weren't worth much more than the publisher's suggested retail price. She flipped open the cover of the next book in the pile. *The Sign of the Four.* It was the same. As were the copies of *A Study in Scarlet* and *The Valley of Fear.*

Realization struck her like a lightning bolt. She

threw her hands up, as not to touch anything else, and danced a step backward from the table. Addie looked over at Charlotte's body slumped in the chair and then back at the Holmes books. This was a crime scene after all.

Chapter 7

Addie couldn't shake the sensation that she was being watched. It was as though the walls in the library had eyes of their own. In her logical mind, she knew that she was completely alone in the room—well, except for poor Charlotte—so she tried to tell herself the feeling was simply her overactive imagination playing tricks. *After all, whose nerves wouldn't be on edge when trapped in a room over thirty minutes with a dead body, right?*

Her phone vibrated in her front pocket. Her arms flailed, sending an antique Tiffany lamp crashing to the floor. The glass shade exploded into shimmering rainbow shards around her feet. "Oh no!"

Somewhere in the horror of what had just happened, she knew someone was speaking to her, but the words were shrouded in fog and floated in and out of her mind until a calloused hand gripped hers. "I said, are you okay, Addie? You're as white as a ghost. Maybe you should sit down?"

"No . . . I'm . . . I'm fine, Jerry, but boy, am I glad to see you. You aren't going to believe what I found out."

"You mean there's more than a dead body and this broken lamp? Or are you saying the body is dead because of this lamp?"

"Well, no, I broke the lamp and as far as I know it has nothing to do with the body—I don't think—but there's more. There's also a set of rare Sherlock Holmes books missing from this room."

"Of course, there is." Jerry, a burly, broad-chested man, fidgeted with the handcuffs on his utility belt. "But tell me, how is it whenever you're involved, a book is missing and a body is discovered?"

"Coincidence?" She winced.

Jerry slid her a look and yanked his notebook from his chest pocket as he concentrated on the desk chair. "I'll get the details later about the books. Right now, I'm pretty sure the chief would want me to focus on the most *obvious* mystery in this room."

"The chief? But isn't that still you?" He shook his head. "Okay then, he's going to love this, because not only are the books missing but they were replaced with copies. Is that mysterious enough?"

"Miss Greyborne." Marc Chandler, Chief of Police, bellowed his greeting over the noise of the eruption of the police presence in the library. "Why am I *not* surprised to see you in a room with a dead body?"

"I . . . umm . . ." Addie was torn by his clipped tone and the breathtaking sight of the lock of sun-kissed chestnut hair dangling over his tanned forehead. "I was just telling Jerry here that—"

"Save it. I'll get back to your statement later. In the meantime, have a seat." He pointed at two reading chairs in the far back corner of the room. "Stay there until I'm ready to question you, and," he added mumbling, "in heaven's name, please don't interfere."

A hot flush spread up her neck to her cheeks. She swallowed to dislodge a lump forming in the back of her throat and scowled at the chairs Marc had indicated. This was humiliating and far too reminiscent of when she was a child, and her grandmother would send her to the corner for a time out.

Without even as much as another glance in her direction, Marc waved his arm toward the door. "Mr. Edwards, now that we're in the room and not in the hallway, run me through again exactly what transpired when you and Miss Greyborne first entered?"

Addie marched over to where Marc stood speaking with Jerry and Blake, his back turned to her. "Excuse me, Chief, but I have new evidence to add to the investigation of this scene."

Marc's shoulders sagged. "I'm certain you do, Miss Greyborne, and when I'm ready for your statement, I will call on you. Now *please* sit down."

Addie opened her mouth to retort but then snapped it shut. *What's the point?* Nothing so far about his reaction to seeing her for the first time in three months, since late February, was how she had envisioned it would be. The fact that he was back in town and hadn't even contacted her probably meant things were in far more of a mess than she realized.

Her heart felt as if it would explode like the lamp shade. He probably wouldn't even care enough to pick up the shattered pieces. They as a couple and, *apparently,* as friends were too broken by their last conversation.

Addie flopped into her time-out chair. Her eyes

held steadfast on Marc as Blake walked him through the movements leading up to when he and Addie found Charlotte dead. Addie kept her ears perked for the slightest variation in the story, but Blake did well. She shifted in her seat. She hated feeling useless. Finally, by the table, they were close enough for her to hear more clearly what was being said about the missing books.

"Sorry, I can't help with that one," Blake said. "I never saw the originals. They were something that Addie and her cousin Kalea came across yesterday when they were cataloguing the books we found earlier this week in the attic."

"So then you can't verify the original books actually existed?"

How dare he dispute my claim! Addie narrowed her gaze, hoping that every last imaginary dart she could conjure in her mind found its way to Marc's cold, cold heart. Blake glanced over at Addie, a look of helplessness in his eyes. "No, I can't, but they would have been put into Charlotte's cataloguing system after they were appraised."

"And where might I find this system?"

"It would be in her computer files on her laptop."

"Do you know where her laptop is?"

Blake glanced over to the desk and shrugged.

"Where was Charlotte staying while she was in town?"

"The Grey Gull Inn."

"Is that where her assistant," Marc said, flipping back through his notes, "Robert Peters, is also staying?"

"Yes, we all are."

"Have you seen Mr. Peters today?"

"No. His car is here on the front street, but I haven't seen him around."

"Could it be possible that he has Charlotte's laptop?"

"I suppose so." Tiny beads of perspiration formed on Blake's brow. "But it's hard to say. I don't recall him ever working on it before. He generally did his work on his own and then would e-mail his reports to Charlotte. She never really trusted him with her personal laptop."

"Do you know why? He was her assistant, wasn't he?"

"Yes, but Charlotte was like that. I was surprised to hear that she gave Addie access to it yesterday, but maybe she felt she didn't have a choice, given the rush job to get this room ready for today's auction."

Marc's eyes narrowed in on Blake's face. Droplets of perspiration now dripped from Blake's brow. He took a hankie out of his breast pocket, dabbed his forehead, and stuffed it back into his pocket.

"Mr. Edwards, why do I have the feeling you're not telling me everything?"

Blake glanced around the room and leaned closer to Marc. "It's just that," his voice dropped, "if there are books missing, it's not the first time things have disappeared from this house."

"Have you reported this to the police?"

"No." Blake plucked his hankie from his pocket and wiped under his collar.

Addie nearly slipped off the edge of her chair as she leaned closer to the two men. This was news to her, and she didn't want to miss a word.

"May I ask why you haven't reported these thefts?"

Blake's knuckles shone white from the death grip he had on the hankie. "I was afraid that the culprit was one of my staff, and I wanted to find out who it was before it got out of hand. News of the thefts could have destroyed the reputation of my company."

"Did you discover who was stealing from the estate?"

"No. I tried everything. I even submitted the staff to bag checks before they left for the day, but things still disappeared."

"How did your staff take to being searched?"

"Not well at first, but I showed them news articles about some of the larger retail businesses that had adopted the same procedures to help them with loss prevention. I told them it was just a good precaution considering the value of some of the items they were working with."

"Did that stop the thefts?"

Blake shook his head. "No, and then they started reporting other strange occurrences."

"Such as?"

Blake glanced at Addie. "Such as things like . . ."

"Like what?"

Blake squashed the balled-up hankie in his fist. "After they had finished setting up the displays in a room and came back the next day, everything had been moved back to its original place, and they had to start all over again."

Marc tapped his pen on the spiral coil of his notepad. "These missing books that Miss Greyborne mentioned to one of my officers could be part of this same ongoing heist."

"More than likely."

"Tell you what, Mr. Edwards. See that officer over by the door? Before you leave, I want you to give him a detailed list of everything you've discovered to be missing from the estate collection."

"Everything?"

"Yeah, we'll need a full report so we can start investigating."

"This whole thing about the ongoing thefts won't become public knowledge, I trust?" Blake whispered.

"I can't promise that, but I will do my best."

"I understand."

"Thank you, Mr. Edwards, you've been very helpful." Marc flicked a glance at Addie and then drew a card from his police-issue jacket. "I may have more questions for you, but in the meantime, if you think of anything else, please call me. That's my cell number on the bottom."

"I will. Thank you, Chief." Blake trudged toward the young officer by the door.

Addie's phone vibrated in her front pocket. She jerked it out fumbling it like a football in the air. Six missed text messages. All from Serena:

What do you mean it's too late?

What's going on?

Are you ok?

Why aren't you answering?

I'm on my way to Hill Road House!

And the last one:

I'm outside, they won't let anyone in. Are you ok?

Knowing Serena would storm the gates and probably get arrested, by her brother, again, Addie swiped out a text.

I'm fine, just a bit of an issue here. The police are looking into it. Don't worry. Go back to SerenaTEA. I'll come by later.

There, that should calm things down for a while. Addie looked up and glanced around the room for Marc. *Surely he's ready to take my statement now?* Her shoulders sagged when she spotted him over by the doorway talking to another officer. She quickly scrolled through her texts and calls but there was still nothing from Kalea. Now she was concerned. Her cousin might be a bit of a flake, but she generally had never been outright rude. Addie held on to the hope that Kalea had been caught in whatever excitement the police presence at the house had caused, and was waiting outside for Addie. She shoved the phone back into her pocket.

When Simon Emerson walked into the library, wearing his coroner's green hospital scrubs, Addie's heart leapt in response to his friendly face, and she grinned when his gaze locked with hers. His blue eyes lit up, and he flashed her that dazzling smile that highlighted the slight dimples in his cheeks. Marc greeted his previous rival for her attentions with a hearty laugh and handshake as if they were old buddies—a far cry from the type of greeting they had exchanged at Christmas, which was the last time they'd seen each other. *Or was it? Did Simon know Marc was back in town and didn't tell me?* It was clear to her that something had changed between the two of them.

Addie tilted forward in her seat, hoping to hear what they were saying. But it was no use. Marc had told her to sit in one of the chairs farthest from the action, and there were so many people milling around the room now it was impossible to hear much of anything. Then Simon nodded at something Marc said, glanced over at Addie, a slight smile twitching at the corners of his lips. He tugged on some blue rubber gloves and joined Jerry, who stood beside the body.

Addie drummed her fingers on the arms of the chair. This waiting-her-turn nonsense was excruciating. After overhearing the conversation between Blake and Marc, she was dying to add her perspective on what happened. Plus, she needed to speak with Blake to try to find out more about the thefts he'd mentioned. As far as she was concerned, that was big news, but Marc didn't appear to be all over it. Her gaze flitted from Marc to the door as she mentally tried to *will* him to see the significance of what Blake disclosed and go after him. Then a smile touched the corners of his mouth as he headed toward the door.

Yes! She edged forward in her seat. He'd finally gotten the message and was going to follow up with Blake himself and not leave the questioning to a young officer. She let out a deep sigh of relief and sank back in her chair. Unfortunately, her elation didn't last long. An attractive, raven-haired woman had entered the library, and when her gaze met Marc's she returned a smile that reached her smoky-dark eyes. By the look on Marc's face as he approached the woman, it was clear to Addie that it was the sight of her and not a revelation about what Blake said earlier that was the reason behind the change in his previous, dour-police-chief demeanor.

Addie studied the woman, trying to figure out who she was. She was fairly certain she wasn't one of Blake's employees, because even though her white, collared, sleeveless blouse and black, slim-fit capris were summer wear, as theirs was, there was nothing casual about their tailored cut. Her red open-toed sandals and matching tote bag even screamed *totally put together professional woman.*

When the woman leaned over and said something to Marc, Addie couldn't help but notice how close they stood to each other. So close, in fact, their shoulders brushed, which didn't appear to create that usual awkward moment for either of them, and then when she laid her hand on Marc's forearm, Addie knew. Whoever she was, she and Marc were anything but strangers or casual acquaintances. Addie shifted and

began to stand up again. Enough was enough. She
needed to know what was going on. Then the woman
looked across the room directly at Addie and nodded
at something Marc said.

Addie's chest tightened as the raven-haired woman
sauntered toward her and she plopped back into her
seat. It appeared that at least one of her questions was
about to be answered.

"Miss Greyborne, do you mind if I have a seat"—the
mystery woman motioned to the neighboring chair—
"and ask you a few questions?"

"Sure, and you are?"

"Forgive me." She held out her hand, "I'm Special
Agent Ryley Brookes."

"Special agent? Like an FBI agent?"

"Yes, and I must say how nice it is to finally meet you.
I've heard a lot about you." Special Agent Brookes
perched on the edge of the other chair.

"You've heard about me? From whom?"

"The DA's office, Chief Chandler." She shrugged.
"You've made quite the stir in the town from what I
hear."

"Coming from the FBI, I'm not sure if that's good
news or bad."

Brookes shook her head with a soft chuckle, her
dark, wavy, shoulder-length hair swinging freely.

"Can you tell me why the FBI is interested in Charlotte McAdams's death?"

"They're not, officially. I'm here on leave and just
helping a friend speed up the investigation process."
Agent Brookes removed a small notebook and pen
from the tote at her side. "Now, Miss Greyborne. Can I
call you Addie?"

Addie nodded, the hold on her chest twisting. Marc
had spent two of the last three months attending a series

of FBI-sponsored training programs for law enforcement officers at Quantico. His last month, if Serena's gossip was correct, had been spent in Italy taking some of his built-up vacation time at the strong urging of the mayor.

Addie eyed her interrogator. Her skin shared the same sun-kissed glow of Marc's. The cold hand twisting at Addie's chest wrenched one more time. Marc had met this woman at the FBI Academy. And then took her with him on vacation.

Chapter 8

Addie's mind reeled at the rapid-fire questions the agent launched at her. She relayed the sequence of events that occurred after she and Blake had entered the room leading up to them finding the body. Except she struggled to remember the exact steps she took after Blake left to speak with his staff. Everything she did after that, until the discovery of the fake books, was a bit fuzzy in her mind.

After Brookes made Addie repeat every detail that she could remember, at least twice, she closed her notepad. "This is all very interesting. Can you wait here for a moment? I'll be right back." Agent Brookes sidled up next to Marc and Simon, who were talking as two paramedics closed the black body bag on a gurney and wheeled it out the door.

The moment Brookes promised turned into five minutes. Ten. Fifteen. The group, now with the addition of Jerry, moved over to the center book table. Addie strained to hear what they were saying.

"I tend to agree with you, Jerry." Marc raked his

hand through his hair. "Given the fact that so many people have come and gone through the house over the last few months, it'll be too hard to determine who left what fingerprints and when, but I also agree with Agent Brookes: We can't let that stop us from looking at all the evidence. Who knows, we might get lucky and find some fresh prints."

Jerry mumbled something Addie couldn't make out at Marc's directive, picked up his black lab case, and began dusting the window ledge for prints.

Marc glanced at Simon. "And you're saying that based on your preliminary examination, Miss McAdams's death appears to be the result of natural causes?"

"At this point, it appears so. There's no evidence of any bodily wounds or a struggle, and as Jerry has determined, because the room was locked from the inside the only sign of forced entry was caused by the work of the handyman to allow Blake Edwards and Addie access to the room. I feel comfortable at this point making that assessment. However, it is preliminary pending a complete autopsy. At which time I'll better be able to make a determination of the mechanism and manner of death."

"Right." Marc rubbed his neck. "Jerry, you finish processing the house. Keep an eye open for anything that looks out of place or someplace someone could have hidden these missing antiques. If we don't find anything, then I'll let the auction go ahead as planned tomorrow. But make sure Mr. Edwards is aware that until we get the final autopsy report back, this room will remain off-limits."

"*What?*" Addie sputtered. She couldn't believe Marc's decision. In her mind, especially after she'd discovered the missing first editions and Blake's tale of other missing pieces, the whole house and grounds should be treated as a crime scene at least until the books were found. *What's Marc thinking?* Addie gripped the arms of the chair and shifted to stand, but stopped when Simon's gaze darted toward her—his eyes clearly telegraphing a warning to stay put and *keep quiet*. Marc glanced over at her, adjusted his police utility belt, and headed directly for her, his arms across his chest, his silence as he stood over her a deafening roar.

She motioned to the chair opposite her, but he didn't move. She struggled to her feet—her frayed nerves caused by the entire events of the morning and seeing him again after so long were the only force willing her legs to cooperate. "Marc, you look well. Time off seems to have agreed with you." She pasted a grin on her face, praying it didn't betray her warring emotions. "I wanted . . . no, I hoped we could talk for a few minutes."

"Unless it's got something to do with what happened here, we have nothing to say to each other at the moment." His eyes narrowed, studying her face. "But I get the feeling that you thought this little reunion would give us time to play catch-up like old friends?"

"No." Addie's cheeks burned as if she'd just been caught with her hand in the cookie jar. "But I did think we could forgo all this formality and talk like we used to."

"After I walk into a room and find you with a dead body? This shouldn't surprise me, though. As it appears, *nothing* with you has changed in the last few months." His gaze flitted over to Simon by the door and then back to her.

Addie winced at the curtness of his voice. "I have some information," she said, trying to regroup her thoughts, "and I think it's important."

"I'm well aware of the additional information you have."

"Oh, I was—"

Simon's hand on her elbow stilled her thoughts and mouth. "I'll call you later." He tilted his head. "You all right?"

She wanted nothing more than to throw herself in his arms. But she had her pride, and the studied attention of Marc, and the added addition of Special Agent Brookes.

"Just peachy."

"You were saying?" Marc brought his attention back to her after Simon left. "Did you have anything else to add to what you've already told Jerry or Agent Brookes?"

"It's just that I couldn't help but overhear"—she ignored Marc's snort—"that you don't feel that it's important to keep the house locked down as a crime scene, and I just wanted to point out—"

"You wanted to point out *what?*"

"Only that even though it appears Charlotte's death might have been natural, I can't help but think that her death coincides with the disappearance of some *very* valuable books . . and I think the two are related."

Marc rubbed his jaw, his eyes fixed on Addie's. "That may well be, Miss Greyborne, but you're forgetting the number-one rule of conducting a police investigation: Follow the evidence. And all the evidence points to a poor woman who had the misfortune of having a heart attack or a stroke or something else naturally occurring and then dying."

"But—"

"So, at this time, I"—he glanced at Ryley—"*we* can only investigate the missing books and the other items Mr. Edwards has reported stolen from the property.

There is no evidence suggesting a murder was committed, if that's what you're implying."

"What if some proof turned up proving otherwise?"

"If that happens, then I would be bound to follow that new evidence, but right now, based on preliminary findings, it was an unfortunate death and a *purely* coincidental event."

"Then don't you think that until proved otherwise the auction should be canceled? Is it really a good idea to allow all those people to traipse through the house until you *do* find the evidence to prove they are connected?"

"Are you questioning my authority in this matter, Miss Greyborne?" Addie shook her head. "Good, because I shouldn't have to explain myself to you, should I? What I'm saying is that unless my officers find any evidence of forced entry into the house or come across the missing items in question while they're completing their search, there is no reason the auction cannot proceed tomorrow."

"Does that mean you're convinced the thief is feeling pretty smug about getting away with it for so long that he or she will return to the scene of the crime by attending the auction? Then you'll be around to catch him or her red-handed?" Addie's smile wilted at the expression on Marc's and Agent Brookes's faces.

Brookes's eyes narrowed in on Addie's. "Tell us why you're convinced that Charlotte McAdams's death is related to a set of valuable first-edition Arthur Conan Doyle books in the first place."

Addie's gaze went from pinning Brookes with a glare to an indignant wide-eyed stare at Marc. "I don't mean to be flippant, but since she's on leave, can she officially be asking me questions?" Marc looked away and nodded.

Brookes didn't flinch except for a short hitch to her breathing. "Yes, even though I am not officially investigating this incident, an FBI agent is really never considered to be off-duty. However, as I explained earlier, I am not acting in the capacity of a federal agent. I'm here as a friend who is familiar with police procedure. This is a matter for local law enforcement—unless, of course, something came to light that would make it fall under federal jurisdiction."

"Satisfied, Addie?" Marc fixed a steely, slightly dazed gaze on her. Addie understood. She had shocked herself, too, with her outburst. "Now answer the question. Why are you so convinced that McAdams's death is linked to those books?"

"Because the books left as replacements would have to have been previously purchased. They aren't something that would be found in *this* collection." She waved her hand around the library. "Whoever exchanged them planned it ahead of time, perhaps in the hope that it would take longer than the next day for the fake books to be discovered."

"And," Brookes said as she studied Addie's face, "what makes you think that this person who exchanged the books wasn't Charlotte herself?"

"Because I had only made her aware of the first editions' existence yesterday. There wouldn't have been time for her to go out and buy the replicas. The closest place where she could have found any would have been Boston."

"And you're certain that the actual first editions and not these reproductions were here the last time you saw them, which, according to your words, was yesterday?"

"Yes, I appraised them myself, and that's where I left them when I was done with them."

"Is there a record of this appraisal?"

"Of course." Addie's tone awarded Marc a dunce hat. "It's all in Charlotte's inventory catalogue. Plus, I left notes for her."

"Which are where?"

"I assume on her laptop. She had left it for Kalea and me to enter our findings into the inventory list."

"Where is the laptop?"

"Her assistant must have it if it's not here." Her eyes narrowed at a thought she'd filed in her memory bank.

Addie had assumed from the two books on the floor by the desk chair that Charlotte had been double-checking the appraisals Addie completed yesterday, but, without the inventory list on the computer, that would have been impossible. The agent had asked a good question: *Where is the laptop?* The room was locked. No one could have come in and taken it—or *had she given it to Robert then bolted the door?* She needed to find Robert and the laptop, and if Ryley hadn't been staring her directly in the eye, she might have shared that thought with Marc, but given the circumstances she shrugged. "I don't know where it is."

Ryley's eyes never wavered from Addie's. "We're to take your word that these first-edition books existed in the first place, and someone made their way into a locked library, perhaps stole the laptop containing the only actual proof that these books had been appraised, and then exchanged the books for fakes."

"Yes." Addie met Ryley's fixed gaze with her own.

Marc tapped his finger on his chin. "Agent Brookes here has an interesting theory that she shared with me earlier. Right now, you are the only person who can verify the books' value, and the only one who had the means or motivation to exchange the books."

"What!" Addie's mouth dropped. "You think I had something to do with Charlotte's death?"

"Murder is something yet to be determined by the autopsy results, but"—Marc pursed his lips—"grand larceny is definitely a possibility."

"And"—Addie fingers curled in her palms—"what are you basing that on?"

"Something you yourself once told me: that *everyone* is capable of committing a crime, even murder, given the right circumstances. " His eyes held steadfast on Addie's.

"I can't believe what I'm hearing." Her nails bit into the tender flesh of her hands. "Okay, say you're right. What would be my motive?"

"If the books are as valuable as you say they are," Ryley said, turning her unfeeling, detached eyes on Addie's, "then my guess is money."

"I don't need money, thank you very much," Addie snapped at her. "And exactly how do you think I got into a room that was sealed from the inside?"

Ryley slowly scanned the room and then rested her gaze back on Addie. "You did admit, and it has been confirmed, you spent the entire day working in this room yesterday. And given the fact that you were in here alone—"

"Correction: I wasn't alone. My cousin, Kalea, was with me. A little fact that can also be confirmed."

"Yes, this mysterious cousin who seems to have disappeared. Tell me, Addie"—Agent Brookes squared her shoulders—"is she your accomplice?"

"What? You think one or both of us smuggled the books out of the room when we left here? No, I left them on the table; Charlotte's assistant, Robert, was looking at them. You can ask him. They were there when I was finished and left for the day."

"Then there's the possibility that you unlocked one of the windows and returned later last night to collect the books and the laptop."

"Why would I remove the only evidence that proves what I'm saying is true, that the books did exist and now there's only fakes in their place? Think about that one, Agent Brookes." Addie forced herself to breathe. If she didn't breathe, she couldn't think.

"What happened? Was Charlotte still in here working, and the shock of seeing you come in through a window scared her into having a heart attack? Or were you aware she was going to be working so you left some doctored tea on the desk for her just in case she was here when you came back to make the exchange? Is that what happened? You drugged her, and then slipped in through the window you left unlatched yesterday."

"Marc," Addie gasped, sputtering out her words, "tell your friend I would never do anything like that. You know me." Her wild-eyed gaze held steadfast on his—her eyes pleading with him to stop this insanity. "Marc, say something. You can't really believe that I had anything to do with any of this."

Her question was met by his stone-faced silence.

"Marc, please! Tell her."

"I believe," Ryley said, her tone as cold and distant as the emptiness in her eyes, "that the cup we took in for evidence will test positive for sleeping drugs or . . . maybe even poison?" Her brow rose with a questioning tic.

Addie sagged back into the chair. None of what she was hearing could possibly be real. She leaned forward, her hands between her knees. This couldn't really be happening. It was all so surreal. The ache in her chest landed in the pit of her stomach like a rock.

"Do you have an alibi for last night, Addie?" Marc's voice rumbled in her ears.

She locked eyes with him. "Are *you* actually charging me?"

"Not at this time, Miss Greyborne." Ryley's smug face swam before Addie. "However, I am fairly certain that after Dr. Emerson completes an autopsy, we'll find the victim was indeed murdered, and the analysis of the contents of the teacup will prove it. You are the person who had the means and motive to pull off such a feat."

"Marc, this is me." Addie jumped to her feet. "You know me. I couldn't have—no, wouldn't have killed Charlotte for some books. No matter what *she* says." She pinned him with a glare. "Now, if you'll excuse me as my head explodes with your sudden U-turn. Because it's getting hard to keep up. First, you said there was no evidence of a murder, and the two weren't connected, and now you're accusing me of poisoning Charlotte?" she snapped, folding her arms across her chest. Her gaze shooting from Ryley's to Marc's. "Explain that sudden turnaround, Officers."

"We're not saying you did at this point. Only that I have to follow the evidence, and right now, as Detective Brookes has made apparent to me in her investigation so far, all the evidence about this particular set of missing books points directly to you. The final determination of the cause of death will decide if other charges might be pending."

Addie's cheeks burned as if Marc's words had slapped her. "I see. Well then, *Officers*, if I'm not being charged right now, I assume I'm free to leave."

At Marc's head nod, Addie bolted past them and ducked under the crime-scene tape. Serena's words of warning, *"Don't go to Hill Road House,"* rang clearly through her mind as she made a dash for the front door. This house had become Addie's own personal horror story, and it was smothering her right now. She needed air. When she passed the study on her way to the front door, she heard men's voices. Jerry's and Garrett's.

She skidded to a stop. "Garrett, have you seen Kalea today?"

"No, I thought she was meeting you this morning."

"She was supposed to. Do you know if she's still at the Grey Gull?"

Garrett shook his head. "We had dinner last night, but then she got a call and said she had to take care of something. That was the last time I saw her."

"Is everything okay?" Jerry closed his notepad.

"Yeah, I just have to find my cousin. Knowing her, she's still sleeping, though. Thanks, Garrett."

It was past noon the last time Addie had checked. *Surely she still wouldn't be sleeping, would she?* Addie gave herself a mental shake. None of what just happened made sense. Fresh air. She needed fresh air. She flung the door open to Blake announcing the cancellation of today's auction to a large gathering of brokers on the lawn below him. His words were met with whispers and jeers. Even his explanation that, by all indications, the public auction would proceed tomorrow as scheduled didn't appear to silence their annoyance. Addie slipped past him and sidestepped her way past the bidders, searching faces for Kalea. When Addie made her way through the group with no sign of her cousin, panic snaked up her spine. Something had to be wrong. Even the flake she knew ten years ago wouldn't have disappeared like this. A cold hand clasped her forearm.

"Leaving so soon, Miss Greyborne?"

Addie spun at the Irish lilt behind her. "Philip Atkinson."

"Is everything okay?" An amused gleam twinkled in his eyes.

She yanked her arm free and darted past him. *Simon.* She needed Simon. He was always there to pick her up when she fell, and right now she was spiraling down a rabbit hole.

Chapter 9

Addie parked in the loading zone in front of the hospital and raced inside the revolving door.

"Whoa, what's the rush?" Catherine Lewis—Addie's father's old friend and now hers, too—cried out, her usual light-peach complexion spiking to fifty shades of cherry red on the color palette chart. Her brunette, shoulder-bobbed hair swung across her face as she darted out of Addie's path.

"Oops, sorry." Addie steadied the tottering woman. "I have to find Simon."

"An emergency just came in."

Addie stopped in her tracks. "I guess he'll be busy then."

"You look upset. Is there anything I can help you with?"

As much as Addie adored her friend, somehow telling her that she was the prime suspect in a grand larceny and possible murder investigation wasn't something she wanted to share at this moment. The stab wounds of

Marc's words were still too fresh. "No, it's nothing. I only wanted to ask him something, but it can wait."

"I'm finished up in the volunteer office for the day and was just heading out to do a bit of shopping before I go home. But a coffee right now would certainly hit the spot." Catherine rested her hand on Addie's shoulder. "Care to join me?"

"No, I should really get back to my shop. Another time, though, soon," Addie said and dashed back out the door, leaving her friend of two years slack-jawed. Addie would deal with the guilt and fallout later. Her heart couldn't take another beating right now.

Addie pulled into her parking space behind her shop and pounded on the back door of SerenaTEA. "Serena, it's me, Addie."

The door flung open. Serena grabbed her wrist, pulled her inside, and shut the door.

The spicy, seductive aroma of Chai tea embraced Addie, calming her. "Hi."

"Hi? Is that all you have to say? I've been worried sick. What's going on?"

Addie glanced at the desk in Serena's office. "Is that a fresh pot of Chai tea?"

"Tea? You want tea *now*? I want some answers. I thought you'd been murdered by a ghost."

Addie flopped down into a chair. "No, as you can see, I haven't been. But . . ."

"But what?" Serena glanced over her shoulder into the tearoom, closed the door leading into it, and studied her friend. "But what, Addie? You're scaring me. I heard rumors that a body was discovered there and when I didn't hear back from you—"

"Marc and his new *girlfriend*," Addie said, choking on the word, "think *I* am a murderer or, at the least, a book thief."

Serena's face paled. "That's ridiculous. You a thief and a murderer?" She leaned her narrow hip against the edge of the desk. "Wait. Marc's new what?"

"Girlfriend. Didn't you know?"

"He doesn't have a girlfriend."

"Well, he and Agent Brookes looked pretty cozy to me today."

"Agent Ryley Brookes?"

Addie nodded.

"Is a woman?"

"Yup, and a very attractive one, too."

Serena plopped her butt on the desk.

"You didn't know about her?"

"I didn't even know he was back in town until this morning when Mom and Dad called me from Cape Cod. They wanted to know if Marc's friend, Ryley Brookes from the FBI, got settled in their guest room okay the other day."

"The other day? And you didn't even know he was back in town until this morning?"

Serena shook her head.

"I wonder why she's staying at your parents' house and not at his." Maybe she'd been way off, assuming they were a couple and were, in fact, just good friends.

"You know how everyone in this town talks. Wouldn't the chief of police having a woman move into his house make a quick round of the coffee-shop gossip circle?"

"Yeah, I hadn't thought of that."

"Remember last month when your neighbor, Mrs. Thornburg, stopped me when I was on my walk and asked me if you were sick?" Addie chuckled, knowing where this was going. "And when I told her you were just fine, she asked me why the doctor was making so many house calls, then. That one took off like wildfire, didn't it?"

"Yeah, she notices every time Simon comes over, but last year when my house was being broken into she didn't see a thing."

"I guess a real crime isn't coffee-shop worthy," Serena said, absently swinging her legs back and forth, the heels of her Skechers softly thudding against the side of the desk.

"Is something wrong?"

"Oh, I was just thinking about Marc being back in town for a couple of days and not calling me. It kind of hurts. We used to be so close."

Despite her own issues this morning, Addie ached for her best friend. Nothing she could say would take away the betrayal Serena felt right now by her one and only brother, a brother she idolized.

A knock on the tearoom door jerked both of them from their thoughts.

Serena hopped from the desktop, wiped a tear from her cheek, and opened the door a crack. "What is it?"

Her part-time shop assistant, Elli Hollingsworth leaned into the slight opening of the door. "Marc and another detective are here," she whispered. "They want to speak to you."

"Tell him I'll be out in a minute. I have to put the cash back in the safe." Serena closed the door and turned the deadbolt.

Addie leapt to her feet. "Don't tell him I'm here."

"I won't. That's why I said I was counting cash. I knew he wouldn't come in if he thought there was cash all over the desk. He wouldn't risk a customer seeing it."

"Thank you." Addie rested her hand over her chest to still her heaving heart.

"But you'd better give a condensed version of what happened this morning in case he asks me anything I should know about."

"Maybe he just wants to introduce you to *her.*"

"The time to have done that sailed two days ago when he got back in town after being gone for three months," Serena hissed.

Addie hated seeing her friend like this, and it made her pretty darn close to hating Marc and the FBI hussy he dragged around with him. Addie refocused and poured out a condensed version of the morning's events.

By the time Addie was done with her tale, Serena stood taller, and with shoulders back she stepped out into her teashop, leaving the door open just a slight crack.

Addie took the cracked door as an invitation. She peered through the small opening. Even though she couldn't see much, there was no mistaking Marc's voice as he greeted his sister.

Serena gave a frosty "Yeah, it's good to see you, too."

Addie turned her ear to the voices. Eavesdropping wasn't beyond her. After all, in the past it had been a good source of vital information about a murder case she was looking into—unofficially, of course.

"Serena, I'd like to introduce my friend, Ryley Brookes." Marc's words were met with Serena's silence.

"I'm so happy to meet you at last," Ryley's voice chimed in. There was something in her voice Addie hadn't detected earlier. It had a soft Southern California intonation. "Marc talks about you all the time. Just yesterday he told—"

"Elli said you wanted to talk to me. I'm here now, so talk, Marc." Serena's voice wielded an edge.

"Serena."

"Sorry, but I'm pretty miffed with you."

"What have I done?"

"According to Mom and Dad, you got back to town two days ago, and you didn't even call. I had to hear you were back from Mom when she called to ask me if your friend here got settled okay."

"That's my fault, I'm afraid," Ryley's silvery voice faltered. "I suggested we take a couple of days to reacclimatize being back in the States after our holiday in Italy before . . . before he went back to work."

"You went to Italy with Marc?"

It appeared Addie's first instinct was right after all.

Serena gasped. "You're more than friends, then? That's interesting, Marc, when only a few months ago you proposed to Addie."

Addie clamped her hand over her mouth to keep a snort from escaping. Judging by the silence in the room, Serena's words had hit like a bombshell. What she wouldn't have given to see the looks on everyone's faces at that moment.

"Enough." Marc's voice sliced open the silence. "You and I will talk later. Right now, we're here on police business."

"What police business could you possibly have with me?"

"Just a few questions." Brookes's interrogator's voice replaced the laid-back girl from Southern California tone. "You are friends with a Miss Addison Greyborne, is that correct?"

"She's my best friend," Serena snapped. "Really, Marc, you know the answer to that so is all this necessary?"

"Just answer her questions, honestly, please, for me?"

Serena groaned.

"And it's also true that you live on the same property as Miss Greyborne?"

"Yes." Serena replied curtly, clearly. She was frustrated by Ryley's inane line of questioning, but it didn't stop there.

"And you own and operate this teashop?"

"Yes, I plead guilty to all that." Her tone cut the air like a knife. "What's it got to do with anything?"

"You also blend your own teas that do not come prepackaged from a distributor for customers."

"Yes, sometimes." Addie could imagine her friend's red blotches rising to meet the grinding tone of her voice. "I use a variety of tea leaves and herbs to make unique blends that I think my customers will enjoy or ones they request."

"Has Miss Greyborne ever requested you make her a special blend?"

"What are you getting at, Agent?"

"Just answer her question, Serena." Marc's voice held an edge of tension.

"I'm simply asking you if she ever instructed you to make a blend of sleeping tea . . . or something perhaps a bit more potent."

"What are you suggesting? That my friend would ever . . . ? I can't believe what you're implying. Marc, really, you're going to let her get away with this? Do you really think that Addie or I could . . . could ever . . . ? I'm speechless."

"Here."

"What's this?"

"It's a warrant to search your shop for any illegal herbs or lethal substances."

Addie struggled to breathe.

"Really?" Serena's voice rose to an ear-penetrating pitch. "You think—"

"Calm down, sis. It's just a matter of covering all the bases. Simon said he would need samples of any suspected herbal products to test against the blood and tissue specimens to determine an exact cause of death."

All Addie could hear was jagged breathing. From Marc or Serena, she couldn't tell, but it didn't matter. Her own lungs were struggling to gather even the smallest molecules of oxygen.

"It's part of conducting a thorough investigation, Serena. No guilt is being implied at this point."

"Maybe that's the way you as an FBI agent see it," Serena snapped, "but in Greyborne Harbor—"

"Come on, Serena, let's get this over with, and then we can all get back to our daily routine," Marc said, his tone strangled. Clearly, he was losing patience with his sister. "Now, if you can open the bins back here behind the counter for Agent Brookes, she'll take a small sampling of each of them."

"By the way," Agent Brookes's smug tone echoed through the shop, "the warrant covers the entire shop. We'll need access to the back room as well as your place of residence."

"That's just my office. I don't keep tea stored in here."

"We still have to search it. Now if you can step aside, please."

Fight or flight? Part of Addie wanted to stay and fight. Drive a fist through Cali-girl's face. But she wanted to protect Serena, not make things worse. Her eyes focused on the dark shape of Serena's rigid back protecting her, she slipped out into the alley, thankful she had at least one friend in a newfound sea of enemies.

Chapter 10

Addie rested her elbows on the top of the desk in the storage room of her shop and massaged the bridge of her nose. A migraine squeezed her skull. The day had not gone as planned. Becoming the number-one suspect on a theft and/or murder list wasn't exactly what she'd envisioned.

Neither was learning that Marc had become a stranger. She'd been so eager for him to return in the hope that they could salvage a friendship after what took place in February, but from his actions and words today that seemed impossible. She could forgive many things, but him even considering her a thief or murderer—or both—snapped the frayed lines connecting her heart to his. She plucked a tissue out of the box on her desk and blew her nose.

"Oh, Addie, you *are* back here."

Addie jumped. "You scared the heck out of me, Paige."

"You did look a little lost in your own world."

"Yeah, I was."

"It's only that I thought I heard you come in, but when you didn't come up front, I thought I'd better make sure the wind hadn't caught the door or something."

"Yeah, sorry, I've been . . . I don't know what I've been doing, to be honest." She rubbed her temples. "It's been a long day. Unless you need me for something, I think I'll just sit back here for a few more minutes."

"No, it's quiet right now." Paige leaned through the doorway and whispered, "But, what do you want me to tell Catherine?"

"Addie?" Catherine swept past Paige. "I thought I heard your voice."

With a tic of Addie's head Paige disappeared back into the shop.

"Catherine, pull up a seat." Addie patted a wooden book crate beside her desk. "What brings you in?"

"I know when something is upsetting you." Catherine dropped onto the box beside Addie. "Remember, I've known you since you were a toddler." Catherine tucked a wayward strand of Addie's hair behind her ear, her warm hand lingering on Addie's cheek. "I wanted you to know I'm here for you. You need someone to talk to, and it can't wait until Simon's free."

Addie's bottom lip quivered.

Catherine clasped Addie's hand in hers. The tender expression that filled Catherine's brown eyes tugged at Addie's chest, and the tears she'd dammed behind anger and disbelief broke free. Catherine snatched a tissue from the box, pressed it into Addie's hand, and then listened until Addie sat back, exhausted, her tenth tissue pressed to her nose.

"I can see why you looked shattered today. But I also know that Marc, deep in his heart, knows you had nothing to do with either crime."

"How can you be so sure? He certainly didn't put up any argument when what's-her-name stood there suggesting that if she was in charge of the investigation, I would be her number-one suspect."

"Perhaps, but he didn't charge you with anything."

"Not yet, but they were at Serena's, gathering tea samples because this woman is convinced it will prove that I did have something to do with all this."

A soft smile played at the corners of Catherine's mouth. "How many times did Marc go along with you as you tried to prove your theories to him?"

"That was different."

"Was it?" Catherine arched a brow.

"Of course," Addie sputtered. "We were . . . Oh. I see what you're getting at." A knowing smile touched Catherine's lips as Addie grasped what she'd meant. "But it was different with me because he generally knew in his gut that I was right, but he needed the evidence to do anything about it, and following up on my theories usually gave him exactly what he needed for proof. You can't think he feels in his gut that she's correct and is looking to prove that her theory is right?"

"Or maybe he's waiting for her to prove herself *wrong* because he knows you would, could, *never* do what she accused you of, and once her evidence doesn't pan out, he knows that will be the end of it."

"I never thought of it that way." Addie drummed her fingers on her knees. "But why would he go to all that trouble to prove my innocence if he already knows I am?"

"Because Marc is obviously falling for Ryley and doesn't want you to become a wedge between them.

So by going along with this, he's not jeopardizing what they have by taking his ex-girlfriend's side over hers."

"Do you think he . . . he loves her?"

"It sounds like it's a possibility. Why? Would it bother you if he did find someone else and fell in love?"

Addie couldn't answer around the tightening in her throat.

"Would it? Be honest."

"I didn't think it would at the time, but seeing him today with another woman did make me ask myself if I'd made a mistake when I let him slip away. On the other hand, is what I felt today only a matter of me wanting what I can't have anymore?"

"Have you figured out which one it is yet?"

"I don't know," Addie said, twirling a pen on her desk. "After Christmas, when we started to spend more time together, I thought I really cared for Marc. He was like going home. He was comfortable, everything I knew and missed. He was like a memory of my past, and it felt right and safe."

"That's to be expected. You'd had a couple of rough years and suffered a lot of losses. We were all thrilled to see you finally moving forward again . . . but . . ." Catherine caught her lip between her teeth and then fell silent.

"But what?"

"Nothing, go on."

"Okay." Addie shifted, eyeing Catherine's masked face, but it was no use. She had withdrawn and wasn't going to finish her thought. "Yes, I was moving forward, and it felt freeing, but that was part of my problem. Was I really moving forward? Sure, I'd finally accepted David's death and part of that could have been because Marc made it easy for me to fall for him—which is probably why I did so quickly. He made me feel the way David used to: safe. Naturally, I gravitated toward that. Then I started to question if the reason I was attracted to Marc in the first place was because I had simply replaced David with him. They were so much the same."

Addie stroked her neck, watching Catherine's face for a reaction, but she showed nothing telling. "Well, except David was never as rude or nasty to me like Marc can be sometimes." Her gaze dropped. "Like ever since he's gotten back to town."

Addie looked up and didn't miss the darkening in Catherine's eyes that those words brought, but still she remained silent, listening. "So when Marc pulled the ring out of his pocket and got down on one knee and said he loved me, I panicked. It felt too much like I was going backward." Addie glanced at her ring-free left hand. "Then I thought about Simon, who was only a friend at the time, but he was so different. When I was with him, he seemed to bring out the best in me and didn't try to change me into who he wanted me to be. I wasn't ready to give that up. I *needed* to see where that went. If I said yes to Marc, it wouldn't have been fair to him or me or Simon. So I pulled away."

Catherine leaned closer, her voice nearly a whisper. "Can I be honest with you?"

"Yes, please. That's what I need right now."

Catherine drew in a deep breath through her nose, straightened her shoulders, and clasped Addie's hand in hers. "Don't get me wrong. I'm not making excuses for his . . . sometimes abrupt behavior, but just so you know from someone who has known him his whole life, Marc has a hard time with expressing emotions like other people do. It's partly because of his job and training and partly because of his past with Lacey.

Right or wrong, he's developed the ability to put his feelings in boxes and compartmentalize them." Her fingers tightened around Addie's. "I never thought he was the right man for you. As a friend, yes, you're great together, but as soon as emotions get mixed into it . . . Well, you're too different, and you really don't bring out the best in each other when you're a couple." Her shoulders heaved, and she slid back on the crate. "There, I said it. Something I've wanted to say to you for a long time."

Addie plucked another tissue from the box and blew her nose. "I'm glad you did because I knew that in my heart, too, I guess." Catherine's brown eyes softened with understanding, which was exactly what Addie needed right now and missed in her life—a mother's shoulder to cry on. "I thought that when he got back, we could finally talk about it. Then I could explain how I was feeling and let him know that I really did care for him—just not the way he cared for me. But that I still cared as a friend. We'd been through so much together."

Catherine patted Addie's hand. "And you may be able to one day, but it's going to take some time. You underestimated how hurt he was. His wounds need to heal. He'll come around, but meanwhile you keep moving forward and stop looking back. Make a clean break from each other and stop this dance you both keep falling back into." Catherine placed her hand on Addie's arm. "You and Simon have got something pretty special. You followed your heart in February. Don't risk jeopardizing that now by second-guessing yourself."

A smile tugged at the corners of Addie's lips. She remembered how her heart leapt at the sight of seeing Simon walk into the library today. He was as attractive to her now as he was the first night she'd met him, although, at that time, she was only attracted to his brilliant medical mind. But since then—well, Simon was new and refreshing. Addie swallowed hard. *That's exactly why Marc and I didn't work.* Catherine was right. The past is best left where it belongs: in the past. Forward was the only direction she should be looking.

Addie wrapped her arms around Catherine's neck and hugged her. "Thank you. This talk helped me clear my mind."

"I'm here anytime you need me. I know your grandmother, bless her heart, tried her best after your mother passed. And even though I can't replace either of them, I'm always here for you." Catherine kissed Addie's damp cheek.

"Addie." Paige's head popped through the door. "Sorry to interrupt, but I'm getting slammed out here. About twenty customers just came in."

"All at once?"

"Yeah, I heard one of them say they were on the cruise ship."

"I thought that wasn't starting until next week?" Catherine rose to her feet.

"The regular shore excursions don't start until then," Addie said, "but I overheard something about a preinaugural docking this week for VIPs or something. I didn't think it would affect us. They sounded like they were here for the auction."

"I guess that's why they came in here." Paige glanced over her shoulder to the front of the shop. "They're book dealers and couldn't get into the library over there or something. I gotta go." She disappeared from the door.

"Thanks again, Catherine." Addie swiped at her

eyes. "I'll call you later, but I'd better get out there now."

"Want some help?"

"I couldn't ask you to wait on my customers. You have enough work with running the hospital volunteer program and everything else you do in the community."

"Nonsense. I spend as much time browsing these shelves as you and Paige do. I think I can handle working the floor until it settles down a bit."

"You're a lifesaver today." Addie grinned. "In more ways than you'll ever know."

Chapter 11

Addie and Catherine headed out into the bookstore. Addie made her way around shelving units in one direction, Catherine the other. It didn't take long until the extra hands on the floor were sought out, and Addie was surrounded by eager book lovers. When she pointed them to the area she reserved for her older and rare books, some had no difficulty in expressing their disappointment at the selection they found. One man made it quite clear that he was only interested in *rare* first editions, and he wasn't alone in his request. Addie found herself reciting the same apology line ad nauseum, explaining she didn't keep valuable books in her shop but only editions that were old and well-loved.

It became clear to her that the rescheduling of the auction was having a trickle-down effect that wasn't positive, and she was bearing the brunt of it. Brokers and dealers knew what they wanted, and Addie didn't appear to have it. She could only hope that when the regular shore excursions started the passengers would be less discerning. If not, perhaps for the high season she'd have to consider stocking some of her prized-possession books that she kept at home. But she quickly squashed that thought. The extra security that would be required at her store made her shudder and count the tallying dollar signs—which, after the day she'd endured, had her thinking of ingenious ways to give demanding bibliophiles paper cuts.

Nope, this was probably a one-day event, and if Charlotte hadn't died and the Holmes books hadn't gone missing, none of these people, as odd as they were, would have set foot in her little shop, but the news wasn't all bad. The rarer, less valuable books she did have in stock were flying off the shelves. She'd be able to increase her auction budget whenever it was rescheduled for after the autopsy was completed. Fingers crossed it would be soon, and she wouldn't be sitting in a jail cell that day. *Would Marc let me Facetime the auction?*

Addie sought out Catherine as the tour group trickled out of the store. "There you are, and why am I not surprised to see you hiding in the mystery section?"

"Oh, Addie." Catherine echoed Addie's chuckle and struggled to her feet, using the bookcase as a support. "Today was the most fun I've had in a long time, plus"—she held up a book—"I even had time to do a bit of shopping for myself."

"*Sleeping Murder: Miss Marple's Last Case.* I see you're still on your Agatha Christie kick."

"I can't get enough of her, and this one looks fascinating. Apparently, Miss Marple exorcises a ghost from a haunted house." Catherine flashed her a teasing smile.

"You've been speaking to Paige or Serena or both of them, haven't you?"

"Remember, I've lived in this town for a long time and grew up hearing those rumors. Don't be so quick to discard them." She rubbed her right knee.

"Are you okay?"

"Yeah, just not a kid anymore and crouching to restock books, well, let's just say it's not as easy as it used to be."

"I'm thinking maybe it's time for you to head home and put your feet up for a while."

"I can't agree more with you." She grinned and waved the book. "I'll just go pay for this, head home, and see if I can learn some pointers about ghost purging from the expert here to pass on to you."

"I'm not going to let you pay for that. It's my gift to you for all your help this afternoon. We couldn't have done it without you."

"You don't have to pay me anything. I was happy to help."

"I know, and I appreciate that, but please." Addie pressed Catherine's fingers around the book. "Take it. It would make me feel better."

"Okay, I won't argue. This one completes my collection, so it'll soon be time to find another favorite author to obsess over."

"When you're ready let me know. I have lots of excellent recommendations."

"You'll be the first I ask since mystery appears to be your forte." She chuckled and squeezed Addie's hands. "Remember, I'm here for you whenever you need me. I'm fairly busy next week with all the events planned down at the harbor for the inaugural docking, but don't forget I'm always just a phone call away." She kissed her cheek.

"I know, and I appreciate that. You're a good friend. Thank you." Addie waved as Catherine made her way out, the tinkling sound of the bells announcing her departure.

It had been a long time since Addie felt mothered, and she smiled to herself as she inched her way toward the front of the store, uprighting books that had fallen over. Judging by all the empty shelf space, she'd definitely been wrong about the VIPs: they weren't as discerning as she'd first thought. Some of them, at least, appeared to be just as happy with quality old and used as they were with rare and valuable.

When she rounded the end shelf by the door, she came to a stuttering stop. Philip Atkinson was sitting at the counter, bent over a book. Her cheeks puffed out as she released a deep breath. *Keep it together, Addie. Right now he's just a customer.* "Philip, I see you found something you like."

He raised his head. "Miss Greyborne." His steel-gray eyes softened to dove gray, small crinkles forming at their corners. "How lovely to see you again so soon, but I must say, you are popping up everywhere today, aren't you? Although . . . " He closed his book, his eyes holding a gleam of deviltry. "If I didn't know better, I'd say you were following me."

"I own this bookstore. Therefore, I'm exactly where I should be. Shouldn't you be in Dublin or Madrid or New York, or wherever?" Heat crept across her cheeks. "What brings you to Greyborne Harbor of all places? Or did you know I live here and came by just to torment me again?"

"You own this delightful little shop? That's why you were at the auction." A soft laugh escaped Philip's lips. "I was afraid when I saw you that you had changed careers and were now my competition. Because I do remember how tough you were to deal with, and I didn't relish the thought of going head-to-head with you again." The corner of his lip turned up in a half smile. "And to answer your question, I had no idea where you were living. My appearance in your quaint little town is purely coincidental."

"Okay, that's fair." Addie made her way around the counter and stood beside Paige. She glanced down at the book Philip had been reading. It was her book-club edition of *A Study in Scarlet.* "I see you're a fan?"

Philip glanced down at the book cover, then back up to Addie. "Why, yes I am. It is disappointing only to find this reproduction in your shop." The muscles in his forehead tightened. "You don't happen to know if there are any *first editions* of this around, do you?"

"No, I don't," she said, struggling to keep her voice even. *Did he know about them or is he fishing?*

"That's too bad." His fingers stroked the book cover. "What I wouldn't give to have an original copy of this."

"Is that what brought you here to the auction? Were you hoping to find one?"

"One could only hope." He tossed some cash on the counter. "Fifty should cover this." He tucked the book under his arm and headed out the door, the overhead bells expressing their delight at his leaving.

Chapter 12

Addie went through the motions of closing the store for the day. To say Philip had unnerved her would be an understatement. She'd even gone as far as double-checking the classic murder mystery books. It was exactly as she'd thought. There were still two other editions of *A Study in Scarlet* on the shelf. It was interesting to her that Philip had selected the book-club copy, a similar edition to the replacements she'd found at Hill Road House.

All the way home, she replayed their conversation in her head. What haunted her wasn't so much what he said but how he said it. He seemed so certain and smug. It was possible, in her mind at least, that he did know the collection of Holmes books had been discovered and then gone missing. The question then became, how? No one except Kalea, Charlotte, Robert, and her even knew the Doyle books had been found in the barrister's case. It made Addie wonder how he had known because by every indication of his reaction to the reproduction he *did* know, and was also aware that they were lost and replicas had been left in their place. But Charlotte was dead and Robert and Kalea were both MIA. *Does that mean he's the thief? Is he the person Kalea texted right after we discovered them?* That could explain why her cousin had disappeared. Addie hit her brakes.

Coming up her driveway directly toward her was Marc's cruiser, followed closely by Jerry's. Marc's car pulled to the side and slowed down to let her pass, but she couldn't even glance over to acknowledge her thanks for the gesture. Her fingers tightened around the steering wheel. She knew exactly why they had been at her house.

Serena stood, arms crossed, at the bottom of the staircase that led up to the garage apartment. The look on her face reinforced that this had not been a social visit. Addie pulled up in front of her door, and by the time she got one foot out onto the pavement, Serena was at her side.

"Can you believe the nerve of them searching my apartment?"

"Did they find what they were looking for?" Addie slammed her car door.

"Of course not." Serena's eyes widened. "You know I don't keep any inventory here."

"How did Agent Brookes take her wild-goose chase, then?"

"She didn't say a word, but I could tell she was disappointed when all she could find was cooking herbs and spices."

"Did she take samples of those?"

"Of course. I'm pretty sure she was trying to save face in front of Marc. I hope she chokes on them when they come back negative for whatever poison she thinks I have stashed away."

"Yeah, but she seems really determined to find something to implicate me. It's too bad she hasn't stopped to think that by doing that with this poisoning theory, she's implying you were the supplier. She'd also be taking down Marc's sister. I wonder what he's said to her about that."

"Probably nothing. Remember, he never told me one word about her, their trip to Italy together, or her staying at Mom and Dad's. So, all I know is that if either of them expects me to welcome her into the family with open arms, they'd better think again."

"But doesn't it make you wonder why she is so bent on proving I had something to do with this? And why bring you into it? And why is Marc letting it happen? There has to be a reason that we're not seeing."

"Oh, that's easy. She knows Marc was in love with you and is probably afraid he might still be."

"I doubt that. You didn't see the way he treated me and the way he looked at her. There's no question of who he's in love with now. But if what you're saying is even partially true, why involve you and risk causing a rift between her and Marc?"

"Because I'm your best friend and biggest advocate, and maybe she thinks if she can prove you poisoned Charlotte, it might sway how I feel about you."

"I'm just guessing, here." Addie shifted her weight and shoved her hands deep into her pants pockets. "Just hear me out for a minute. She doesn't want to alienate you and cause an issue with Marc. All this sample collecting is just a show to prove to him that no stone was left unturned in finding the evidence to prove that I did whatever she thinks I've done. That way she can clear you and then say to Marc that she knew all along that you could never have knowingly helped me in such a devious plan, and that I must have used our friendship to learn some of your knowledge to make my own concoction."

Serena burst out laughing. "You should have been a writer, not a bookseller, because that's the craziest conspiracy theory you've ever come up with." She snorted, covering her mouth, still giggling.

"What?" Addie looked sideways at her. "It's a sound theory. Why else would she be so determined to prove I'm behind all of this?"

"Are you sure," Serena gasped, fighting her urge to laugh, "that finding out she went to Italy with him and then coming to Greyborne Harbor isn't bothering you more than you let on? Because I think you're losing it."

"I am not, and no, I'm not bothered by it. At first maybe a bit—I mean, he only proposed to me three months ago, and I couldn't believe he'd replaced me so quickly. Then seeing the two of them together made me realize that he'd found someone perfect for him: she's professional, she plays by the rules, she's everything I'm not. And then I thought about Simon. I realized that I'd found someone perfect for me. Because we're both—"

"Rule breakers?"

"Rule *benders* is more like it. We never actually *break* the rules." Addie chuckled softly. "But that's not what's concerning me."

"What is then?"

"Doesn't it seem strange to you that an FBI agent would let her emotions rule her actions? You'd think with all her training, she'd be a little less—"

"She's still a woman, and maybe in her mind since she's on vacation, this is her way of marking her territory. The only way she knows how is through an investigation."

"Maybe, but she did tell me today that an FBI agent is really never off duty."

"Do you think she's on leave for some other reason than vacation time, *or* not on leave at all and still very much working?"

"I don't know, but it does seem odd to me the way she's jumped into this investigation, and how Marc seems to be letting her take the lead in it. I get the feeling there's something else going on either with this case or with her."

"Is there something about Blake Edwards or Charlotte that you don't know? Like a reason either of them might be a person of interest to the FBI?"

"Not as far as I know. I didn't know Charlotte personally, except by her company's reputation, but I've known Blake most of my life. But then again . . ." Addie hesitated and glanced at Serena. "How well do we really know anyone? We might think we know someone, but then something happens and we discover that we really never did know that person." Serena's eyes flew wide open. "I wasn't talking about you and me. I only meant people in general."

"Are you sure? Because I don't want to find out you've got a skeleton in your closet that's going to come back and bite me one day."

Addie threw her head back laughing.

"It's not funny. It would break my heart if I found out you weren't who I thought you were."

"Don't worry. There are no deep, dark, sordid secrets about me waiting to be revealed." Addie draped her arm across Serena's shoulder. "Look, we've both had a lousy day and need to take our minds off all this. Is Zach working at the Grey Gull tonight?"

"Yup."

"Would it make you feel better if you saw him?" Serena's eyes lit up. "I thought so. Let's go say hello, and we'll grab dinner while we're there."

"Perfect, let me get my purse." Serena bolted up the stairs to her apartment and was back before Addie had fastened her seat belt.

Serena hopped in and Addie put the car in drive. Serena let out a horrifying squeal. "What's wrong?" Addie slammed on the brakes.

"My phone's dead."

"Is that all? I thought you were dying."

"I might as well be because there's no time to charge it before we go." Serena's voice teetered on panic. "What am I going to do?"

"Take mine out of my bag and use it."

"Oh . . . I never thought of that." Serena snatched Addie's phone and scowled at the lock screen. "Could you please put in your password?"

Addie stopped at the top of her driveway, punched in her password, and handed Serena the phone.

"Thanks, I thought we should call ahead and ask the manager if he could squeeze us into Zach's section."

"I'm glad it was life and death," Addie mumbled under her breath as she pulled out onto the road. "Speaking of Bruce," she added, "I better ask him about my cousin when we're there."

"What about her?" Serena asked, phone plastered to her ear. "It's busy. I'll try again in a minute."

Addie glanced at her with her peripheral vision. "What are you doing? Going through my phone?"

Serena's finger stilled on the screen. "Just looking at these pictures." She flashed the phone screen in Addie's face. "Is this your cousin? She's gorgeous. Wow."

"I'd forgotten we took those photos yesterday."

"What were you guys doing? Here's one of you almost standing on your head."

Addie took a quick glance at it and giggled. "Yeah, that was our silly break yesterday afternoon. We were both feeling like we were suffocating in that stuffy library and I tried to open the window. When I couldn't get it unstuck, Kalea tried, and it got sillier from there. I think we both had a mini mental breakdown for about fifteen minutes." It had felt wonderful to have fun with her cousin. They had been like kids again without a care in the world. "Hey, I don't know why I didn't think of this before, but you didn't happen to see that woman hanging around out in front of the house when the police had it closed off, did you?"

"No, I'm pretty sure I didn't. If I had, I would have remembered how intimidated she'd have made me feel."

"Looks aren't everything." Addie slipped into a parking space in front of the Grey Gull Inn. "She's one of those people you aren't really sure of how well you know them, which is exactly why I'm going to head over to the registration desk. I need to find out what *they* know about her. You go make your sad puppy eyes at Bruce and get us a prime table in Zach's section." Addie closed her door. "I'll come find you as soon as I find out if Kalea's still registered."

Addie strode in the direction of the hotel lobby and paused. Marc's police cruiser was parked at the curbside. It appeared she and Marc had the same notion of checking out her wayward cousin's registration status.

Not knowing what to expect when she entered the lobby—probably a reprimand for interfering in *his* investigation—she straightened her shoulders and pushed through the door. Half expecting to be greeted by his mocking voice, she blinked when the manager's wife, Millie, greeted her.

"Hi, Addie, I haven't seen you in a long time. How have you been?"

The small lobby was empty. "I'm . . . I'm fine, thanks. Yeah, it has been a while. Since the Founders' Day parade, wasn't it?"

"Yes." Laugh lines played beside her eyes. "And I must say you made a lovely Betsy Ross."

Addie laughed and curtsied. "Thank you so much, but I feel it did pale in comparison to your Martha Washington costume."

"Don't be silly, I'm just a middle-aged woman. Who else could I have gone as?"

"Millie, you know you're more than just a middle-aged woman. Look how you keep this place running. Bruce would be lost without you."

"Now that is true. The poor man can't find a bottle of ketchup in the fridge unless it jumps out and bites him on the nose."

Addie snorted. A tendency she hated, but for the next few minutes she relished in the silliness of shared laughter—with the occasional snort—with Millie.

Tension released, she was ready to put her sleuthing hat back on. After regaining some semblance of composure, she inquired as to whether Kalea was still registered.

"You know we can't give out information about our guests." Millie held up a finger to quiet Addie's brewing retort. "But she did tell me when she checked in that she was here to visit you, and you were her cousin. So, on account of that, I will tell you that she is still registered but only because she paid for three nights and didn't check out when she left this morning."

"What time did she leave?"

Millie shrugged. "We have no idea. When house-keeping went in to refresh her room, everything was gone. She must have left sometime during the night."

Addie bit her bottom her. This wasn't what she'd hoped to hear, but it made sense if she followed her theory about Philip and the book-club copies. *Oh, Kalea, what have you gotten yourself involved with?* "Thanks, Millie." Addie tapped the desktop. "You've been a big help." She wheeled around and froze. "Marc, what are you doing here?"

"I was just on my way out and saw your car."

"I see. So . . ." Addie glanced behind him, expecting to see Ryley lurking in the background. "What brings you to the Grey Gull tonight? Business or pleasure?"

"Most likely the same thing that brings you here."

"And what's that?"

"If you're looking for your cousin, it appears she's gone. We just checked her room."

"I see. Millie just told me that when housekeeping went in this morning, it looked like she'd packed up and left."

"That's what it looks like. Any idea where she was heading?"

"No, but I have a suspicion that when you find Robert Peters, he might know something."

"What makes you say that?"

"He took an . . . How should I say this? An unnatural liking to her yesterday, and now she's disappeared, and there's no sign of him, either. You put two and two together. To be honest, I'm getting worried that he—"

"Relax, we found him."

"Where?"

"He was upstairs sleeping in one of the bedrooms."

"And Kalea wasn't with him?"

Marc shook his head. "Millie gave me her license plate number from the registration form, and I've issued an APB on her and her car."

"Kalea did mention to me she had a boyfriend. Maybe that's a lead, too?"

"What's his name?"

"Nolan."

"Nolan what?"

"She didn't say, but she did tell me he was the senior partner in his law firm."

"Thanks, I'll get somebody to check it out."

"What about Charlotte's laptop?" Addie cleared her throat in the hope it would distract from her change of subject. "Did Robert have it?"

"Nope." Marc eyed her warily. "He said last time he saw it, Charlotte was using it in the library. Apparently, she told him to go get some sleep because she wanted him to do the morning setup, but she stayed in the library to finish up some paperwork."

"Then she must have bolted the door after he left?"

"It looks that way." Marc's jaw tightened. "Look, Addie, I can't talk to you any more than I have about the case, but I do need to talk to you about this morning." He glanced at Millie, who was on the phone, and motioned with his head toward the window, his voice dropping. "I think I owe you an apology."

"You think? You were downright rude and mean. You always did have a tendency to overreact when it came to you and me, but your behavior this morning was unbelievable."

"Yes, it was," he said, clutching the brim of his cap. "I admit it. But I wasn't prepared to walk into a crime scene and find you there, and I didn't know how to handle it. It definitely isn't the way I had planned on seeing you for the first time since . . ."

"I know. It didn't turn out to be exactly the greeting or conversation I thought we'd have either when you got back."

He raked his hand through his hair. "I really don't know what to say except I'm sorry for the way I behaved, and I'm sorry you had to find out about Ryley the way you did."

"As far as Ryley is concerned . . ." Addie bit the inside of her cheek to keep her tongue from unleashing what she was really feeling toward the agent.

"What about her?"

"Nothing." She dropped her gaze, entwining her fingers. "I think we both have to admit it all turned out the way it was supposed to, for both of us."

"I guess yes, in the end it did. But it took a while for me to see it, I have to admit."

"I'm sorry, Marc. I never meant to hurt you that night."

"I know you didn't." His expression softened. "It's just that after Christmas I thought we finally were both on the same page. For the first time since we'd met. You had changed and seemed ready to move forward. We had two wonderful months together, and I saw a future I didn't want to end. But when I pulled that ring out of my pocket and saw the look on your face, it told me nothing had changed. I realized that in all the time we'd known each other, we've *never* been on the same page at the same time. Heck, when I look back now, I don't even think we were ever even reading the same book."

"But I didn't reject you. I just told you I needed more time."

"Yeah, because Simon was still hanging around."

"He and I were—*are* friends, Marc."

"Pretty close now, too, from what I heard. As soon as I told you we both needed time to figure out what we really wanted and I left, the only reports I got back were about Addie and Simon. Addie and Simon went here. Addie and Simon did this, Addie and Simon over and over. I guess it didn't take you long to figure out what you really wanted, and that didn't include a future with me. I went from being hurt and numb to finally accepting it and moved on . . . at least until I saw you again this morning. And then the anger I had fought against all those months bubbled to the surface."

"Marc?"

Addie jerked and darted a look at the doorway. "Hello, Agent Brookes."

She nodded curtly at Addie and quizzed Marc with a raised brow. "Is everything okay?"

"Yes." Marc straightened his shoulders. "Addie, if you hear anything from your cousin, please call the station and let us know. We have a few questions for her." He tipped his hat at her and walked toward Ryley, gesturing with his head to the main door.

"What was that all about?" Ryley leaned into him, lowering her voice.

"We're both looking for her cousin." Marc swung around. "Addie, you don't by any chance have a photo of Kalea, do you?"

"Yeah, on my phone."

"Can I see it?"

"Sure." Addie dug around her bag. "Oops, Serena must still have it."

"Where is she?"

"In the dining room. I'll go get it from her."

"No, just text it to me later, that's fine."

"*Actually* . . ." Ryley laid a predatory claw on Marc's arm. "Why don't you send it to me?" A distinct undertone of venom wove through the silky-smooth tone. She thrust her business card into Addie's hand. "I can run it through our database and see if it can locate her. You know, the last place she used a credit card or something."

Marc gave Ryley a side glance. "Do you think that's a good idea, considering?"

"Maybe you're right."

"Considering what?" Addie's gaze flitted from Marc to Ryley. The protective way he looked at Ryley made Addie realize it had nothing to do with the fact that she was still a suspect, but was a reference to something else.

"Nothing," Marc said. "Just send it to *me* later." He placed his hand on the small of Ryley's back and ushered her through the main door. "What were you thinking with that comment about running the information through the FBI computer?" He lowered his voice. "Do you even have access right now?"

"I wasn't thinking. It's just an old habit. I've never been in this situation before."

"If your field supervisor got wind of you using FBI resources while you're on mandatory—" The door closed.

Mandatory what? Considering what? Addie needed to hear more. She hurried into the warm summer evening, not certain how she would explain to Marc why she was chasing after them. It didn't matter. His cruiser was already pulling away from the curb.

Chapter 13

Addie scanned the dining room. Bruce told her he'd seated Serena by the wall of windows overlooking the harbor, but there was no sign of her redheaded friend. Then she spotted her in the corner by the server's coffee station locked in a hug with Zach. Her eyes fought the sting of tears. What she wouldn't give to have Simon's arms around her right now. It had been one of those days when just feeling the beat of his heart in rhythm with hers would have fixed everything. Even if only temporary. She swiped a budding tear from her eye.

"Yoo-hoo, Addie, over here."

She glanced in the direction the voice had come from and took a detour around a table of six to get to the grinning faces of Maggie Hollingsworth, a member of the book club, her mother, and a man Addie didn't know. "Hi, Maggie, it's nice to see you." Addie nodded her greeting. "And Vera." She paused when her gaze fell on the striking silver-haired gentleman seated with them.

"Addie"—Maggie gestured toward the man—"this is Art Dunbar. He's one of my real-estate agents at Hollingsworth Realty."

"Nice to meet you, Art." Addie extended her hand. "I'm sorry, you didn't look familiar. I don't think I've seen any of your signs around town."

"You will soon." Art returned her gesture with a firm shake.

"Are you new to the business, then?"

"Heavens no!" Vera, an equally as graying-haired woman, piped in. "Arty's been a Realtor for years."

"Don't mind my mother." Maggie slid a side-glare at Vera and flicked a wave of bleach-blond coiffured hair over her shoulder. "Art is relatively new to Greyborne Harbor, but he was a Realtor for years in Seattle."

Addie's skin tingled at the tension between mother and daughter. On the other hand, she thought some mothers and daughters did often rub each other the wrong way. Not having had much to do with either woman outside of the book club, maybe this was normal for them. "Well, it's nice to have met you, Art, and welcome to Greyborne Harbor. I hope you come to love this town as much as I have."

"Oh, love won't be an issue." He reached his arm around Vera's shoulders and gave her a light squeeze.

"Please, both of you control yourselves," Maggie snapped, and glanced around at the tables surrounding them. "We're in public," she hissed. "I don't need the whole town seeing one of my agents carrying on with my *mother* in a restaurant of all places."

"Really!" Vera gave an exaggerated eye roll. "Is that all you care about? What the people in this town think of the *Queen of Real Estate*?" Vera picked up her wineglass and swigged a large swallow. "Art, maybe it was a mistake to bring you back to Greyborne Harbor with me."

"Nonsense, my dear." He patted Vera's hand. "These last eight months here with you have been the happiest of my life."

"Oh, Arty," Vera cooed and leaned her head on his shoulder.

"Mother, stop!"

Addie took that as her cue to leave, voiced her pleasure at seeing them all, and made her way to her own table, reaching it just as Serena sat down. "I need a drink—now." Addie flopped into her chair and scanned the room for Zach to take her order.

Serena's big, round, brown eyes locked on hers.

"What?"

"Are you okay? Did something happen since I last saw you, about twenty minutes ago?"

"Yeah." Addie dropped her bag on the empty chair beside her. "The whole darn world's gone crazy, that's what's happened."

Serena barked out a laugh that mimicked a sick seal. The foursome at the table behind them turned in unison to look at her. Serena smiled at them and they, obviously uncomfortable with her acknowledgment, returned to their meals. She turned her freckled face back to Addie. "And you've just come to this realization?"

Addie glanced at the two women, who still appeared to be sniping at each other. "You know," she said, turning back to Serena, "I never had my mother growing up, but I do hope that if I had, we wouldn't have ended up like those two."

"If you're talking about Maggie and Vera, they've always been like that. Vera is practical and down to earth, and Maggie . . . well, she's always been full of herself and worried more about keeping up appearances than anything else."

"I just feel sorry for that poor man with them."

"Art?"

"You know him? I've never seen him before."

"Yeah, he works for Maggie."

"I got that part from my brief introduction." Addie scanned her menu. "How come he doesn't have any signs around town?"

"Gloria told me at the last book-club meeting that he had to write his state exams. I guess he was some hotshot Realtor out west, but each state has their own licensing requirements or something to that affect." She waved her hand in a fluttering motion. "I don't know. I wasn't really paying attention to what Gloria was saying because . . . I really didn't care." She flipped her menu up, chuckling.

"No, neither do I. It's just the animosity between those two really got to me, especially after having just dealt with Marc and Ryley."

Serena pushed down the top of Addie's menu. "What? Where did this happen? Are they tailing us now?"

"Don't be silly." Addie lifted her menu back up. "Marc was checking out the lead I gave them about Kalea staying here, and we happened to run into each other, that's all."

Serena pressed Addie's menu back down and locked eyes with her. "Are you sure that's all?"

"Actually . . ."

"I knew it. What happened? What did Miss Special Agent say to put you in this world's-gone-crazy mood?"

"That's just it. She didn't say much to me, other than openly displaying her displeasure with Marc and I speaking to each other. It's the whispered conversation that I managed to overhear most of as I tailed them out the door." Addie leaned over the table and told her what she'd heard.

"And that's it? You have no idea what followed 'mandatory'?"

"It could mean a lot of different things. Like mandatory leave, mandatory—"

"Assignment." Serena sat back. "But you're right. It's a weird thing for him to say."

"I know, and it makes my conspiracy-theory mind run wild with all the options."

Serena snapped her menu. "The world hasn't gone crazy tonight—you have." She held it up, covering her face to hide a giggle she couldn't suppress.

Addie pulled Serena's menu down and made a googly-eyed face at her, then pushed it back up to the sound of a hearty laugh from behind her friend's shield.

"Let's order. I still need that drink and I'm starving," Addie laid her menu on the table as she searched for Zach.

It didn't take long for their drinks and entrées to arrive and feeling much better than she had earlier, Addie pushed her plate away and moaned. "Now I need to sleep. Hopefully, when I wake up this nightmare will all be over."

"When you ran into Marc, did he say anything about where the case against you is at?"

"No." Addie wiped her mouth and dropped her napkin on the table. "The days of him telling me anything in relation to a case are long gone, I'm afraid."

"You mean all those times he protested about sharing details of a case with you, but then did it anyway?"

"You know as well as I do he only kept me in the

loop when it was clear that if he didn't, I was going to investigate on my own. So by sharing some of the information with me, he thought I'd keep my nose out of police business."

"Yeah, right." Serena wiggled her eyebrows. "But he still knows you. And in spite of how your relationship has changed, he also knows full well that you're going to do some sleuthing on your own now, too. So that hasn't changed, has it?"

"No," Addie said, chuckling, "that hasn't changed, especially when Ryley is trying to make me appear to be the number-one suspect of the day. I just have to figure out who else to add to that list."

"Do you have any names in mind?"

"A few, but I'd have to really take a look at them and see if it adds up. I mean, Simon says that everything indicates that Charlotte's death was the result of natural causes, which has everyone—well, except Ryley and her ridiculous theory about me—believing her sudden death and the missing books aren't related, that it's a coincidence but—"

"You're not convinced?"

"No, I'm not. One thing my father always used to say about a criminal investigation was, 'There is no such thing as coincidences. Everything is related, somehow. You just have to find the missing piece of the puzzle to make the whole picture come into focus.'"

"Does that mean," Serena said as she finished off her wine, "that we're going back to your shop to pull out that blackboard of yours?"

"Not tonight." Addie rubbed her hands over her face. "I'm exhausted. Let's just go home and call it a day."

"Sounds good to me." Serena waved Zach over for the bill.

When he placed it on the table, Addie scooped it up. "I'll get this tonight."

"If that's the case, then I'll leave the tip." Serena gave Zach a saucy wink, crumpled up a bill, and closed his fingers around it.

He glanced at the bill and let out a husky laugh. "Are you trying to buy me, Miss?"

Serena batted her lashes. "Not in the least. I'm just wondering if you could . . ."

"I could what?" Zach leaned forward, hanging on her every word.

"Stop and pick up some milk before you come home."

Zach playfully swatted Serena's behind with a napkin from the table as she darted out of the line of fire.

All the way out the door, Addie stifled her laughter, not wanting to create a scene. She loved watching her friend's playful antics. It reminded her of the silly banter she and Simon often exchanged. She had made the right choice for her, and she couldn't wait to get home to call him. At least hearing his voice today would help lift some of the weight off her day.

When Addie turned down her driveway, she squealed at the sight of the silver Tesla parked by her front door.

"It looks like you're going to get that hug you needed so badly today after all." Serena nudged Addie with her elbow.

Addie beamed as she parked the car, waved good night to Serena and dashed up the front steps to her porch. She flung the door open and stepped into waiting arms that swept her off her feet. Simon planted a tender kiss on her lips and rested his forehead against hers. "Welcome home."

She snuggled her head into his arm as he walked her down the hallway to the kitchen. If she were a cat, she would have purred. This is exactly where she had wanted to be all evening. When he waved his hand over the chocolate fondue he'd arranged on the island for them, she couldn't suppress the tiny squeal that snuck out. "I thought you might need some comfort food after your day." His eyes glistened as he popped a chocolate-dipped strawberry into her mouth. "So please don't tell me you've already had dessert."

"No, I saved the best for last." She kissed his cheek and nestled her head against his shoulder. "Thank you," she whispered. "I knew there was a reason I gave you that key last year and said come over whenever you want to use my gourmet kitchen."

"If I didn't use it, you'd have to knock the cobwebs out of the kettle just to boil water."

"Hey, I cook, too."

"When?"

She paused.

"See? You can't even remember the last time you actually used this kitchen, can you?"

She grinned her concession. How on earth, after all she had been through these last couple of years, had she managed to get so lucky in finding Simon?

She remembered her feeling of despair when Marc abruptly left town and Serena, her go-to person, had her free time consumed by Zach. It was only natural that she and Simon gravitated toward each other. In the past, he'd been a good friend to her, and they had a lot of fun together. Being with him these last few months made her realize that Simon was the whole package. She eyed the feast of cut fruit and decadent melted chocolate, her mouth watering—for more than just the lake of chocolate. It was little things like this that he managed to pull off every day that reminded her how different he was from anyone else she dated previously. He didn't just make her feel safe, he nurtured her, and made her feel more loved than she could ever have thought possible.

"I don't know where to begin." Her gaze landed on Simon's lips.

"Here." He handed her a small fondue fork and plate. "Just dig in."

Addie stabbed her fork into a juicy chunk of pineapple.

A bang on the door caused them both to jump.

"I'll get it." Simon patted his chest as if he were having heart palpitations. "I'll get rid of whoever it is, so we can gorge ourselves in peace on doctor-prescribed melted chocolate."

She could hear him chuckling all the way to the front door. She dipped the pineapple chunk into the chocolate and popped it into her mouth, soon followed by a piece of strawberry and then a large section of orange. By the time Simon returned, her mouth was stuffed, and warm chocolate oozed from the corner of her lips. But when she looked at him, she swallowed hard. "What is it? What's wrong?"

She glanced over his shoulder, her chest tightening. "Marc? Jerry?" The two somber-faced officers entered the kitchen. "What brings you by?" Addie's voice cracked. "Would you like some fondue?"

"They're not here on a social visit." Simon's voice was barely audible.

She searched each of the men's faces. Her heart tumbled to her toes.

Marc stepped forward. "Miss Greyborne, I need to inform you that I have a warrant for your arrest for suspicion of committing grand larceny."

A cold hand squeezed Addie's chest, and she couldn't get enough air to speak. She saw more than heard his monotone voice droning on, fulfilling the requirements of his duties.

"You have the right to remain silent. Anything you say can and will be used against you in a court of law. You have a right to an attorney . . ." The remainder of Marc's words were lost in a blur as Jerry walked toward her, asked her to turn around, and snapped the cold steel handcuffs around her wrists.

Chapter 14

Addie shivered and clutched the rough wool blanket tighter around her shoulders and wiggled her frozen toes. Sandals were great summer footwear unless sitting in a police station's basement interrogation room. She silently cursed the architect or engineer who had designed this small space with an air-conditioning vent that blasted cold air directly down from the ceiling. The desk sergeant, Carolyn, Simon's sister and her friend, thankfully had provided Addie with this blanket or the rest of her would have been as numb as her toes were right now.

She cupped her icy hands together and blew into them, then stopped. She imagined she already looked a frightful sight, and it probably wouldn't be a good idea to show up in front of a judge with black smudges across her face.

After taking her fingerprints, Carolyn had offered her some wet wipes. Unfortunately, the booking process was run like a well-oiled machine, and Addie was asked to stand and have her mug shot taken almost immediately, giving her no time to remove the ink stains. As she examined her fingertips now, she wondered if the taint of the night would ever wash off her.

She puffed out a deep breath and studied her prison walls—at least that's how it felt. It was nearly an hour since she'd been taken from a holding cell, led in here, and told to take a seat at the small table, with the promise that someone would be with her shortly. *Yeah, right.* She glared at the large mirror on the opposite wall. Addie had seen her fair share of police dramas and was aware that mirror wasn't there for aesthetic purposes. Someone was on the other side watching her every move, and if she was a betting woman, she would have placed her money on it being none other than Special Agent Ryley Brookes.

Addie stared unblinkingly at the mirror, a slight curl winking at the corner of her upper lip. As if on cue, the door flew open and Agent Brookes, carrying a black briefcase, and Marc, with some papers tucked under his arm, entered. Neither of them said a word as they took their seats in the two chairs across from Addie. Marc set a beige file folder on the table. Without looking up at her, Marc asked if she was certain she didn't want her lawyer present.

Addie shifted on her hard wooden chair and shook her head.

"I'm sorry," Brookes said, "you'll have to verbally answer the question."

"Yes," Addie sighed, "I waive the right to have a lawyer present at this time." She leaned her elbow on the table and glared at Marc. "You know as well as I do that I have done nothing wrong, and this whole thing is ridiculous."

Marc cocked his eyebrow. He didn't speak. He just stared at her. This was a bad sign.

"Can you account for your whereabouts on Wednesday evening?" Brookes asked, the line of her mouth set firm.

"I was at home."

"Can anyone verify that?"

Addie's lips twitched. She had seen this part too often in the movies. The suspect lives alone. No one can corroborate the fact that she was home as sworn, and that's it. No alibi for the time in question. Addie's heart knocked against her ribs as panic skittered up her spine. Then she remembered. "Serena. Yes, Serena came over Wednesday evening."

Stifling silence filled the room as Agent Brookes jotted something down on the notepad in front of her, her brow creased. "What time did she arrive, and what time did she leave your place of residence?"

Addie struggled to remember. Keeping track of these kinds of trivial details wasn't something she ever thought she'd have to recall to prove she was innocent in a crime. Who did anyway besides maybe someone who was planning to commit a crime? Certainly not the average citizen. Addie drummed her fingers on the table as she replayed that evening over in her mind. She recalled that she hadn't been home long, so Serena must have made her entrance around . . .

"Six thirty," Addie blurted out, "and then she was there for roughly an hour, so she left about seven thirty."

"And after that?" Agent Brookes tapped her pen on her notepad.

Addie shook her head.

"Simon wasn't there?" Marc's voice sounded strangled. Its accusatory edge seemed to be at odds with his professional-cop demeanor. It had echoes of the jealousy present last year when he and Simon had both vied for her affection. Normally, she would have tried to smooth his ruffled feathers, but as she and Marc were strangers now, not even friends, she would let him suffer.

Agent Brookes's jaw clenched as she wrote something on the paper.

"No." Addie's lip quivered. "He was working."

An uneasy silence spilled back over the room.

"He did call later to say good night, though." Addie made a point of watching Marc's reaction to that. His cop face cracked, but only a tiny sliver of the man she used to know peeked through.

"On your cell phone or landline?" Ryley cocked her brow without looking up from her notes, her non-actions clearly indicating that she chose to ignore the rising tension between Addie and Marc.

"I have a cell phone only." Addie's voice wavered.

"So, in reality," Agent Brookes said, leaning toward her, "you could have been anywhere when that call came through, right?"

"I suppose. Yes, but I wasn't. I was at home." Addie racked her brain. There must be some way she could prove she was at home and not lurking around an old house that had given her the creeps. "I was doing some research on my laptop." She gave a shaky smile. "You can check it for IP addresses, my search history, and the times I logged in and out. That should prove I was at home, too!"

"Unfortunately for you, Miss Greyborne"—Ryley's eyes flashed and narrowed to tiny slits—"laptops, like cell phones, are portable, and it could have been accessed from anywhere."

"What are you thinking? That I sat out on the road in the middle of the night in front of one of the creepiest houses in town and researched the value of two books that aren't even missing from the library? But then I broke in so I could steal a set of *other* books?" Addie swallowed, but it was no use. Her mouth had gone too dry to dislodge the lump lodged in her throat.

Marc flipped open the file folder in front of him. Without a word, he pulled out a photo the investigation team had taken of the window latch in the library. Then slapped a photo of a fingerprint on top of it. This was repeated with a series of other pictures taken in the library of the center table, the desk, and the fireplace hearth. Each one had a corresponding photo of fingerprints. The last picture he tossed down on the pile showed notched markings around the exterior of the bottom window sash.

Ryley reached down beside her chair and retrieved a small plastic evidence bag from her black case and pushed it across the table. "Does this look familiar?"

Addie swallowed and then swallowed again. Nothing seemed to be able to dislodge the lump. "That looks like the tip of an acrylic fingernail."

"You'd be right." Agent Brookes studied Addie's hands. "I'd say it might just be a perfect match to the one that's missing from there." She tapped the tip of her pen on the desk in front of Addie's index finger.

"I know how this appears, but there's an explanation, for all of this," Addie said, waving her hand over the pictures. "First, my nail broke when Kalea and I were moving boxes of books. I thought it had dropped into one of them and wasn't about to go digging around for it. And all these fingerprints? Yes, I was in the room and did try to open the window. I have pictures of Kalea and I fooling around, trying to get it open when the stuffiness in the room started to make us both dizzy."

"Where are the pictures?"

"On my phone."

"Your phone wasn't in your possession when you were brought in, and it's not at your house."

"Wait." Addie glared at Ryley and Marc. "You searched my house, too?"

He nodded. "Standard procedure when an arrest warrant is issued. A search warrant is, too."

"We have your computer, and we'll check out your search history, but where's your phone, Addie?" Ryley pinned her with a glare. "Is there a reason you don't want us to find it? Are you hiding something on there?"

"It's . . ."

Marc leaned forward. "Why are you hesitating in answering the question?"

"I'm not," Addie snapped. "I'm trying to think where it could be, and . . ." She couldn't help but notice the sideways glance between Marc and Ryley. "Wait, I remember! Serena had to borrow it last night before dinner because hers was dead. She must still have it. But I can tell you, I did not, nor did Kalea, ever get that window opened."

"How can we be so sure?"

"Because if you go back and look closer, Agent Brookes," Addie said, crossing her arms on the table and leaning forward, "you'll see that it's impossible. The sash is too old and warped. It won't open even with this evidence that you think you have." She pointed to the photo of the damaged exterior window frame. "Someone, not me, has tried to jimmy the window open from the outside."

"How do you explain your broken nail being found outside at the base of the wall under the window?"

Addie wanted to slap the smug look off Ryley's face but held herself back. After all, Brookes was an FBI agent and not just some regular woman who happened to be marking her territory with Marc.

"I can't. But was there any evidence of my footprints in the soil?" Addie's gaze darted from Ryley to Marc. "Remember, it rained earlier that evening, and if I'd been there breaking in as you are suggesting by all this, I would have left some trace outside other than that." Addie stabbed her finger on the evidence bag. "You both surprise me. As trained detectives, you've missed one crucial element here that even a *fiction* writer such as Sir Arthur Conan Doyle employed in the writings of his detective character, Sherlock Homes."

Marc's jaw flinched. "And what might that be, Addie?"

"An acute observation of even the smallest, seemingly unimportant details at a crime scene can hold the key to unraveling the entire mystery, preventing the investigator from being misdirected by following other irrelevant or red-herring clues meant solely to take the investigation in the wrong direction."

"What are you talking about?" Marc's strangled voice rumbled in her ears. Obviously he was losing patience with her.

"It's elementary reasoning and deduction. Since none of your photos show a woman's size-eight footprints outside the window, it stands to reason that the fingernail was planted at the scene by someone who, not wanting to muddy their own shoes, stood on the gravel path running beside the house and tossed the nail below the window."

Ryley stabbed her finger on a shot of the damaged exterior of the window frame. "It would be difficult, if not impossible, for the perpetrator to pry the window open from the footpath as depicted in these."

"Very true, *Detective.*" Addie stressed her final word

as she thumbed through the photos of the exterior scene. "However, if you'll notice there are *no* footprints of any size or shape beneath the library window." She sat back, crossing her arms over her heaving chest. "Curious, don't you think?"

Ryley's eyes held steadfast on Addie's. "And what is to say that you didn't go to great lengths to sweep away the tracks?"

"Because, there is one important detail missing from these photos. There is no indication that a branch or other object was used to rake over the wet soil to hide footprints. Besides . . ." Addie pushed her chair back, raised her leg, and thumped her left foot on the tabletop. "Do you see any sign of embedded soil in the tread of my sandal?"

"How are we to know those are the shoes you wore Wednesday evening?"

Addie dropped her foot to the floor with a thud and met Ryley's gaze with one equally as penetrating. "Then I guess you'll have to test them, plus every other pair of shoes I have. Here." She kicked off her sandals and shoved them under the table with her foot toward the detectives. She gave Marc a saucy grin. "You might also want to examine my pink fluffy slippers since they're what I *was* wearing Wednesday night, and perhaps you should also swab the bottom of my bare feet as they were most likely tucked into my bed at the time of my supposed cat-burgling adventure."

Ryley choked back something between a snort and a gasp.

Marc's lips slightly twisted at the corners as though he was willing himself not to laugh. "Just the shoes are fine." The tips of his ears turned red as he bent over and scooped up her shoes into an evidence bag.

"But I think the most important piece of evidence

you have regarding the window frame is this particular shot." Addie pulled a photo from the pile in front of her. "Notice the extensive weathering around the wood scratches and indentations in the frame. None of these marks were made recently. Someone just took advantage of them being there and decided to plant my nail at the scene to make you think the two were recent and connected." A sense of victory swept through her. "A perfect example of a red-herring clue meant to misdirect you."

Ryley reached into her black case. "Then how do you explain your fingerprints all over this?" She shoved another evidence bag across the table.

"That's the pry bar Brian used to open the library door."

"Correct, and one he later reported as missing from his tool bag, and the same one we found in the bushes with your fingerprints all over it."

"My prints are on it because he asked me to get it from his tool bag, then he had me hold it while he forced the study door open. You can ask Blake Edwards and half his staff. They were standing right there."

"Did you have reason to go into his . . ." Ryley glanced down at her notepad ". . . tool bag later in the day?"

"No, I never saw him again after that."

"So what you're saying is that all this evidence is wrong. Yes?"

"That's exactly what I'm saying. Someone is trying to make it look like I did it. Someone is setting me up."

There was a knock on the door. Marc opened it and came back with Addie's phone in his hand. Addie glanced at the mirror. Whoever was on the other side of the glass just provided her with the proof she needed to argue at least one of their allegations against her. *Wait a second.* Her phone had appeared rather quickly from the time they asked her about it.

"Did one of your officers already go to Serena's house and get that?"

"No, she's upstairs in the waiting room."

"Oh, that's nice and convenient for you." Addie grinned at whoever it was behind the glass listening.

Marc turned the phone screen toward Addie. "Here, punch in your password, please." He pulled it away when she reached for it. "I'll hold it. You just enter your code."

Addie pressed the digits and sat back, crossing her arms over her chest.

Marc and Ryley huddled head-to-head as they scrolled through her photos. "And you have no idea where Kalea is now?" Marc looked up at her.

Addie shook her head.

Ryley took the phone out of Marc's hand and studied the pictures. "I can see now why none of Kalea's fingerprints were found inside the library around the window."

"Why's that?"

"Because," Ryley flashed the screen in Addie's direction, "in all these pictures she's wearing white gloves."

"Yeah," Addie said, "those are customary to wear when handling vintage books, finger oil on the pages and stuff."

"So why aren't you wearing them?"

"I had been taking my shift doing the data entry on the computer. Kalea was reading off the information about the books to me: publisher date, edition, things like that. We took turns doing the research because there was only one computer." Addie shrugged. "I really couldn't have typed with them on. Plus, it gave me a better grip on the window latch when I was struggling with it."

"But Kalea didn't follow your lead and take hers off when she tried, like in this photo?" Agent Brookes showed Addie the photo where Kalea was lying prone on the window seat, feigning death with her attempt to force the window open.

Addie smiled at the memory, and then her face stiffened. She remembered the conversation her and her cousin had about the gloves. When Addie suggested her cousin take her gloves off so she could get a better hold on the small latch, Kalea changed the subject, and that's when the silliest photo was taken with her trying to open the window with her foot. Then another memory of the day flashed into Addie's mind. When they were leaving, Kalea set her handbag on the table, took everything out looking for her cell phone, and then repacked it. Had she also slipped in the Beeton's first edition of *A Study in Scarlet*? *Was Kalea setting me up for the theft of the books all day?*

"Are you okay?" For the first time since her arrest, Marc's face showed signs of concern for her.

She nodded. "I was just thinking about how silly we were behaving. It felt like the walls were closing in on us, and I guess we just needed to relieve some of the tension."

There was a tap on the glass. Marc glanced questioningly at Ryley and left the room. A moment later, there was another rap. Ryley remained staunch, but the slight reddening on her neck gave away the fact that even she thought this interruption was unusual during an interrogation. Without a word, she gathered up the folder, Addie's phone, and evidence bags from the table and exited.

An uncomfortable feeling nestled in Addie's gut as

a headache snaked up the back of her neck and made its home at the base of her skull. Probably a common side effect of spending nearly twelve hours locked in windowless rooms. The only way she did know exactly how much time had passed was because she'd managed to catch a glimpse of the time on her cell phone when she had entered her password. Twelve hours that felt more like eternity. This must be what purgatory was like. She moaned and rested her forehead on the cool tabletop.

The door flew open and Addie jerked upright. "You're free to go." Marc shoved her phone across the table toward her.

"What do you mean?"

"I mean the charges against you are pending right now."

She grabbed her phone and stood up. "And you're done with this?"

"Yes, we have all the pertinent information from it that we needed."

Addie glanced over Marc's shoulder. "Does your sidekick know I'm being released?"

"Yes, Agent Brookes is fully aware."

"Really?" Addie straightened her shoulders as a sense of vindication shored up her throbbing back. "So, if I have this right, you're not charging me?"

"Not at this time." Marc lowered his gaze. "It's a pending charge. The DA said when he stopped the questioning that he'd like to see more evidence before he can make a decision on the charges. He mentioned"— Marc's jaw tightened—"that you had pointed out a couple of holes in the investigation. Therefore, he wants us to take another look before he decides to file charges or not."

"You mean Jeff Wilson, the DA, is here?"

"Yeah." His eyes held a suggestion of a twinkle. "As you were acutely aware throughout the course of the interrogation, there was someone else watching from behind that glass."

"But I thought his office was in Salem?"

"It is, but when I called last night to have the arrest warrant issued, I guess he took a special interest in learning firsthand how strong of a case we had against his star contract book expert."

"He drove here to witness my interrogation?"

"Yup."

"Well, I'd like to thank him for saving me the humiliation of having to appear in court this morning for a bail hearing."

"I'm afraid he's gone now. He had to be in court for a nine a.m. hearing."

"Oh, I was hoping I'd have the chance to talk to him."

"He wouldn't speak to you now anyway, Addie. Just so you know, it's not over yet. Ryley took the investigation team back to the house. If she finds signs of those footprints or an attempt to cover them up, a point you clearly made was missing from our case, or anything else tying you to the book thefts, well, we'll have no choice but to pick you up again."

Addie tilted her chin up. "Can I have my computer back now, too?"

"We aren't done with it yet."

She opened her mouth to protest, but knew by the look in his eyes it would be no use. "Fine, then. Am I free to go *now*?" Her voice had an edge to it, but she didn't care.

He opened the door and stood back, allowing her to pass. She heard nothing more after that and raced barefoot down the hall, up the back stairs, and burst through the door behind the information desk. Jerry jumped up, his hand on his holster.

"Relax, Jerry," Marc said from the doorway, "she's been released. She's not escaping."

Jerry sat back in his chair as Serena jumped up from hers in the waiting room. "Oh, Addie, you look—"

"Don't say it." Addie raised her hand as she made her way around the desk. "Please, just get me out of here so I can go home and burn these clothes."

"Can I have that blouse? I always did like the tiny pink and white polka dots."

"It would clash with your hair."

Serena's gaze halted at Addie's bare feet. "Where are your shoes?"

"It's a long story. I'll tell you on the drive home."

"Okay, and then I'm staying until you're safely tucked into bed."

"I can't go to bed, as much as I'd like to. I have to have a shower and then get to my shop. I can't even think about leaving Paige on her own again, there's too much to do."

"Then I'll wait for you and drive you. There's no way you should be driving after a night without sleep."

"Okay, sure, I'm too tired to argue. Thanks."

"But it'll cost you." Serena's eyes danced with an impish sparkle.

"What?"

"That blouse." She grinned as she opened the door.

Chapter 15

Addie's fingers tightened around her steaming cup of elixir. She closed her eyes, savoring the full-bodied aroma that removed the last tainted residue of the night. It was one thing to shower and put on fresh clothes, but her soul also needed to be refreshed. She sipped long and slow, allowing the nutty blend to settle on her tongue and then glide like warm silk down the back of her throat. This would no doubt go down in her memory as the best cup of coffee she'd ever had. Maybe. She set the cup down on the counter. But it definitely beat the police station swill Marc had served her at three in the morning.

"Addie?"

Addie swung around on the counter stool and met Paige's questioning gaze.

"Sorry to interrupt." Paige winced. "I know how much you need that coffee right now, but . . ." She leaned her blond, curly head toward Addie, dropping her voice. "Dapper Dan wants to talk to you."

"Who?"

"I don't know what his real name is. That's just what I call him. I see him every morning when I take the sandwich board out to the sidewalk. I think he works up on Main Street because it's the same time every day, and he always wears his white hat and carries a cane umbrella."

Addie chuckled. "I guess I'm off to see Dapper Dan, then." From her vantage point, all she could see was a woman perusing the sale rack by the front door. "Where is he?"

"He's over by the History and Mystery sections."

"I should have known. Where else would a suave gentleman be found?" Addie primped her hair and smiled at the woman as she sidestepped around her and made her way to the wall of shelves on the far side of the shop. "Art? How nice to see you again?" She held out her hand in greeting.

"Good morning." He closed the book he'd been examining and glanced at his gold wristwatch. "Or should I say almost good afternoon?" he said with a crooked grin.

"Yes." Addie rubbed her hand over her middle. "And my stomach tells me it must almost be lunchtime."

"That's exactly where I was headed when I decided that you might just be the one person in town who can help me."

"Oh?"

He gestured with the book in his hand. "I understand from Maggie and Vera that you are the expert on this local ghost legend book."

She looked at the copy of *The Ghosts and Mysteries of Greyborne Harbor* and shook her head. "I would never call myself an expert, but I have read it in depth. Why?"

"I'm not sure if you're aware"—he tucked the book

under his arm as he pulled a business card from his inside jacket pocket—"but I am the listing agent for Hill Road House."

"No, I wasn't." She turned the card over, glanced at it. "Congratulations?"

His laugh rumbled in his chest. "Some might not think I should be excited by it, but since it's my first listing in town, I have to make the best of it. Besides, I'm really under the gun with it to prove myself worthy to Maggie."

"Really?"

"Yes, she only hired me because Vera insisted, and then she had to wait until I took the Massachusetts real-estate course and then pass my state licensing. She kept me on as an office employee even when I couldn't do anything for her but write advertising copy and fetch coffee."

"I'm really confused now. I thought you were already a real-estate agent—or did I misunderstand last night?"

"I am, but each state requires agents to be licensed in their region regardless of the years' experience I had in Seattle. It didn't count for anything out here."

"I vaguely remember hearing something about all that. But how can I help you today?"

"You see, in this industry it's all about the money." He rubbed his thumb and forefinger together. "And so far, I haven't brought any into the agency. I feel like this listing is a test, not only of my sales abilities but also to prove to Maggie that I'm worthy of dating her mother."

"How would it be a test?"

He leaned in closer. "Because none of the other agents in the office would take the listing . . . It's considered a tough sell, and Maggie . . . well, let's just say she made it clear if I didn't she might not have a position open for me much longer."

"I see." Addie rolled her bottom lip between her teeth. "What does this book have to do with any of this?"

"Because, my dear"—he waved the book in the air—"I believe I've hit on the perfect sales campaign, and *this* book, and a few of these others about local hauntings and pirate legends, will help me sell a house that is rumored to be haunted."

Addie's brows knit together. "But isn't that something you'd want to *downplay*?"

"Not when the house's reputation has spread up and down the eastern seaboard. I can't get ahead of it, so my thought is to exploit it for all it's worth."

"That's an interesting sales tactic."

"So far, it's working." A tiny smile touched the corners of his lips. "I have two potential buyers coming to view it later next week."

"And in full disclosure, you did tell them the rumors about the house?"

"*That* is exactly why they are interested in seeing it. Now I just have to make sure the auction house is cleared out by then."

"That shouldn't be a problem. Tomorrow the yard sale starts, which should clear out a lot of the inventory." She rubbed her forehead. "Or did Blake extend everything because of the library being closed down as a crime scene?"

His startled gaze set on hers. "Didn't you know? The private bidders' auction will be moved to his auction house in Boston."

"No, I didn't know. I've been . . . indisposed for a while, I guess." Her skin crawled at the thought of her night at the police station. "I guess I'm out of touch."

"Yeah, and from what I heard, there were a lot of irate bidders who came strictly for the private auction, including that cruise ship that made a special port of call to be here. I heard that a few of them did stay on for the public auction today and are planning to attend the yard sale tomorrow. I guess they hope that some of what should have been sold at Thursday's private bidders' sale will find its way to the tables." He raked his fingers through his hair, causing silver tufts to stick up. "It's only that it looks like, with all the commotion of that poor woman's death and those missing books, that the turnout for any of the sales hasn't been what they anticipated, and sales have been low. I heard there was still a lot of stuff to pack up and ship to Boston."

"Isn't it better to have some furniture in the house like all those staging shows on television say?"

"Normally, yes, but in this case, with what I'm trying to sell, I was hoping the house would be empty for viewing. It would help prospective buyers really *feel* the creepiness of that big old empty house as I relay the tales about the previous deaths." His lips twitched. "Although, I guess now there's one more mysterious death to add to that story."

"And that's why you're so interested in that book? Hill Road House isn't mentioned in it."

His face lit up with a smile that reached his eyes. "I understand that from Maggie, but I'm selling the whole Greyborne Harbor region, not just the house, and one of my buyers is thinking of capitalizing on the rumors around town and turning the estate into a tourist attraction. Especially now since the cruise line will be stopping here every week. He said it would be the perfect location and might give some of the attractions in Salem a run for their money." Art's eyes filled with a hint of a twinkle.

"Okay," Addie chuckled softly, "I have to give you credit for thinking outside the box and making the best of what might prove to be a tough sell. Anything I can do to help, let me know."

"All I need from you is about six more copies of this book." Art handed her *The Ghosts and Mysteries of Greyborne Harbor.* "And about six of each of these." He pulled books from the shelf. "Do you think you can get them in by next week so I can make up some marketing packages?"

Addie took the five books from his hands and glanced at the titles. "I can place the order and hope my distributor has them in stock."

"Can you put a rush on it?" He gave her a boyish grin that seemed to erase twenty years off his sun-weathered face.

"I'll try my best. That's all I can promise."

"That's all I ask." He retrieved a white straw fedora from a bookshelf and placed it on his head, picked up a cane umbrella from its resting place against a bookshelf and hooked it over the crook of his arm, and smiled, turning to leave.

"Are we expecting rain today?"

He glanced back at her. "I really don't know, why?"

Addie pointed to his umbrella.

He glanced down at it and chuckled. "Force of habit, I guess, after living in Seattle. I never leave home without one now. You never know when you'll need it."

"I guess it's best to be prepared for the unexpected."

He grinned and walked out, umbrella twirling in one hand.

She shifted her armful of books and started for the front counter, but came to a full stop. Standing at the counter was none other than Martha. Addie wondered if she'd ever get used to seeing her old nemesis in her shop. Although things between them had been a little less prickly over the past months, Martha Stringer still had a cactus personality. One was never quite certain what to expect when confronted by her, and Addie glanced up the row to see if there was any sign of Paige. Martha's daughter could always be counted on to act as a buffer between them. Her heart sank when she saw her shop assistant busy with a regular customer.

Addie took a deep breath and pasted on the friendliest smile she could muster. "Martha, how nice to see you." Addie set the books on the counter. "I'm surprised to see you in at lunchtime, though. Paige told me that since you started your new select-your-own-toppings sandwich bar, it's become your busiest time of day."

Martha fanned her round, flushed face with her hand. "I needed to get out of that heat for a few minutes. Those ovens have been going since five a.m., and the air-conditioning is on the fritz. I feel like *I'm* the one getting baked in there."

Addie didn't know whether to offer support or laugh, but when Martha erupted into a deep belly laugh, she had her answer.

Paige popped her head around the corner of a bookshelf. "What happened, Mom? Why are you here?"

Martha swatted a tear from her cheek as if it were a mosquito and tried to answer, but it was no use. The heat of her shop had obviously made her dizzy in more ways than one. Addie choked, stifling her laugh, and looked at Paige.

Paige glanced from one to the other. "I guess I missed what the joke was."

Addie pawed at the air, trying to regain her composure under the watchful eye of a customer by the end sales rack. "It's just that your mother is half-baked."

"Yes, what she said." Martha jerked her thumb at Addie and wiped her eyes with the corner of her white apron. "But seriously, Paige, you didn't take a lunch with you this morning when you dashed out of the house for work, and that useless girl I hired, well, she made way too much egg salad, so I brought you both in a few for lunch." She held up a brown paper bag, a flush spreading across her apple cheeks. "That is if you want them?"

"Of course we do." Addie grinned and took the bag. "How did you know my stomach was rebelling against starvation?"

"I guess when I heard what happened last night"— her gaze dropped—"that if Paige had to get in early to open and didn't have time to make anything, then you probably didn't, either, considering . . ." She snapped her mouth closed. "I just hope you like egg salad."

Paige threw her arms around her mother's neck. "Thank you."

Martha's eyes glittered with unshed tears, proving her tough exterior was slowly cracking. The old Martha would have insisted that Paige quit working for a troublemaker who went off and got herself arrested. This new version of Martha was one Addie hoped was here to stay.

"Thank you so much, Martha. You're a real lifesaver," Addie called after her as the doorbells jingled with her departure.

Paige opened the bag. "It's full. There are at least half-a-dozen sandwiches in here."

"Really?" Addie peered into Martha's bakery bag. "Why don't you take a couple and go next door to Serena's and have lunch with Elli. I'll eat mine when you get back."

"Are you sure?"

"Yeah, I'm fine. I'm hungry, but I'll wait." Addie scanned what she could see of the shop. "It's quiet in here for the time being. You go ahead and take your break now because you opened this morning when I was . . . indisposed." She hoped Paige didn't see the hot flush that spread across her cheeks.

But there was no worry about that as Paige pulled three wrapped sandwiches from the bag. "I'll see if Serena can get away now, too, and come have hers with you," she called as she scampered out the door.

Thirty minutes later, Paige burst back in through the door, giggling. Addie looked up from the consignment account book she'd been balancing. "I take it you had a good break."

"Yeah, Elli's such a hoot. She's not all that bright sometimes, but what she doesn't have in smarts, she sure makes up for with her sense of humor." Paige took one look at the books Addie had refilled the stocking cart with. "Where did all these come from?"

"Wendy came in with a couple of boxes. She sold that old house she and her husband had."

"The one over on Juniper?"

"Yeah, and she doesn't have any room in her new apartment for even half her book collection, so she's going to donate them to the store."

"Donate them? Not consign them?"

"She wouldn't hear of making money off them. She just wanted them to find good homes." Addie pivoted around the end of the counter toward Paige. "I think this move is very hard on her. She and her husband had lived in that house for nearly fifty years, and now that he's gone she seems a little lost."

"She was a good friend of Mom's. I'll ask about her and make sure she's doing okay."

"That's a great idea. In the meantime, I told her we couldn't take the books unless she let me give her a store credit, so I've marked that in the consignment book and made a note under her account on the computer. She said she had about eight crates of books to bring in yet, so after she does, I'll enter how much of a credit we'll give her."

"That's nice, but if she's looking to downsize her book collection, won't that defeat her purpose?"

"I'm one step ahead of you, because that's exactly what she said," Addie said with a laugh. "I pointed out our wide selection of children's books and told her the store credit would make her the most popular grandmother *ever* at birthday parties and Christmases if she accepted it."

"Good idea. I bet she jumped at that. I think she has about a dozen grandkids."

"Fourteen at last count. Plus, I also suggested she join the book club. I thought it might be good for her to get together with some of the other members who have lost their husbands, too."

"Yeah, she and Ida might hit it off. I'm pretty sure they know each other, but maybe not socially."

"I was thinking . . ." Addie twisted her fingers together. "Maybe you could ask your mom if she wants to join, too."

"My mother at a book-club meeting? That'll be the day. Unless they're cookbooks, I don't think she's ever read anything else."

"It might be good for her, then, don't you think? Since she's started to come into the store, she does seem to be taking more of an interest in what you're doing. It might be good for both of you to do something like read and review books together."

Paige shrugged and pushed the cart up the aisle. "I'll ask her, but don't hold your breath."

"That's all we can do, is ask," Addie said with a chuckle. "Oh. Wendy said she'd be back later with those other books if she can get her sons to help her with them."

"Sounds good," Paige called back and then stopped. "Did you eat yet?"

"No, I haven't. What was Serena doing when you were in there?"

"She was on the phone with her suppliers trying to get her orders sorted out for next week. I saw her eating her sandwich while she was on hold."

Addie peeked at the wrapped sandwiches in the bakery bag. "There's a couple left in here. Maybe I'll take one over to the hospital and see if Simon's hungry. I haven't seen him since last night." She recalled the haunted look in his eyes when she was led out the door in handcuffs and then ushered into the back of the police cruiser. "Yeah, I better go see him." She called out as she grabbed the sandwich bag, her purse, and headed out the front door through the park to the hospital.

Addie raised her hand to knock on Simon's hospital office door and froze when voices drifted through the partial opening. She edged closer, not averse to eavesdropping. As a matter of fact, this was a skill she had learned to recently embrace.

"What you're saying, Simon, is that there is *no* cause of death?"

"No, Marc, I said there is no indication of poison, trauma, or any other weapon used that would have caused a sudden death in this manner."

"Same thing, isn't it?"

"Not exactly." Simon let out a labored breath. "It only means I have to run more tests before I can determine an actual cause of death and file my report."

"I need to know if I have a murder on my hands or not."

"At this point, I can't say for certain."

"Come on, you have to give me more than that. I have a suspect who is convinced that the death and the book thefts are related, and a special agent who feels that particular suspect is guilty of both crimes."

"I can only tell you, *again,* that I have run the standard toxicology tests, plus I've tested all the herbal samples you brought me, and they all came back negative in the blood and tissue samples. Nothing that I've tested for induced sudden death. Unless you can bring me exactly whatever it is that you think poisoned this woman, it appears to be just as I said: She died as the result of a heart attack."

"Okay, so based on that, you're saying that the two aren't related. The victim just *happened* to die, and the books just *happened* to disappear at the same time?"

"That's what the autopsy evidence indicates at this point, yes. You can tell your *agent* friend"—by the exasperation in Simon's voice, Addie pictured him raking his fingers through his hair—"that she's got it wrong on all accounts. You know as well as I do that *suspect,* as you called her, is no more capable of killing someone or stealing those books than you or I."

"I can *believe* that, but the problem is . . ." Marc's

voice moved closer to the door ". . . I don't *know* that based on the evidence. There's just too much right now to prove that Addie is responsible for the books going missing, and I need to know if there is any evidence to prove that she may have had something to do with Charlotte's death, too. But you're saying the death was natural causes, so that just means that unless something else comes up, the theft charge still looks like it's going to stick."

"Can you hear yourself, Marc? What happened to you? This is Addie. The woman you once loved and proposed marriage to."

Marc cleared his throat. "Unfortunately, I have to follow the evidence."

The door opened, and Addie slid around the corner into a cubby, crouching on the far side of a linen supply cart. She didn't hear Simon's reply to Marc's last remark, but judging by the quick pace and thudding force of Marc's boot steps leading away from her, it wasn't what the chief had wanted to hear. She counted . . . seven . . . eight . . . nine . . . and ten, before she crept around the cart and edged toward Simon's office door. She had to be certain she'd given Marc enough time to round the corner to the elevators at the end of the hallway. When she came fully out of hiding, she stopped short as she caught sight of Simon traipsing off in the same direction.

Chapter 16

Addie needed to process the conversation she'd just heard between Marc and Simon and a brisk walk in the sunshine offered her the perfect means in which to do that. The summer sun beating down on her warmed the coldness of Marc's words that was coursing through her veins. She'd opted to take the longer route to give her the breath of fresh air she desperately needed and cut up the alley off Birch to the back alley to her shop. When she yanked the handle to open the door, she was stopped dead in her tracks by a wall of boxes.

"Oops, wait a minute," Paige called from the other side, followed by muted scuffling sounds. The door swung partially open and Paige popped her head out. "I didn't expect you back from lunch so soon. Wendy's two sons just dropped off these crates of books, and I haven't had time to move them from in front of the door where they left them."

Addie eyed the narrow opening between the door-frame and the crates. "No problem, I guess we're about to see if those crunches I do every morning have been worth it." She sucked in her tummy and grinned at Paige when she managed to squeeze around them and through the doorway.

Paige pushed another box to the side and collapsed on the lid. "How was lunch?" She eyed the bulging bakery bag Addie clutched in her hand.

Addie brushed a strand of hair from her eyes. "Simon was busy, so I never saw him."

"You haven't eaten yet?"

"No, I lost my appetite, but if you're still hungry help yourself." Addie gave the bag the sniff test. "On second thoughts, don't bother they've been out too long." She winced tossing the bag into the trash can.

"I can go next door and pick you up a fresh one, if you like."

"I'm good, but if you want to go get yourself something, go ahead."

"Thanks, but no, I think I should finish going through these books to see exactly what we have. At first glance there seems to be a lot of the summer beach reads we needed."

"Perfect. Since I didn't get a chance to pick up those classics from the auction, at least we'll have something for the tourists."

Addie surveyed her disorganized storage room. She knew she'd have to pull up her big-girl pants, stop feeling like the *suspect* for a moment, and stop thinking about how she could prove her innocence. Now wasn't the time to think of all the what-ifs. She needed to concentrate on what had to be her main priority, and that was keeping Paige employed and her shop open. It was less than a week until the first official cruise ship was scheduled to dock. Fingers crossed, she'd still be here and not rotting away in some prison cell.

"If you want to work back here," Addie said, her gaze surveying the boxes, "sorting through these, maybe you can select the books you think we can sell and just jot down the titles and publishing information. Then when you take them up front to shelve, give me your list and I'll enter them into the inventory records on the computer." Addie smiled when she glanced over at Paige, whose nose was already stuck in a box. "If we work together, it might not take too long to get through all these."

"What do I do with books I don't think we can sell? Do you want me to put them aside for you to look at?"

"Naw, you know as well as I do what our customers like. I trust your judgment. Just start another box for them. We can donate them to the school annual book drive or something."

"Sounds good."

Paige didn't waste any time delving into the first box as Addie headed to the front of the shop to look after business. For the next few hours her plan clicked along like a well-oiled machine, and by five o'clock closing Addie and Paige high-fived each other when the last customer left for the day and Paige had shelved the last of the new books. Addie locked the door behind her assistant, flipped the door sign to CLOSED, leaned her back against the warm, sun-kissed glass door, and gazed longingly at the coffeemaker.

She wondered if she could reach it, after no sleep last night. The prospect of placing one foot in front of the other long enough to make fresh coffee and then walk to the back room was daunting, but she was resilient and motivated. She had to prove to Marc that his evidence against her was completely wrong and to find equally as strong evidence proving her innocence. *What's a few more hours without sleep?*

She shook out her arms and hands to wake herself up, launched herself off the door, made herself a cup of coffee, and then went to the back room. She tugged the covering from her blackboard mounted on the wall. "Hello, old friend, where do we start today?" she said, staring at the blank surface of the board.

"Problem: police evidence points to me. Solution: figure out who else it points to." She picked up a piece of chalk and scribbled the word *Suspects.* Then she wrote *Kalea* under it. As much as she didn't want to believe it—her cousin was at the top of her list because she appeared to have left town without a word and there was the whole thing about the gloves and emptying her purse onto the table—Addie stabbed the chalk, marking an exclamation point after Kalea's name.

Then she added *Blake.* After all, she had witnessed the argument between Charlotte and him and could see that there was no love lost between them. There was also Charlotte's assistant, slimy *Robert Peters,* who hadn't kept his feelings about his overly demanding employer private.

Addie examined the names she'd written and then drew a line from Kalea to *Garrett Edwards,* Blake's nephew. Kalea had canceled their dinner to meet up with him, so as far as Addie knew he was the last person her cousin was in contact with before she disappeared. *Is he part of the theft?* He probably knew about the books, and he had access to the house. She wasn't sure about him but decided that, for now, his name would stay. She tapped the chalk on her hand.

Think, Addie, who else knew about the books or had access to the library? Bingo! She almost shouted as she jotted down *Philip Atkinson.* He was at Hill Road House and had been in her store and even insinuated that he

knew the missing books had been swapped for reproductions.

"Okay, now I have a starting point, but what do I
know?" She paced in front of the board, occasionally
glancing sideways, shaking her head, and pacing some
more. "Think, Addie, what would Dad say right now?"

She jumped at a sharp knock on the back door.
"Who is it?"

"It's me, Marc."

She flung the door open. "Are you here to arrest
me again?"

He shook his head.

"Then what?" She glanced over his shoulder at his
empty cruiser parked in her Mini's spot. "You're
alone? No shadow tonight?"

"Can I come in, please?"

"It depends. Is this business or pleasure?"

"I just wanted to return this." He produced her laptop from behind his back.

"And did you find everything you needed? Did it
prove to you that I was researching Wednesday night
and couldn't have been at Hill Road House?"

"Unfortunately, it's just as Ryley said: It's a laptop,
and you could have been anywhere when you logged
in and did a search. We can't pinpoint an exact location."

"Then what you're saying is that I still don't have an
alibi?"

"That's exactly what I'm saying."

Hurt and irritation welled up in her. She snatched
her computer from his hands and started to pull the
door closed. His hand pulled back against it.

"Addie, it might be time to think about finding a
good lawyer because with the evidence we have against

you, it won't take the DA too long to reinstate that arrest order." Addie blinked, fighting back the tears burning behind her eyes. "I'm sorry, but as a friend, I thought I should give you a heads-up—"

"As a friend? You arrested me for theft and possible murder. Is that someone I could really have as a friend?"

The muscles in Marc's jaw tightened. "You're right, but personal feelings aside, I hope you understand that I'm just doing my job and have to follow where the evidence leads."

"Then if you're not here to arrest me right now, you'll excuse me so I can go back to proving all that evidence you think you have against me actually leads to the real thief—and if I'm not mistaken, *killer*, too."

"Not so fast." Marc wedged his boot in the crack of the door and stepped inside. He scanned the board. "Addie, how many times—"

"Don't say it. You lost the right to tell me not to get involved when you arrested me and made me your prime suspect. What do you expect?" She poked him in the chest, pushing him back toward the door. "That I'm just going to sit back and let it all come out in the wash?"

"I'd hoped that you'd see the seriousness of this and let it all play out according to the official investigation." He removed her finger from his sternum. "You have to stay out of this, more than ever before, because you *are* the suspect right now."

"Then I have nothing to lose, and it makes it more imperative that I do a little digging on my own."

"No, Addie. I can charge you with interfering in a police investigation."

"How is me trying to prove my innocence interference? Really, Marc, are you afraid I might show up that girlfriend of yours? Is that the real issue here?" She bit back a laugh as his face reddened. "Tell me why Ryley is so bent on proving me guilty that neither of you can see that I've been set up."

"That's not what's happening. It's that so far all the evidence points to you, and unless something else comes to light . . ." He pushed his cap back, revealing a damp brow glistening under the overhead lighting. "It's like always. You just don't know when to back down and leave well enough alone, allowing the police to do their job."

"Yeah," she huffed, "I can see firsthand how well you're doing your job. I think you should go now." She opened the door and rested her hand on the doorframe. "Unless you *are* going to arrest me for interference in your investigation, I want you to leave."

"Addie, I—"

"Now!"

She slammed the door behind him and swallowed back a sob. If he thought her capable of what he was accusing her of, then there would be no going back for them. Maybe one day they could become friends again, but that wouldn't be today.

She stared at the board. This wasn't only about proving her innocence now. It was personal. Someone had gone to a lot of work to set her up as the suspect, and she needed to know what the next move was, so she could call checkmate and stop being a pawn in his or her game. One person who appeared to be bent on proving her guilt and ruining her good name came to mind. She made her way to the board, picked up the chalk, and scribbled *Ryley* above her cousin's name.

A knock on the door sent her sleep-deprived nerves skittering. She whipped the chalk at the door. "Marc, this is harassment!" She flung the door open. "Simon?"

"I take it that harassment greeting was meant for none other than the chief of police, whom I saw pulling out of the alley?"

"You'd be right. Come in."

"Do I dare ask what happened?" He glanced around the back room, his gaze resting on the blackboard. "I take it he didn't like seeing his girlfriend's name at the top of your list of suspects?"

"I added that after he left."

"By the glassy look in your eyes, I'd say it's time to get you home. You need food and sleep." He kissed the tip of her nose.

"I can't right now. Marc told me to get a lawyer, and that the DA would probably be reissuing that arrest warrant because I don't have a concrete alibi."

"Addie, it's late, and you've had no sleep. Leave this. You can work on it tomorrow."

"But Simon . . ."

"No buts." He placed a finger over her lips. "You can't even stand up right now you're so exhausted. Come on, I'll drive you home."

"Good, because I don't have my car," she said with a saucy wink.

"I saw that, so it's a good thing I dropped by or you'd be hoofing it up that hill. But one look at you right now and I have a feeling we would find you sleeping at the end of the alley tomorrow morning." He returned her sauciness with a playful swat as she fetched her handbag.

Simon steered her to the sofa in her living room. "Now sit. Stay. And no more about suspects and being set up and because you don't have an alibi, you're going to jail."

"But—"

"I said, no buts. I heard it all the way here from your shop. You're so tired you're not even making sense. Your mind is reeling in every direction." His lips brushed across hers in a whispered kiss. "Now relax and forget about it all. You can't solve it when you're in this state. I'm going to make you some tea and toast and then you're going to bed. Doctor's orders."

Addie only had the strength to kick off her shoes and nestle into the sofa. Her heavy eyelids fluttered, and she fought to keep her eyes open enough to watch the simple, homey actions of Simon shoving the clutter of books on her eighteenth-century Marquetry coffee table aside to slide a small tray in front of her.

"Smells amazing." Addie forced those words over the cotton-ball feeling in her mouth.

"You still have this?" He sat beside her and picked up a blue wristwatch off the table.

"Yeah, of course I do. You gave it to me. You said I had to become more *aware* of my health." She propped herself up on one elbow and reached for a cup of tea from the tray. "I tell you, dating a doctor comes with a lot of responsibilities. Like wristwatch monitoring and tracking what I eat," she said, inhaling the earthy-musky camomile scent.

"Then why haven't I seen you wear it lately?"

"I do. Not during the day, though. I got tired of it beeping at me, telling me when to move and all that. I only wear it at night now."

"Do you?" He studied the device in his hand, his brows furrowing. "Were you wearing it Wednesday night when you went to bed?"

"I never forget it. It helps me see how deeply I've slept. Why?"

"Because this tracks your sleep, hours, quality of your sleep, and movements based on your heart rate."

"I know. You showed me all that when you set it up for me."

His piercing blue eyes focused on her.

"What?"

"If you were wearing this Wednesday night, the data stored by it will prove you were home sleeping and not out committing a burglary."

Chapter 17

This was the second time in as many days that Marc had treated her like a child, sending her from the room for a time-out. Addie leaned forward on her elbows and rubbed her palms together. She and Simon had arrived at the police station at precisely 7 a.m., the start of Marc's shift. He had cordially greeted them both, and he and his sidekick, Ryley, listened as Simon explained about Addie's fitness watch and showed them the data stored in the app on her phone. That was when Marc dismissed her to the waiting room—nearly two hours ago.

Her gaze bore into the closed door. It was times like this she wished she had x-ray vision or could be a fly on the wall. She'd have given anything to know what they could still possibly be debating. Simon was relatively an expert on the health app data they'd presented. It made her wonder if it was Marc or Ryley questioning his explanation. Surely they could see by now she had an airtight alibi. It was all there, logged into her phone. She rose to her feet and started pacing.

Marc's office door opened, and Simon stepped out.

"Simon, finally. What's going on? Why is this taking so long?"

Marc and Ryley, hot on Simon's heels, exited down the back staircase without even a glance in her direction.

"Simon, what's happening? Am I free of the charges?"

His drawn face said it all even before he spoke, she knew the answer. "No, but I'm pretty sure you will be soon. Hang in there a while longer."

"What do you mean? Can't they see I couldn't have been the one that broke into the library? We have proof now."

He brushed his lips across her hot cheek. "I think you were right to add Ryley's name to your suspect list," he whispered in her ear.

Her eyes widened. He rested his forehead against hers, drawing her closer. "For some reason, she's trying to find a loophole in the data program and refuses to believe you are innocent. It didn't matter what I said. She won't be convinced. I'd say something else is driving this, but I don't know what."

"So now what?"

"She wanted to wait to do any follow-up on this until after the weekend because the DA doesn't generally work Saturdays, but I made Marc call him and run this new development past him."

"And?"

"And he's agreed to meet with us at his house in Salem."

"You're going, too?"

"Yeah, she said a couple of things that made me wonder how much she could be trusted to present *all* the facts about this program and its capabilities. I want to be there just in case she tries to brush any of it off. Then it will be completely the DA's call if he wants to pursue charges against you or drop them, and he won't be influenced by a partial report."

"I thought she was a professional. Wouldn't she want to get to the bottom of this?"

"You'd think, but as I said, I get the feeling that there's something else going on here, but I have to go. They're waiting." He squeezed her arms and gave her a light kiss. "I'll call you as soon as I know anything."

Addie plopped onto one of the waiting room chairs. She couldn't believe it. When she'd added Ryley's name to her suspect list, she had done it out of pure spite and anger but never really had any intention of following through with an investigation on her. Now she wasn't so sure. Maybe her gut instincts knew more than her head, and she better think twice about dismissing the agent's actions so quickly.

Addie gathered up her bag and headed out the door. Since Simon had driven them to the station first thing this morning, Addie was on foot as she made her way over the two blocks to her shop. But she didn't mind. It was a beautiful summer morning, and the warm breeze off the harbor gave her just the lift her spirits needed as she mentally processed all the information rattling around in her head. There were too many questions and not enough answers. She was in the middle of writing a mental to-do list when Martha came out of the bakery, brandishing her famous broom.

"Morning, Addie." She swept the sidewalk in front of the bakery door. "It looks like it's going to be a quiet Saturday down here."

Addie blinked. She'd been so wrapped up in her thoughts, she hadn't even noticed, but Martha was right. It was nearly ten, and there were still plenty of parking spots. "It's like a ghost town this morning. What's going on?"

Martha stopped her sweeping and leaned both hands on the end of the broom handle. "I hear half the town is at that yard sale today. I guess there's not a parking spot for over six blocks around that house."

Addie glanced up the deserted road. She had completely forgotten that this weekend was the public sale.

"Mildred was furious. She was late opening the Emporium on Main Street this morning because she couldn't even get out of her driveway." Martha resumed her sweeping with renewed vigor.

Addie bolted past her shop door and burst through the door of SerenaTEA. "Serena!"

A red head popped out of the back room.

"What are you doing today?"

"Not too much by the look of it. Why?" Serena dried her hands on a towel as she came out of the back.

"Do you want to play hooky with me and go to the Hill Road House yard sale?"

"Not really. I have no intention of going anywhere near that place and don't think you should be either, considering."

Addie waved off her friend's look of concern. "Not to worry. The charges are going to be dropped. At least I hope they are."

"I didn't mean because of that. I meant because of *her.*"

"Who, her?" Addie's brows bumped together.

"Kathleen Gallagher."

"Serena, don't be silly. There are no ghosts in that house."

"Then how did someone get into the library, kill

that woman, and then steal those books?" She crossed her arms. "Answer me that one, Miss Smarty-Pants."

"That's why we have to go there today. I need to talk to Blake. He told me other things have disappeared from there, too, over the last months, and I want to check a couple of things out."

"Well, you can count me out. I won't set foot in that creepy old house."

"But that's the beauty of the yard sale. You won't have to go in the house. Come on, please." She gave Serena some puppy-dog eyes and even clasped her hands together in supplication.

"Okay," Serena heaved out a breath. "Anything to make you stop that pitiful begging. Also, under no circumstances am I going in that house. Do. You. Understand?" She set the towel on the counter. "I was kind of curious to see what deals I could find anyway, but didn't dare go by myself."

"That's the spirit." Addie grinned. "What time can you get away?"

"Elli will be in anytime now. So whenever."

"Great, I'll let Paige know, and then I'll meet you out back."

"Sounds good."

Addie paused, her hand on the doorknob. "Martha just told me parking is at a premium around the house. Do you trust Paige or Elli to drive your jeep so one of them can drop us off?"

"What's wrong with your car?"

"I don't have it. Simon drove this morning."

Serena's eyes popped wide open, and a grin covered her freckled face. "You finally had a sleepover with him?"

"No." Addie's cheeks burned. "It's a long story. I'll

tell you later. But could one of them drive your jeep, please?"

"Yeah, sure. Elli drives it for deliveries all the time." She cupped her hand in her chin and leaned across the counter. "But I want the full details of last night in exchange for this."

Addie ignored her friend's remark and hustled next door to tell Paige her plan for the day. Her young assistant was seated at the counter reading the morning newspaper. Addie glanced around the empty shop and waved off her employee's jump to action. "It looks the same in here as the street does."

Paige stared at her blankly.

"Like a ghost town," Addie said with a chuckle. "And speaking of ghosts, since it's so quiet around here today, Serena and I are going to head over to the yard sale at Hill Road House for a while."

"You actually convinced her to go with you?"

"Yes, she's adamant about not going inside, but I won her over when I promised she could stay in the yard."

"Yeah, I guess the yard is probably free of wandering spirits."

Addie muttered to herself about foolishness all the way to the back of the shop, and stopped short as she passed the last row. From here she had a clear view to the local history book section on the back corner of the far wall. "Paige, why are all these books on the floor?"

"What?" Paige skittered up to her side and peered down the row. "I . . . well . . . I don't really know."

"We were both pretty exhausted when we closed up yesterday. I guess we just missed seeing this before we left."

"But usually I do a quick store inspection after I

come in." Paige frowned at the books scattered on the floor.

"Did you this morning?"

"I did what I do every day: I came in, went to the back, turned off the alarm, hung up my sweater, if I have a lunch I put it in the fridge, and went to the bathroom. Then I head out front and set up the sandwich board on the sidewalk, pick up the newspaper from beside the door . . . darn it!"

"What?"

"This morning the front-page headline caught my eye. It was about Hill Road House, and I started reading the article and didn't do my inspection." Her gaze dropped. "I won't let it happen again."

"Don't worry about it. I just can't believe that someone threw books on the floor." Addie bent down to retrieve one and then stopped. "Paige, look at this." Her cheeks burned with righteous anger. "All the books down this aisle in the supernatural mystery section have been tossed, too!"

"It looks like someone ran down here with their arm out in order to fling all the books to the floor." Paige picked up a copy of *The Ghosts and Mysteries of Greyborne Harbor.* "Who would be so disrespectful to books?"

"I don't know. None of our usual customers would do something like this." Addie picked up a book and re-shelved it. "Sometimes they're not interested in it after reading the cover blurb or reading the first few pages and leave them in a pile beside the reading chairs, but to just throw them on the floor? This is a new one."

"I think with all the new tourists coming in, we're going to have to keep a closer watch on things."

"You're right. All books, but especially some of the older, rarer ones need to be treated with respect." Addie slid another book into place. "And when I get my hands on the person who did this . . ." A pounding resonated from the back room. "That must be Serena."

"You go ahead. I'll finish cleaning this up." Paige struggled to stand under the load of books in her arms.

"Are you sure?" Addie helped her to her feet.

"Yeah." She glanced down the aisle. "I'll get the cart. It won't take long."

"Okay, thanks." Addie squeezed Paige's hand and trotted out the back door.

As they approached number 555 Hill Road, Addie bounced excitedly on the backseat. "Look at the floor lamp that woman is leaving with." She flung her arm out between Elli and Serena. "That would be perfect in the back corner of my shop. I wonder if there's another one?"

Elli pulled over at the front entrance. "I hope the best deals haven't gone already." Serena cast a leery gaze at the haunted monstrosity.

"I know. It's nearly eleven, and the sign said it started at nine." Addie joined her on the sidewalk.

Serena spoke to Elli through the open car window as Addie made her way toward the gate. She relaxed her shoulders. Today it was propped open so there'd be no eerie responses from it. Serena joined her, and they made their way around the house, following the signs and the noise to the back garden. Addie whistled. "I think Martha got it wrong this morning."

"Why? What did she say?"

"She said half the town was here. I'd say it's more like the whole town." Addie looped her arm through Serena's, and they navigated through the crowd to the closest table set out under a large tent.

"Look at those teapots." Serena made a beeline over to a table of kitchen goods. "Aren't they precious?" She examined a delft blue porcelain one. "This would be perfect in my shop. And look at this Chinese stoneware one." She set down the blue-and-white-flowered one and picked up a beige pot with Oriental markings on the sides. "This is beautiful and would be perfect in my store."

"If I'm not mistaken," Addie said as she inspected the pot, "that's either a nineteenth-century or early-twentieth-century Chinese Yixing teapot. You can probably get it for a decent price since it's out here on the sale tables."

Serena went full-seasoned garage-sale shopper on her, gathering items together and group-price bartering with the young woman working the table. It was clear that Serena was no stranger to haggling, and from what Addie overheard from the nearby booths and tables, the townspeople of Greyborne Harbor matched Serena's vigor in demanding the best deals they could, too.

As entertaining as watching haggling was, Addie wasn't interested in accumulating more stuff for herself and tugged her phone out to check messages from Simon. Nothing. There were still no missed calls or texts from or about her cousin, either. She shook her head. The police had showed their incompetency in investigating the footprints; she wondered if that was also the reason they were still unable to locate Kalea.

It made her question Ryley's involvement in all this even more. She'd set her sights on Addie and didn't appear to be considering any other suspects. This brought Addie's thoughts back to her cousin, the second name on her blackboard. She had pretty much become a ghost, but Addie wasn't thinking of the apparition type; more of the change-your-identity-and-disappear-forever type. Something Kalea could well achieve by living off the hundreds of thousands of dollars from the sale of the Beeton edition of *A Study in Scarlet* and the other original copies of the Holmes books.

She meandered around the tables, noting the crowd expanding with people only looking for later-day leftovers at a reduced price. The professional early-bird shoppers knew what they wanted when they came to these events, when they wanted it, and had the cash to make that happen, but by what she overheard they were long gone by now. As she made her way from one table to the next, her eyes peeled for a floor lamp, she became aware that along with the tagalongs and lookie-loos, there also appeared to be a large police presence. She counted six officers weaving through the hordes of people. At first she thought they were doing crowd control, but then she realized half of them were holding what looked like lists in their hands. They'd check the list, scan the items on a table, and refer back to the list.

Ethan, a young officer she'd come to know, wasn't scanning a list. He was scanning the faces of people. This wasn't normal security, not even for a yard sale with slightly above-average garage sale items. Something else was going on.

Serena slid up to her side, grinning like a Cheshire cat, and nudged Addie. "Look." She opened the large tote bag she'd brought with her as she juggled two more hemp-handled shopping bags. "I can't believe the deals I found. How did you do?" She glanced at

Addie's hand that only held her cell phone. "Nothing?"

"No, I'm only on the lookout for a floor lamp," she replied absently as she continued to scan the crowd over Serena's shoulder. There was something about how the officers were walking a grid pattern that disturbed her. Something was wrong. "You know what? I'm going to go inside and find Blake."

"You're what? You told me we wouldn't go in that house today."

"I said *you* didn't have to. It's okay. You stay out here and shop. I want to find out about the books I saw on Wednesday."

"Addie, don't go back in there. Something bad always happens when you do."

"I'll be fine. I won't be long." What was that people said about famous last words? She shivered as she strode toward the back porch.

Chapter 18

As Addie reached the bottom step, the door flew open and a flustered Art stomped down the stairs. "Is everything all right?" she asked.

"Yeah, but it's not looking like the auction house is going to have everything cleared out before my first buyer arrives next week."

"Is there still lots left over?"

He slapped his white fedora on his head. "The police have the library still cordoned off, so it's not empty and, apparently, there's another issue, but Mr. Edwards didn't elaborate."

"What are you going to do if they're not out of here soon?"

"Not much I can do. Who knew I'd have an eager buyer in the first place? I'll just get Vera to work her magic on the staging around what's left when I conduct the showing." He tipped his hat and hustled off through the crowd.

Addie wished she had Art's positive attitude, the ability to make the best of a bad situation. She took the steps two at a time and excused her way through throngs of people only to come to a traffic jam at the bottom of the haunted staircase. She could just make out Blake and Jerry, heads together, obviously discussing something in the study. Probably not the best time to ask Blake about the police being here.

Sick of waiting for the slowpokes in front of her to get a move on, she spun around to leave and caught sight of a wispy cloud drifting over the top step. The image floated upward, hovering for a moment, and drifted toward the wall, vanishing in a puff of vapor. Addie's chest squeezed, forcing her breath out of her burning lungs. Her quick intake of air congealed into a sob-scream. She clasped her hand to her mouth and glanced at the crowd before her. Thankfully, no one seemed to notice her. Or the ghost.

Addie attempted to think logically about what she'd seen. Smoke and hot air rise, therefore what she'd witnessed was a result of smoke coming from somewhere in the house. Someone had burnt something in the kitchen or had lit a fireplace without checking the damper first. *Don't be an idiot. No one in his right mind would light a fire on a hot summer day.* She circled her fingers on her temples, conjuring another explanation that didn't scream *moron*.

With no other less-stupid idea, she sniffed her way to the kitchen. Nothing but stale old house and mixed scents of people. She peeked into the library, gave a tentative sniff. Nothing. If she couldn't scientifically prove the vapor's presence that left two options: one, ghosts—or this one at least existed; two, she was going crazy. Not a fan of either one of those, she slipped under the yellow crime-scene tape across the door, ducked inside, and then softly closed the door behind her.

Breathing hard, she rested her back against the door,

ears perked for any footsteps. No signs of freshly burned logs in the fireplace. *Shoot!* It definitely wasn't the cause for the smoke she'd seen in the upper hallway.

She edged away from the door and surveyed the room. This was the first time she'd been inside here since *that* day . . . the day that sent her life careening sideways. She had changed but on first glance nothing in this room had. It was as though time stood still. The books were still packed in lot sale boxes. The center table was still a hodgepodge of first-edition novels. The chair was in the exact same position she had left it when she turned it toward her and discovered Charlotte dead. But something was different.

She narrowed her eyes and scanned over every detail she could remember from that day. What was it that niggled at her now? She couldn't put her finger on it. She focused on the desk, her mind replaying Thursday morning.

The teacup was gone. Naturally it had been taken to the lab for testing. However, the stains caused by the spilled contents were visible across the desktop and over the edge. The letter opener and antique inkwell were just as they had been, but the feather pen wasn't there. She tried to remember if there was anything about it that seemed odd or out of place when she discovered the body, but nothing came to mind. It was a regular feather dip quill pen that had sat in the crystal inkpot. *What reason would the police have to take it?* The well was dried out and hadn't been used for years.

"Addie?" A red-faced Jerry loomed in the doorway. "*What* are you doing in here?"

"I was just . . . just looking for signs of smoke. I'd seen some in the hallway and—"

"There's no way you didn't see the crime tape."

"No." She smiled weakly, wringing her hands. "I—"

"Out." He pointed to the door.

She didn't move. "Jerry, I'm not touching anything, I promise. I only had to see the room one more time, besides, there might have been a fire—"

"Out!"

"Please, Jerry. My future depends on me being able to put some of this together. I promise I won't touch a thing. You can stay in here with me to make sure I don't if it makes you feel better. Please."

"What am I supposed to tell the chief when he finds out?"

"We can tell him I saw smoke in the hallway, and we came in to check for signs of a fire." She gave him a shaky smile.

"That might be the reason you *say* you came in here, but we both know that's not why you want to stay and look around, is it?"

She bit her lip, shaking her head. "But now that we are in here . . . please. I'm pleading with you. I've been arrested, and I need to find out what happened because none of it makes sense. You can stay in here with me."

"Why do I let you talk me into things?" He rubbed the back of his neck. "Okay, but I stay, and you don't touch anything while we check for a source of the smoke. Fifteen minutes and that's it."

"Thank you." She crossed her heart and inspected the center table.

"What do you hope to see that we haven't already considered?"

"I don't know. There are just too many things that don't add up."

"Like what?"

"First, the room was locked. Whoever stole the books must have done it earlier in the evening. It makes me wonder if that's the reason Charlotte was working that late and stayed on after Robert left. She'd discovered the replacements, and did this"—she waved her hand over the table—"to see if any others were replicas."

"You know what has stumped me since the start of this?" He moved to her side.

"What's that?"

"Why would someone go to the trouble of replacing the rare books with fakes anyway? Why didn't they just steal them and be done with it?"

"Well, I have a couple of theories about that, but with me being the number-one suspect"—she gave him a sidelong glance and teasing grin—"you probably don't want to hear them."

Jerry glanced at the door. "Yeah, I do. I have questions, too, and the chief sure doesn't want to talk about it."

"Okay, then try this on for size. Because the replica books aren't sold anywhere in or around Greyborne Harbor, and the only bookstore I know that carries this new reproduction collection is in Boston, that means the books—"

"Would have been pre-purchased."

"Exactly, and I didn't discover the set or the original Beeton's copy of *A Study in Scarlet* until Wednesday. As far as I know, Charlotte wasn't aware of their existence until then, either, because I think she was genuinely shocked when I told her what I found in the old bookcase."

"And she died that night. The same night the books were replaced." Jerry stroked his stubbled chin.

"Yes, so even though the books in the barrister's case weren't appraised until Wednesday, someone who had a good understanding of book appraisals had already been through the bookcase and knew of their existence before I or she did. Charlotte couldn't have pulled this off." Jerry nodded slowly, seemingly following her thought process. "The police need to focus on the staff and find out what their backgrounds are. They're the only ones I can think of who would have had access to the library earlier in the week."

"What makes you think it was earlier in the week and not before that?"

"I overheard a conversation between Charlotte and Blake, and she distinctly said that Blake's crew had only discovered the barrister's bookcase this week in a storage space in the attic."

"That means it was sitting in here unopened for almost a week before you worked on it."

Addie nodded.

"And you had no access to this room before Wednesday?"

She shook her head.

"Then, realistically, the first person to come to mind would be Robert. Wouldn't he have the background to appraise the books and learn their value?"

"You're right, but he never left the house that night and was upstairs sleeping." She snapped her fingers. "Unless . . . the books are still stashed away somewhere in the house and the thief is waiting until this all settles down for him or whoever to safely get them out?"

"Interesting." He fidgeted with the handcuffs on his belt . . . "And you're convinced Charlotte's death wasn't a coincidence?"

She shook her head again.

"It still doesn't answer my question about why someone would swap the books."

Addie puffed out a breath. "Whoever it was didn't count on someone like me discovering the ruse. Remember, I stepped in at the last minute to help. My being here wasn't planned. Whoever pulled this off might have hoped that the auction would be canceled because of the discovery of the body, and then no one would be the wiser to the missing books. To the untrained eye, it would appear that they were still here, and a theft investigation wouldn't have been launched."

"Maybe . . ." Jerry said, drawing out the word as he slowly scanned the room and then focused on the table.

"What are you thinking?"

"I know Simon's preliminary report shows she died of a heart attack, but . . . what if . . . ?"

"What if someone killed Charlotte to stop the auction from taking place?"

"Yeah."

"But why?" Addie strolled around the perimeter of the room, taking in every detail. "We must be missing something important here. Is this room exactly the way it was when you took your photos?"

Jerry moved over to the desk and looked at the books on the floor by the desk. His gaze rested on the fireplace, and he took a step toward it. "Not exactly." He bent down, resting on his haunches.

Addie crouched down next to him. "What do you see?"

He pointed. "Those track marks in the soot from the fireplace. See how they've fanned out? It looks like something's been dragged across here in front of the hearth. I'll have to check the photographs at the station, but I don't remember it being so pronounced on Thursday."

Addie stood up, her hands on her hips as she studied the fireplace. Three notches were etched into both carved wings of the eagle in the center of the marble mantel's frieze.

"Jerry, do you have any gloves on you?"

"Yeah, why?" He brushed off his hands.

She pointed to the intricate carving. "Can you press these notches and see if anything happens?"

He tugged on a pair of blue rubber gloves and pressed on the spots she'd indicated. Nothing happened. He ran his fingers over the area. "Nothing. The holes are recessed too deep."

"Maybe." Addie worried her bottom lip between her teeth as she scanned the carved marble pilasters on either side of the firebox opening.

"What about the roses carved in the top corners? Could you please press on those and see if anything happens?"

"Nothing; they don't budge. They're carved into the marble by the feel of it. They're not castings that were added."

"So much for that theory."

Addie focused on the portrait, rumored to be of Arthur Gallagher's father, the man who designed Hill Road House, hanging above the fireplace. An original gilded frame encased the man's imposing pose, complete with muttonchops and tailored waistcoat.

A slight quiver prickled across her shoulders at the man's daunting expression. There was something alluring and menacing, haunting yet captivating about the look in his eyes. As if he knew a secret.

She shook off her momentary mesmerization. "I don't think there's anything else to see in here . . ." A thought struck her, "Jerry, did you find any tea stains under the book by the desk or were they only on the cover?"

"On the cover. Why?"

"There were no stains underneath it?"

"Nope, there were tea stains around it where it splashed, but nothing under it."

Addie narrowed her eyes and examined the area around where the book had been found on the floor. "We all assumed that Charlotte was working with the book, and then had chest pains, and as she clutched her chest, the teacup got knocked over, and the book slipped from her hands, plummeting to the floor, right?"

"That's what we figure happened."

"But that would mean the tea spilt first, and the book landed on the stained area. But since only the cover is stained—"

"That means she dropped the book first and then knocked over the cup."

"Right. Does that seem odd to you? I mean, it's like something startled her, causing her to drop the book, then after that tip over the cup." Addie looked at the position of the chair facing the desk, which is how Charlotte would most likely have been seated. She envisioned the position she found her facing, the fireplace, and then the book covered with tea.

"What are you thinking, Addie?"

"I don't know. Nothing, I guess."

"Maybe she bumped the teacup over, grabbed for the book so it wouldn't get damaged, and it slipped from her fingers and fell under the desk."

"Then there would have been some sign of the tea under the book." She frowned. "No, it looks like the book fell first, then she bumped the cup." Addie played in her mind what may have happened. "If she heard something behind her that startled her, she would have dropped the book as she spun the chair around to see what it was. Her left elbow might have smacked the cup over, which caused the staining on the cover." Addie returned to the fireplace and frowned at the first notch in the carved eagle wing. "Jerry, can I have some gloves, please?" She held out her hand.

"Yeah, I think I have more in here." He dug around in his pocket. "Here."

She pulled them on and traced her finger over the hollowed notches. The center one was recessed deeper than the two on either side. Her fingers were still too large to see if there was a button or if it was an ornate part of the design.

"Find anything?"

She shook her head. "It's exactly as you said."

"You doubted me?"

"No, but my fingers are smaller. I was only hoping they might be able to feel something yours couldn't."

"I really don't like being in here." He glanced around the room.

"You feel it, too, don't you?"

"What?"

"That chill in the air and the sensation of being watched."

"I think it's just that I feel so guilty about allowing you in here that I'm afraid Marc will walk in. We better go."

"Okay, I don't want to get you into trouble." She pulled the gloves off and stuffed them into her jeans pocket. "But thanks for indulging me." She glanced at the desk on her way past. "Is there a reason the police took the antique feather pen for testing?"

He ran his fingers through his hair. "We didn't take any pen for testing."

"Interesting. I swear it was on the desk in that old inkwell Thursday morning."

"I can check the crime-scene inventory list and take a look at the pictures to be sure." He reached for the door handle. "I guess it's one more thing to add to the list of missing items."

"What do you mean?"

"I mean, that's why half the police department are here right now. Overnight, there were a number of other antiques stolen."

"Even with the security guards Blake hired to secure the yard sale merchandise and patrol the grounds?"

"It's baffling, to say the least." He headed out the door.

Addie followed but hesitated when a rush of cold air wrapped its wisp-like fingers around her. This wasn't the first time in this room that inexplicable cold surrounded her. The intensity of it reminded her of the air-conditioning vent in the interrogation room. But there were no AC ducts in this room, and since the house had sat empty for over seventy years, she doubted there were any anywhere in the entire mansion.

She swept one last glance at the room and gasped. A faint vaporous mist floated before the fireplace. *It's just the dim lighting.* Old man Gallagher's eyes drew in Addie's gaze. They appeared to have grown darker, emptier than they looked just a few minutes ago. A quiver raced up her spine. She blinked. Twice. The vaporous image dissipated and just as quickly so did the bone-numbing cold. She fled through the door, Serena's story replaying in her mind.

Chapter 19

It seemed to take forever to herd Serena away from the yard sale and load her purchases into the jeep once Elli came to pick them up. The guilt of having deserted Paige for another day ate at Addie, and she dashed through the back door of her shop. She looked longingly at the blackboard covered by the drop cloth, her fingers itching for the chalk.

Jerry had given her a few more things to consider: the ashes having been spread around and the fact that the police had not taken the feather pen. It was time to fit all the puzzle pieces into place. This craziness had gone on long enough, and there was no way she was going to allow her reputation to be ruined, again. The evidence she needed to prove her innocence had to be hidden in at least one of the clues. She just needed time to work on it. *When?*

Knowing that Paige, despite the slow day and repeated assurances through text, would need a break by now, Addie dropped her bag on her desk and scanned the shop for her assistant.

It was eerily silent. There wasn't even the telltale squeak of the book cart wheels that generally meant Paige was restocking shelves. She peered down aisle after aisle. No Paige. Given Paige's fascination with mystery and paranormal lately, she headed to the far wall and screamed.

Paige lay in a heap on the floor, her slight body covered with books. Addie fell at her side and placed her fingers on Paige's neck. She stifled her sobs. Paige did not need her to panic. She needed Addie to be strong. Paige's pulse thrummed against Addie's fingers, and her chest rose and fell with shallow breaths.

Addie pushed books off Paige's head and turned her young friend onto her back.

"Paige, can you hear me?"

The girl's eyes fluttered but remained closed.

"Paige, it's me. Open your eyes."

Addie dialed 911. Within minutes an ambulance arrived, and as the two paramedics loaded Paige onto the stretcher, Marc marched through the door.

Addie eyed him. "You're back from Salem?"

"Yeah, we'll talk about that later. Right now"—he glanced at the books on the floor—"we need to deal with what happened here. Are you okay?" He placed his hands on her upper arms. His eyes searched her face, concern written in his expression.

She blinked back tears and swallowed an expanding sob.

"Come on. Let's sit down so you can tell me what happened."

A squeamish sensation settled in the pit of Addie's stomach as Paige was wheeled out the door on a stretcher. "I don't know what happened. I don't know if she was attacked or a heavy truck went by and tumbled the books off the shelves, but I have to go with Paige." She started for the door. Marc's clasp on her arm tightened.

"It's okay, Martha's going to the hospital with her. It's best you stay here and tell me what you do know, because by all appearances it looks like a deliberate attack during a robbery." Addie struggled to release his grip on her, but it was no use. His hand tightened, and she relented. "Come on, let me make you a coffee and we can talk."

Out of the corner of her tear-blurred eye, she caught sight of the stretcher being loaded into the back of the ambulance and a paramedic assisting Martha up the steps to join her baby girl. Addie's sobs came fast and furious. Marc held a tissue out for her. She clutched at it, and he pulled her into his arms. They sat together not saying a word until the last of her tears dried up.

When she pulled away from Marc, a warm blush rose up from under her collar. She couldn't believe she had buried her face in his chest and wept her eyes out, and he let her. When she glanced past him and saw Ryley standing at the end of the sale rack, the look on Ryley's face confirmed it had happened. Ryley didn't say a word or take a step toward them, but the malicious look in her eyes sent a tremor through Addie. Ryley sent one last death glare before joining the other officers.

Marc, seemingly oblivious to the unspoken exchange between the two women, pulled his notebook from his jacket pocket and clicked his pen. "Do you think you can tell me now what happened?"

Addie blew her nose into the tissue. She relayed what little she knew, how she and Serena had been at the yard sale all morning and had only returned to the store. She didn't mention the part about being in the library with Jerry. She couldn't see the point of getting

either of them into trouble. After all, nothing that occurred there had anything to do with what had happened here—did it?

When she'd finished telling him what she could
about her discovery of Paige and the tossed books, he
had her check the cash drawer and the rare book inventory for any indication that whoever did this might
have gotten away with something. After she took a
quick inventory and established that nothing was missing, he snapped his notepad closed. She took that as
her cue they were done, mumbled something about
Paige, and started for the back room to collect her
purse. Marc grasped her arm and spun her toward
him.

"You have to stay here until the officers are finished
investigating. They might have more questions." His
eyes echoed what used to be his longing to take her in
his arms and kiss her until neither of them could
breathe anymore.

"Marc, are you done?" Ryley's dark eyes flashed. "I
think we have everything we need from here."

Marc dropped Addie's arm as if it burned him and
raked his hand through his hair, causing it to stand up
in chestnut tufts. "Yup." He tucked his notepad back
into his jacket pocket. "If you think of anything else,
call me—"

Ryley cleared her throat.

"I mean, call the station." He placed his cap on his
head. "Oh, by the way, the DA is looking at the evidence Simon presented to him giving you an alibi.
When he makes a decision, he'll let me know if he's
going to drop the charges or reinstate them."

Addie slumped down on a stool as the two of them
left and pulled her phone out of her pocket. Her

thumbs flew over the keyboard as she sent a text to the one person she needed.

Paige is on her way into ER. She was attacked in the shop. I heard you were back from Salem. If you're working now, call me as soon as you know anything about her condition. If you're not working, COME NOW! I need you.

"Addie!" Serena careened around the bookshelf corner. "Are you okay, sweetie?"

"Can you believe this?" Addie fought back a sob. "Paige was attacked right here in my shop."

"I heard. Is she okay?"

"I don't know. I just texted Simon but haven't heard back yet."

"Was anything stolen?"

"No, that's just the thing. Nothing was taken—no books, none of the money in the till, nothing. None of this makes sense. Who would want to hurt Paige for no reason? She's so sweet, and everybody loves her."

Serena hugged Addie. "Let's get you out of here."

"I can't go now." Addie jerked her head toward the officers by the door. "I have to wait until they're done."

"Unfortunately, I have to get back to my shop. Elli's in a tailspin over all this and was terrified about me leaving her alone just to pop in here."

"I think we'll need to reevaluate our working alone policies after this episode."

Serena's gaze went to the floor. "Do you think this is related to the book thefts?"

"Not when nothing was stolen. I think, if it is related, it's more like a warning."

"About what?"

"I don't know. I've been so consumed with my arrest I haven't had time to look at any of the evidence yet." She glanced at her back-room door. "Maybe it's time I start to try to put some of these pieces together."

"Well, stay out of trouble, and as soon as the police leave, lock your door. We don't want another attack happening in case the person comes back. Maybe the first time was just a recon so they could see what was in the store and how many staff was in here." Serena gave her a quick squeeze and trotted out the door.

"I'll be in the back room if you need me," Addie called to an officer by the door.

He ticked his head in acknowledgment, and she marched toward the storage room. Maybe if she got lucky, she'd discover who the book thief was and figure out if Charlotte's death and the missing books were related. The same theory she'd originally presented, and one that Marc had yet to embrace. She flipped the drop cloth off the board, picked up the chalk, and tapped it on the black surface. He said he needed evidence before he could ever consider that her hunch was right, so evidence is what she would find. "Okay, girl, start with what you know."

Library door bolted from inside

Windows securely latched from inside – sash warped, unable to be opened without breaking window

No other entrance to room

Tipped over teacup

A tipped-over teacup. The contents had obviously dripped down the side of the desk onto the book below it. Charlotte must have been working on these books when . . . *When what?* The stains weren't evident under the book, so the book was dropped first, and then the tea was spilt.

Heard something behind her

Dropped the book

Spun the chair around

Her left elbow knocked over the cup
Contents spilled across the desk onto the book on the floor
???

She drew a vicious line under the question marks. *How did everything play out?* She needed proof, not conjecture.

Reading over what she'd written, Addie added:

Books on floor dropped after tea spilt. She circled the word *after.*

Feather pen from inkwell on desk missing

Missing laptop? She'd have to ask Marc next time she saw him if it had been recovered yet.

Rare books and original magazine edition of debut story exchanged for cheap reproductions

Angle of the desk chair turned toward fireplace

Books on center display table, disturbed missing price/info cards

Firebox ashes smeared across hearth and floor

Faint footprint on throw carpet by desk – stepping in spilt tea?

My fingerprints on window ledge and pry bar and broken acrylic nail found outside of window!

Books in shop on floor???

Paige attacked in the store!

She smashed the chalk onto the board, sending bits flying.

"Addie?"

She spun toward the door. "Marc?"

"I hoped we could talk for a minute." He stood in the doorway, cap in hand, a sheepish look on his face.

"Where's your partner?"

"She's at the hospital, taking a statement from Paige."

"She's awake?" Addie checked her phone for a message from Simon. Nothing. "I'm not sure what we have to talk about. After arresting me, you made it very clear about what kind of relationship we have now: you the cop, me the perp. So unless you've come back to accuse me of something else ridiculous like knocking Paige out and are going to haul me into the station again, we really don't have anything else to say to each other."

"I'm just trying to make sense of all this. Of me, what I'm feeling." His gaze met hers. "Of us? When I held you, I . . ." He slumped back against the doorframe.

His gaze locked with hers, but instead of feeling what she would once have felt, that shiver of excitement about being captured in his deep brown eyes, she only saw a haunted expression of a man she no longer knew.

He must have sensed their distance, too, and picked up on the fact that unless what he had to say was related to the investigation. The look in her eyes told him this wasn't the time or place. She was in no mood for it. His gaze darted away from hers, and his body stiffened. "What are you doing there?" He scanned over what she had written. "Addie, I already told you, you can't get involved in this investigation. You're the prime suspect, and all the evidence points to you."

"I think I already blew a few holes in that evidence you so smugly thought you had. Tell me, is it your 'off-duty' FBI agent girlfriend who's calling the shots?" Her fingers hooked air quotes. "From how she's conducting herself, I'd say she's trying to smear my name instead of finding out who's really behind what happened."

"Why would she do something like that?" Marc pierced her with a glare. "She's as professional as they come. I've *allowed* her to become involved because she offers a new perspective on investigations from her experience working with the FBI. She's been very valuable in pointing out some areas we should take a closer look at."

Addie crossed her arms over her chest. "She missed the lack of footprint evidence in the soft soil under the window."

The tips of Marc's ears turned cherry red.

"Plus," she said, waving her hand at the board, "if you look at this with a logical eye and not an emotional one, it's clear that someone has gone to a lot of trouble to make it look like I am the thief. A position she appears far too ready to embrace, for whatever reason." She leaned across the desk, her eyes fixed on his. "I'd say she's too emotionally involved with this case because she's emotionally involved with *you*. This is the perfect way for her to squash any feelings you might still have for me that could cause you to second-guess your commitment to her."

"Addie!"

"Think about it. She knows you're dedicated to your law enforcement career, and by accusing me of theft and possibly murder, it's a heck of a way to make sure you wouldn't have any temptation or thoughts about trying to make things work between us again."

Marc's gaze dropped. His fingers slid across the brim of his cap. "Is there a chance that could ever happen?" he asked, looking up, his eyes searching hers.

"Look, Marc, part of the problem with us was that as long as I played by *your* rule book, we were good, but as soon as I didn't, you had an issue with it and could turn downright nasty, like now. You could never handle the thought that I might have a few rules of my own, and they may not be your idea of protocol but they did get results, didn't they?" Her eyes flashed. "So that's exactly what I'm going to do here, with all this." She waved her hand toward the board. "I think we both knew deep down that it would never work out between us in the long run. We wanted different things in life. And here we are now, and it looks like we both ended up getting what we wanted, just not together."

"You're right."

"Yup, and Ryley seems perfect for you."

"She is," he said, squaring his shoulders, "and I'm hoping you and I can move past what happened between us and at least go back to being friends."

"Friends?" She snorted. "I wanted that, too, but then you arrested me for theft and possible murder. Not to mention the horrible way you've treated me through all this. And now . . ." She shouldn't have enjoyed Marc's flinching jaw as much as she did. "I don't know, maybe we will be friends again in the distant future. Until that frosty day comes, I first have to prove to you that the evidence you *think* you have against me actually leads to the real thief and killer."

"As your *friend*, I'll tell you again: Stay out of this— more than ever before because you *are* the suspect right now."

"Then I have nothing to lose, and it makes it more imperative that I do a little digging on my own."

"I think I'd better leave now because I really don't want to have to cuff you again, and if I stay any longer and you say much more, then I'll have to." Marc spun around and thumped into Simon's chest. Marc's head ticked in a curt nod as he pushed past him.

Chapter 20

"What was that all about?" Simon studied Addie's heat-reddened face.

"Never mind him. Did you see Paige? How is she?"

"I'm off this weekend so I didn't go into the hospital after we got back. But as soon as I got your text, I went in to see what was going on."

"And?"

"She's awake. It appears she has a mild concussion and a small contusion on the back of her head. Other than that, there are no injuries but Dr. Phelps wants to keep her overnight for observation." He glanced into the front of the sales floor as an officer strode past the door. "When I was there," his said, voice dropping, "Ryley came in to take her statement."

"Did you hear any of it?"

"Yeah, and it doesn't make much sense. Her head injury might be more severe than Phelps thought, so I'm glad they're keeping her in a bit longer."

"What did she say?"

"She said she was dusting bookshelves and was

keeping her ears open for the door chimes because she didn't want to get startled by any customers who might come in. She swears she never heard anything, and then out of the corner of her eye, the books along the wall shelves started flying off in every direction. She said it was like something out of the movie *Poltergeist*, and when she started to turn around to investigate, all she saw was a dark blur. Her head exploded with a sharp pain, and then everything went black."

"Wow." Addie paced back and forth in front to the blackboard. "This isn't the first time the books in that aisle have been found on the floor, but definitely the first time Paige saw it happening."

"What do you mean this isn't the first time?"

Addie filled Simon in on the tossed books on the floor that morning before she headed off to the sale.

"And you have no idea how it happened then?"

"I thought maybe a truck went by. The building's so old it shook the books off the shelves, but"—she shrugged—"who knows now." Her thoughts replayed finding Paige's body limp on the floor, covered in books.

"That's a good theory, though."

"Yeah, the first time it happened, but this time? It seems something else is at play."

"Do the police have any theories?"

"Just that maybe it was an attempted robbery, except nothing was stolen."

"Interesting." Simon rubbed his jaw. "Anyway, what was that whole scene with Marc all about?"

"I basically told him that I was tired of everything happening *to* me and, of course, pointed out how despicably he's been treating me since he came back. I also made it clear, I think, that from now on I was going to start making thing happen on *my* terms, not his or *hers*!" She picked up a piece of chalk and under-lined *Ryley Brookes*. "Proving my innocence is number one."

"You really don't think she's a person of interest, do you?"

"Yes, I do. The more stuff that keeps happening *to* me, the more I'm thinking I was set up, and she has the strongest motive for that."

"You're not being realistic. Why on earth would an FBI agent set you up?"

"Because there's something fishy going on with her, and she seems to be the one pushing my guilt."

"She is that. When I presented the sleep app to the DA, she tried to poke holes in all the cyber evidence I provided. She tried to tell the DA that someone else could have been wearing your watch while you were performing the thefts. I pointed out that the heart rate would have changed. Good thing this particular model stores a record, and I could show him how that night's heart rate was consistent with the three weeks preceding."

"Why is she so bent on me being the thief?"

"Did you know she was with the cyber security department of the FBI?"

"No. Isn't she still?"

"What I could gather, from overhearing snippets of their conversation from the backseat, is she was trans-ferred to teach at Quantico. That's how she and Marc met."

"Did she say anything about being on a leave of ab-sence?"

"No, but there were a few unfinished sentences and some glances between the two of them today."

"What kind of glances?"

"I don't know. Does it matter?"

"Just wondering. I'm trying to figure out their relationship."

"Do you really care about it?"

"No, I don't care. Whatever it was that he and I had is over." She gazed into Simon's eyes and forced her heart back into her chest. He *was* her person, him and Serena, the two people in the world who actually got her. "Did the DA give you any indication of which way he was leaning after you presented him with my alibi?"

If Simon noticed the change of subject, he didn't show it. Perhaps he was just as relieved as she was not to talk about Marc anymore. "Not really, but my gut says he was going to look into it deeper. All we can do is wait now and see what he decides."

"I can't wait anymore. So far this week that's all I've done, and I can't help but think that this attack on Paige was a warning."

"What makes you say that?"

"All the books that were on the floor that covered her were ghost story books or books about the supernatural. Someone is really trying to make this look like a paranormal event."

"Especially given that Paige didn't hear or see anyone behind her when the books started to fly around."

"Yeah." She pressed her lips tight. "But I just can't see how they could have pulled it off, though. The police didn't find any strings running along behind the books. You know, something someone could have planted earlier that they could tug on to make the books fly off, and I can't figure out another way it could have worked."

"The culprit might have taken any trace of the threads or other props they used when they left?"

"You're right." She shook herself. "But regardless of how this was staged, my gut tells me it was a warning sent to scare me off."

"Scare you off of what? So far you haven't done anything except get arrested for robbery and spend the night in jail."

"I know. That's why it doesn't make sense. Tonight was the first time I've even written any of the clues on the board, so it's not like someone has seen them and got scared because I'm on to something."

"But you did have names on there before."

Addie blew out a deep breath. "You're right."

"Do you think Paige's attack and the book thefts are related?"

"My instincts tell me they are, just like they tell me Charlotte was murdered and didn't coincidentally die."

"Addie, I still haven't completed the autopsy, but what I have so far shows no indications of any cause of death other than what I reported to Marc. It appears to have been a heart attack."

"Okay, then what can cause a heart attack?"

"Poor lifestyle choices, hereditary factors, illness, disease. There's a number of factors that can contribute to heart failure."

"Poison?"

"Yes, but I haven't found any indication of that."

"On the upside that means at least one of Ryley's theories about me giving Charlotte some tainted tea was wrong."

"The woman died, and someone took advantage of her death to steal the books. That's what happened."

"Okay, Sherlock, then how did they get into the library and achieve that?"

His face went ashen.

"Exactly. We need to get back into that house without Jerry hanging over my shoulder."

"What are you talking about?"

"Nothing, come on. It sounds like the police are finishing up out front. We need to take a drive."

Addie locked the front door after the last officer left and hopped into Simon's Tesla Sport Coupe. He drove to the corner, turned right up Main, and then a few blocks down he turned left on the winding street toward Hill Road House.

Addie glanced at the dashboard clock. She was pleased to see that it was past six. That meant the yard sale had been over for a couple of hours and shoppers would be long gone. Simon pulled into a space in front of the main gate. They started up the sidewalk but stopped midway under a bough of the old maple tree when the front door burst open. Blake appeared, his hands clenching the shirt collar of a short, balding man.

"I told you to stay away from here!" Blake hauled him out onto the porch and shouted mere inches from the man's flustered face. "You've caused enough trouble for all of us lately!"

"She was my sister, and that means I now have the legal right to the money you still owe for the work she did." The man poked his finger into Blake's chest.

"Exactly. The work *she* did. Remember that and get out of here. I already told you that the firm will receive what's owed to them *after* the private bidders' auction is completed."

"But that's not for weeks, and I . . . we have bills to cover."

"Your gambling debts aren't my problem, and they should never have been Charlotte's, either." Blake shoved the man and he tumbled, arms flailing, down the stairs.

The bald man sprung to his feet, brushed off his beige trousers, and pointed at Blake, his finger, thumb and hand mimicking a cocked gun. A sardonic chuckle rumbled in his chest.

Blake's eyes smoldered black as he planted his left foot on the top step and pointed his own finger at the man. Addie winced at the transformation in the character of her old family friend. This threatening side of Blake was one she'd never seen before. "Get out of here now and consider yourself lucky that Robert called you a taxi and not the police after that scene you created with him in the library."

"Go ahead, call the police," the man taunted. "I want to report *you* and *him* for stealing my money." He shook his fist in the air.

"*Your* money?" Blake hissed and descended another step. "If I remember correctly, your father still holds the controlling shares in the company."

"Pfftt!" The man sprayed spittle as he wobbled on unsteady legs. "That old coot. He doesn't even know what day of the week it is anymore. What do you think he's going to do?"

"You'd be surprised at what he *does* remember. One call from me and—"

"And what? He'll disinherit me?" A short humorless laugh erupted from the man.

"If you know what's good for you," Blake hissed between clenched teeth, "you'll shut your mouth now and get in the taxi. Never come near me or my employees again because then you will find out just how far my reach goes." He stomped across the porch and into the house, slamming the door behind him.

The bald man whizzed by Addie, his elbow grazing her ribs, leaving both her and Simon in a wake of lemon gin.

"Who do you think that is?" Simon watched the man weave an unsteady path down the sidewalk.

"I think that's Charlotte's brother, Duane, and I hope he's not driving and takes the taxi."

"Why?"

"He's obviously drunk. Look at him, and he reeked of alcohol."

Simon peered around the stone pillar gate post. "Don't worry. He got in the cab."

"Good." Addie breathed a sigh of relief. "Well, shall we go and see if we can find out what that was all about?"

Simon tucked her hand in his as they ascended the creaking porch steps. She gave him a sideways glance. His chiseled features never failed to make her heart thump a little stronger, and she smiled to herself. After everything she put him through, she was grateful he'd waited for her to be ready for him, and gave his hand a gentle squeeze as they stepped inside. Thankful he had channeled his inner Rhett Butler to her challenging Scarlett O'Hara last year when she struggled to lay David's ghost to rest and was torn between him and Marc. Now if he would only do what Rhett couldn't in the end: be patient a little longer. She was coming to the realization of what he meant to her, just like Scarlett eventually did, but for Scarlett it had come too late. Addie gave his hand another squeeze.

Chapter 21

The front entry was a buzz of activity. Staff members appeared and disappeared, carrying antiques and collectables from the front rooms to the back of the house. A young man Addie had met before came down the stairs, carrying a Victorian floor lamp. "Jeff, wait! Are you taking that out to the back for the yard sale tomorrow?"

"Yes, I am, Miss Greyborne. As the items out there sell, we're moving more leftovers out. Mr. Edwards wants as much as possible sold by the end of the sale tomorrow."

"Could I buy that lamp now?" Not waiting for an answer, Addie fished around in her large handbag for her wallet.

"There is no way I'll take your money." Blake's voice echoed across the foyer. "You earned that lamp with the work you did on the appraisals."

"Honestly, I couldn't."

"Yes, you can and will." He grinned and glanced at Jeff. "Jeff, could you please put a sold sign on that and leave it by the front door so Miss Greyborne can pick it up on her way out?"

Jeff scrambled into the front living room and moments later returned with the lamp, a red SOLD tag dangling from the fringed lamp shade.

Blake reached for Addie's hand, squeezed it. "It's just a small token of my deep gratitude, my dear."

"Thank you so much, Blake." Addie batted at a fringe with her finger. "It will look perfect in the dark corner of my shop."

"What brings you by this evening?" Blake signed a sheet of paper on a clipboard a young staffer handed him.

"I've been"—Addie cast her eyes to the Oriental hallway runner—"preoccupied the past few days with—"

"The arrest?"

"Yes." Heat crept up her face. "Yes, my arrest, and I haven't had much time to talk to you since that horrible morning."

Blake's attention was distracted by a young man carrying a box down from upstairs. "Is that from the master bedroom?"

"Yes, Mr. Edwards."

"Did Robert check the contents of the room first? I don't want what we've set aside for the Boston auction to go for pennies at the yard sale."

"I don't really know."

Blake gestured with a tic of his head toward the kitchen. "Then I guess it's a good thing he's back there checking the inventory before any of you remove it from the house."

"Yes, sir, I'll find him straightaway."

"Nothing goes out without him or me approving it for the yard sale first, got it?"

The young man nodded and hustled down the hallway.

"Sorry about that." Blake rubbed his hands together as if to warm them. "Yes, we do need to catch up. However, as you can see, we're trying to get ready for the last of the sale tomorrow. Did you want to walk while we chat?"

Addie looked at Simon, who gave a slight shoulder shrug.

"Actually, I can see from here that the police tape is removed from the library door. Does that mean they're finished their investigation?"

"Yes, just about an hour ago. There was some concern about a missing feather pen, but with all the other stuff that's gone missing lately, they really couldn't find much reason to keep the room locked up for that one little item."

"Is that why there was such a strong police presence here today? I saw you speaking with Jerry, one of the officers, and the grounds were crawling with police."

"Yes, we discovered more thefts this morning when we came in."

"What kinds of things were missing this time?"

"Well, there was an old tumbler music box, some old photos, an antique vanity hairbrush and hand mirror set, an old record player, and some vinyl albums. All things we had set aside for the yard sale. Oh, and a few other books—"

"From the library?"

"Yes. When we discovered the other missing inventory, I called the police. When they came in, they wanted me to check the library with them to see if anything had been disturbed in there. That's when I noticed that a number of other books had been removed from the table."

"Which ones?"

"I'd have to check the inventory list, but by my recollection of what Charlotte had told me earlier, there should have been copies of the *Wizard of Oz*, *Ulysses*, and an 1882 edition of Victor Hugo's *Les Misérables*. I remember those because she was beside herself with their discovery."

Addie whistled. "All books worth some serious money at auction."

Blake set his lips in a firm line.

"Is that why you told Duane McAdams you weren't going to pay the appraisal bill now?"

"You heard that?"

"Not intentionally"—she glanced at Simon—"but you were arguing on the porch when we arrived."

"I'm sorry you had to witness that scene." Blake cast his eyes downward. "But can you believe that little twit expects me to write him a personal check for Charlotte's appraisal work?"

"That's an unusual request, isn't it? I mean, to pay him now and not wait until the sales contract is complete. As I imagine, all funds would have to be distributed through the courts since the estate auction was ordered by them for repayment of back taxes?"

"Darn right it is, and when it's all cleared, the payment will be going directly to the McAdams firm, *not* to Mr. Duane McAdams. How he ever got that idea in the first place is beyond me."

"He must be desperate for money." She recalled the argument she'd witnessed between Blake and Charlotte about Duane. It made her wonder if he would be desperate enough to take his own sister out of the picture and steal books worth a fortune.

"He and everyone associated with this hapless contract. We're all going to lose money on it. With all the thefts, I can't be expected to pay for the inventory we don't have anymore to sell. I tried to tell him that an insurance claim will have to be filed once we find Charlotte's laptop to get her appraisal inventory list to compare the lost products to. Until that's done, the McAdams firm will just have to wait until after the final sale in Boston next month to receive even a partial payment."

"Did Duane contribute in any way to the hours involved in sorting and appraising the stock?"

"Never worked a day in his life, that one." Blake's face twisted in a mock laugh. "Since you're here, would you mind going into the library to look through the books? I couldn't give the police a complete report because, without Charlotte's list, I had to go on memory of what I'd been told she and Robert discovered. Maybe there's more missing that you might remember appraising or seeing on Wednesday."

"Sure." Addie bit the inside of her cheek to keep her excitement in check.

One corner of Simon's mouth twitched. "Did you notice any other books missing when you were in here earlier?"

"When were you in the library?" Blake asked Addie, his brows bumped together.

"This morning, Jerry, one of the police officers, and I thought we saw smoke in the hallway. We went in to make sure there wasn't a fire."

"That's happened to me and a few of the staff a couple of times, too." The creases in Blake's face deepened. "But we never found anything. I guess it's just a quirk of this old house."

"Yes, that must be it." Addie held her voice even as

she fought to contain the excitement bubbling up in her chest. She wasn't seeing things. Others had seen it, too

"So, you'll take a look at the books?"

"Yeah, no problem."

"Wonderful. Let me look after a few other things with the staff and check on Robert's progress in the kitchen. I'll come and find you as soon as I can."

Butterflies swarmed her stomach at Blake's request. This was exactly what she'd hoped for when she dragged Simon along. As the threesome stood in front of the closed library doors, a cold air current enveloped them. She shivered and noticed goose bumps rising up on Simon's arms. He obviously felt it, too. *A least I'm not going crazy.* "I assumed this house had never been updated with air-conditioning, but judging by how quickly it got cold, I guess I was wrong."

"No, you're not wrong," Blake said. "There's no AC, and we've found it weird how it will suddenly get unbearably cold in spots. I never take my sport jacket off despite it being seventy degrees outside. Now, if you'll excuse me for a few minutes."

Addie rubbed her arms to keep warm, and Simon flung the doors open. Bitter cold air encased them. "What on earth?" She peered inside. "This is weird. How can it be this frosty in here when the sun's still out and we're in the middle of a heat wave?"

"The chill we felt in the hallway must have been the cold air seeping from under the door of this room."

"But where's it coming from?"

"Some of these old houses do stay rather cool in the heat."

"I know. The construction back then was far more solid than new construction is, but this is ridiculous. I can almost see my breath," Addie said, tiptoeing into the room.

Simon followed her in. The goose bumps on his arms were amplified tenfold as he came to her side. "You got lucky with Blake asking you to check this room, but I suspect that even if he hadn't, you would have found an excuse to get back in here. Mind telling me what we're looking for?"

"You heard him. He wants me to check through the books."

"Yeah, but you only found out about that a few minutes ago. Before he provided you with an excuse, there must have been something you wanted to check out." Simon held her gaze. "Mind telling me, so I keep my eyes open, too? Because to me, everything looks exactly as it did on Thursday morning."

"No, there's something different. I sensed it this morning. I can't put my finger on it, but I'll know when I see it." Addie thumbed through a pile of books. She dug around in her tote bag and pulled out a small memo pad and pen and began writing.

"What did you find?"

"It's what I didn't find. There are four other books, aside from the ones Blake already mentioned, that aren't here now. I'm just making note of the titles for when he finds the inventory list, so he can cross-reference them."

"And you're sure they were here."

"Positive. Kalea and I talked about them, and I showed her the publishing dates, how to search them in the various rare book online catalogues, and how to calculate their worth based on their current condition."

"You told her all that?"

"Yes, it was part of her training for the work we had in store for us the rest of the day."

"I know she's family to you"—he placed his hands gently on her shoulders—"but I feel I have to point this out: She's gone, and so are some very valuable books."

Addie hung her head. "I know how this looks, but I just can't believe my cousin would have had anything to do with this."

"Before Wednesday, when was the last time you'd seen her?"

"Ten years ago."

"A lot can happen in ten years."

"I know, but—"

"You know what? Just forget I said anything about her." His lips brushed over her forehead before resting his against hers. "Blake said when they came in this morning other things in the house were missing, and the police brought him in here to check this room. Did he say if the doors were locked when they entered the room?"

"He didn't."

"Let me go find him to ask. If they were *unlocked*, like they were when you came in with Jerry, there wouldn't be as much of a mystery as to how someone got in here. But if this morning when Blake came in, they were *locked* . . ." He double-tapped his knuckles on the table. "I'll be back in a minute."

Even though the body was long gone, the feeling of haunted eyes still permeated the room and Addie's soul. She shivered and sorted through the books, creating stacks based on publishing dates from rarest and oldest to newest. It took her mind off the fact she was freezing and alone in a room where invisible eyes cooled one's heart.

There was a scuffling noise behind her, and she relaxed. "Did you find Blake? What did he say?"

There was no answer.

"Simon?"

Nothing.

"Simon?"

Chills raced along her spine. A coil of wispy white smoke billowed in the fireplace, and then poof, it was sucked into the chimney, leaving the room empty and Addie's heart sinking to her shoes.

Chapter 22

Heart back in place, Addie tiptoed to the fireplace. Too embroiled in her thoughts, she almost stepped on the previously missing feather pen. Simon and Blake came through the doors, and she jumped.

"What's wrong?" Simon rushed to her. "You're as pale as—"

"A ghost?" But Addie didn't look at him because her gaze was focused on the feather pen lying by the fireplace. "Blake, did you find the pen today and put it back here in the library?"

"No, but . . . What's his name?"

"Jerry?"

"Yeah, did ask me about it later. But I hadn't seen it. I don't even remember it being here on Thursday, but Jerry confirmed it was because he had photos of it. But when he and I came in here this morning to check this room after the other thefts were discovered, I don't remember seeing it then."

Simon's darkening eyes fixed on hers. "Blake said the police had to unlock the library this morning, but it was unlocked when you came in later because they'd been in and out of here all day."

"You can't remember if the pen was here earlier or went missing later?" Addie asked.

Blake shook his head. "Sorry."

"The pen reappeared"—she pointed to the floor—"but it's funny how the laptop has never turned up."

"No, it hasn't," said Blake, "and Robert has no idea where it is. He has his own. There's a partial inventory list on it. He always sent his work to Charlotte, and then she'd add her own to make a complete list."

"The night she died, did he say why he was upstairs?"

"Yes, he told the police that about two a.m., she got into a foul mood and was snappy about everything. He even made her a cup of tea in the hope it would calm her down, but even that didn't placate the witch. He finally let her have it. They quarrelled and she sent him away, but with strict orders to be back by seven. He decided it was too late to go back up to the hotel for just a few hours' sleep, so he went upstairs and crashed on the master bed."

"Had he done that before?"

"Not as far as I know. The mattresses are fairly old and stale. I wouldn't have wanted to sleep on one, personally. Anyway . . ." Blake squeezed the bridge of his nose between his thumb and forefinger. "I'd better get back to work. I think we've come to the last of the boxes to be moved outside, and I need to get the staff started on boxing up what I've tagged to be shipped back to Boston."

"Will there be much furniture left? The real-estate agent mentioned he was hoping the house would be cleared out by the end of next week."

"That man has been nothing but a thorn in my side. At first, he wanted nothing touched, and then he wanted nothing left over. He'll take what he gets. The bank has given my company until the end of the month to dispose of all the estate holdings. He can wait." Blake approached the doors and then stopped. "You haven't seen my nephew, have you?" At Addie and Simon's head shakes, the line of his mouth set firm. "That boy. Smart as a whip in business but runs like a rabbit away from any hard work." He grumbled all the way to the doors, which banged behind him.

Simon cupped his hands together and blew into them. "Is it my imagination, or is it colder in here now than it was earlier?"

"The sun is starting to set." Addie glanced out the window. "Maybe that's why."

"You're probably right." Simon took her hand from the fireplace mantel and stroked his thumb in small circles over the back of it. "Why were you as white as a sheet when we came in?"

She recounted her encounter with the apparition. As she finished there was a low scraping noise from over his shoulder, and they both turned to look, but there was nothing out of the ordinary.

"You do know that's not a ghost? It's probably just mice," he said. "These old houses are infamous for them, especially ones that have been closed up for nearly seventy years."

"You're right." She remembered the coil of smoke. "But it is getting harder not to believe in the ghost theory."

Simon dropped her hand. "Did you find what you were looking for? Because I think we should leave."

"I still have to find something that proves my innocence."

"I just don't think it's good for you to spend any more time here. You're not thinking clearly with all this ghost talk, and now"—he waved his hand in front of the fireplace—"thinking you saw an apparition?"

"I saw something. I know I did. Just like I did at the top of the stairs the first day I was here. Something weird's going on here. How else do we explain the locked room, the missing books . . . and that!" She pointed to the feather pen lying on the floor.

"I don't remember it being there Thursday. Pretty sure with all the foot traffic around the body it would have been trampled."

"That's because it was in that old inkwell on Thursday when you came. But when I was in here with Jerry earlier, it was gone."

"Now here it is on the floor in front of the fireplace." Simon squatted on his haunches to study the pen and the area in front of the hearth.

Addie snapped a couple of photos of it with her phone. "I'll have to show this to Jerry." She stuffed her phone in her pocket. "I don't know what to make of it since Blake says the room was locked until they came in this morning. Do you have any ideas?" She trained her eye over the marble mantelpiece.

"Nope, sorry. This has me as baffled as you."

She ran her fingers over the scrolled carvings. "Jerry and I looked at this detail earlier and didn't see anything out of the ordinary but . . ." She bent closer, her fingers tingling with anticipation. "Hand me that feather pen."

"What about prints? We shouldn't touch it if you think the police will be interested in its reappearance."

"You're right." She fished around in her pocket and retrieved the glove Jerry had given her earlier. "Ready?" She snatched up the pen.

"What are you thinking?"

"I'm thinking that these little decorative notches,

which I assumed were only part of the pattern, are more than that." She waved him closer. "See how this one in the center of the design has a very slight scratch mark here?" She stabbed the tip of the ink pen into it. The mantelpiece shuddered, and the back of the fireplace slid to their left, wrought-iron log holder and all.

Simon's eyes widened as they stared into a hidden room behind the fireplace.

Addie shot Simon a side glance as she bent down and scrambled into a small brick room. Simon, close behind her, whistled when he stood upright. "I can't believe this. Do you think it was built as a panic room?"

"I don't know. The brick looks old. I'm not sure they had panic rooms when the house was built."

"What year do you think that was?"

"About the same time as mine, I think, so about the mid-eighteen-hundreds."

"But why build a room that doesn't lead anywhere?"

"Who knows? Maybe the original owner had some deep, dark secrets he wanted to keep hidden."

"Do you know who owned it originally?"

"I only know that it's been in the Gallagher family for years. At least that's what the ghost story suggests, so I'm assuming that it was built by the family."

"I can certainly see why a room like this would give credence to ghost legends. But I think we need to do more digging into the family background if we want any idea why this would have been built. It might answer a few questions."

"This could be how the person who stole the books got in and out of the library when the door was bolted from the inside."

"Exactly. I'm guessing that they stayed hidden in here until the police left and the coast was clear for them to make a run for it."

There were no markings on the brick from what she could see, and the room was empty except for something white in the corner just over her shoulder. "Look."

"It's a folding stepladder."

"It's one of those plastic three-step ones. It's not wooden like one you'd expect to find in a seventy-plus-year-old house."

"Which means it's newer."

"Very new," Addie said, opening the stool with her gloved hand. "It's hardly got any dust or grime on it." She took a closer look at the walls. "See that?" She placed the stool at the opening to the hidden room and climbed onto the top step, slid a disk aside, and peered out. "This explains why I always felt like someone was watching me in the room."

"What do you see?"

"Take a look for yourself." She clambered down.

Simon climbed up on the stool. "Wow, that's a pretty good view of the entire room."

"Yes," Addie said from the library side of the hearth, and ducked back into the brick enclosure. "And it's camouflaged by the left eye of the man in the painting over the mantel."

Simon climbed down. "That means while the thief waited for everyone to leave, he could also hear what was going on in the library. That's why he was always one step ahead of everyone else."

"This is probably where he stashed the other things he stole, waited in here until everyone left for the day, and then had no problem slipping them out at night."

"It's also how he learned that you had broken your nail and the value of the books you found."

"Not to mention the existence of the Beeton's first

proof of *A Study in Scarlet,* which alone is worth over a hundred and fifty-six thousand dollars."

Philip Atkinson flashed in her mind. Despite the fact that she had only discovered the books on Wednesday, and they hadn't been advertised in the auction catalogue, she knew by his comments in her store that he was aware of their existence. He did have a reputation as a ruthless broker who would stop at nothing to get what his client wanted. The only reason he would be here in the first place was because one of his clients wanted something in particular from this estate sale. It stood to reason, given that the Holmes collection reproductions would have taken a day or two to locate, someone had to have known about the books' existence before Wednesday. That someone was either Philip himself or someone he was working with on the inside.

"I have to call Marc."

Simon placed his hand over hers. "I will. There's less likely to be as much drama since you're still a suspect, and we haven't heard that the DA has dropped charges."

"You're right. But this can prove that there was another way the books could be stolen. It answers so many questions. I'm just afraid that Ryley will try and make it sound like I knew about this room, and it was me using it."

"I think that one's even a reach for her to prove."

"I hope so."

When Simon stepped out to talk to Marc, Addie paced the small room, studying the shades of caulking between the bricks. It didn't make sense that this space had been so well constructed and great pains had been taken to conceal its existence to have it just end in a dead end. There must be something they were missing. Her toe caught on a board edge.

"Simon, look at this." Crouching, she ran her fingers over an area of the uneven, aging oak plank floorboards. She felt a slight indentation between two planks and pulled. With a groan the board edge pulled upward, revealing a three-by-three-foot trapdoor. As she lifted the door, musty air and decay leeched into the small space. She gagged on the nasty dust motes.

"I'll be darned." Simon peered down the black cavernous hole.

Pinching her nose closed with one hand, she tugged her phone out of her jeans pocket and shined the light over the edge of the opening. "It's a stone staircase." Her nasal tone echoed down into the subterranean chamber.

Simon grinned and gave her a sidelong glance. "Yeah, but judging by the green algae on those stairs, I'd say it hasn't been used for years."

"You're right." She leaned farther over the edge, having to release the hold on her nose to keep her balance, and shone the light deeper. "Yuck, it reeks down there." She pulled back, covering her nose and mouth with her hand.

"It does explain this room in some ways, though."

"I wondered if the original owner was a smuggler, but by the putrid smell coming up the stairs, he could have also been a mass murderer and stashed his victims down there." Bile erupted into the back of her throat.

"I guess that's the stuff of ghost legends." Simon closed the lid. "I think we'll leave the inspection of this area to the police. They have hazmat suits, and we don't."

"I'm not going to argue with you." Addie stood up and wiped her hands on her cropped jeans. "How long did Marc say it would be until they got here?"

"He only said as soon as they could. There's an incident in the town center."

"What kind of incident?" A cold tickle of unease rippled across Addie's shoulders as Paige's colorless face surrounded by toppled books flashed behind her eyes.

Chapter 23

Addie crept back through the fireplace opening into the library and studied the portrait of the aging gentleman. His mutton chops and neatly clipped beard gave him an aristocratic appearance. However, the hollowness of his eyes made her shiver. She couldn't decide if the painting depicted an accurate window into this man's soul, or if the emptiness in his eyes was a result of the sliding peephole behind the wall.

Either way, her curiosity was piqued. Monday morning she'd go to the town clerk's office and see what information they had about him and if there were any original copies of the architectural plans of the house on record. If the fireplace hideaway and the tunnel entrance were any indication of what was built into these walls, somewhere buried in the town archives there might be a clue to other secrets the house held.

"We might be in for a long wait." Simon made himself comfortable in one of the reading chairs by the window and patted the one beside him. "It's a good time to tell me all the details of this ghost story everyone is mumbling about."

Overcome by the haunting expression in the eyes of the man in the portrait, Addie took one last look at the painting and settled into the deep leather chair. "There's not much I can tell you. I never paid much attention to the grumblings I heard about the house."

"Really?" His eyes glistened with amusement. "Addie, the lover of all things pirates and historical, dissed rumors of a real-life haunted mansion?"

"Not entirely. I know the history of the old town haunted buildings that are part of the annual ghost walk. But I never paid much attention to this house until Serena told me what she'd heard, and then Paige verified it, and most everyone in town echoed the same tale."

"I can tell you that after I read the statement Blake gave the police, I can see why the tales did develop over the years."

"What did he say to Marc?"

"He said in his report to the police that when the court order came down to sell the entire estate for back taxes, the court-appointed attorney noted in his report that there was evidence of vagrants having lived in the house, which most likely gave rise to the stories of the house being haunted."

"I guess that would explain the reports of locals seeing glowing lights at night and shadows in the windows."

"Not exactly, because when I asked Marc about it, he denied it. He said the house was locked up pretty tight. Apparently, it was an unwritten rule by every police chief over the years to keep a close eye on the house because of the circumstances surrounding the owners' death and the disappearance of their son. The police knew the house hadn't been vacated, only left unattended and was still full of all the furnishings and whatnot."

"So much for the vagrant theory." Addie's gaze darted around the room, and she rubbed her hands over her chilly arms.

"However . . ." Simon paused for effect as Addie squirmed in her seat, glaring at him for being overly dramatic. "When Blake's company came in some months ago to start the cleanup and appraisal process, the cleaners reported to the police that it was clear someone had been living in the house recently."

"What did Marc say to that?"

"He told Blake to tell them that was impossible because every shift an officer would drive by and do security checks."

"Is that why Blake was so reluctant to report the thefts to the police after that?"

"It most likely played a part in it. Blake also told Marc that he didn't report the thefts because he thought it was a staff member, based on the fact that there was never any sign of someone having broken into the house. So he took actions himself to try and stop the pilfering."

"But they still continued." Addie shivered and glanced at the painting. "I guess that's why the tale of the house being haunted is spreading like wildfire right now. People want an explanation of what's happening here regardless of how ludicrous."

Simon's eyebrows rose with questions.

"Serena told me," Addie said, shifting in her seat, "that Arthur and Maeve Gallagher lived in the house with their son, William, who at the age of twenty-one had a major falling out with his father and left home in 1945 and never came back. Both his parents died five years later in 1950 under mysterious circumstances."

"You mean when William left, he never returned to Greyborne Harbor after that?"

Addie shook her head. "He didn't even come back for their funerals."

"That must have been some falling out."

Addie shrugged. "No one seems to know what happened between them. I guess in William's mind, his actions were justified."

"If he never came back, does that mean the house has been vacant since 1950?"

"Yeah, from what Serena said. William then ordered the house closed up, and it remained so until the court seized it for back taxes. I guess William passed away a few years ago, and the taxes fell into arrears. So the courts ordered the entire property and all contents to go to public sale and auction to pay off the money owed."

"But if he had no intention of returning, why didn't he just sell it so he didn't have to pay the taxes on it for all those years?"

"Who knows, really? But there's more to the story. William had a young wife, Kathleen, who also met with her demise right here in Hill Road House."

"You're kidding. What happened?"

"I guess it was during the young couple's first year of marriage in 1945 and shortly after the birth of their son. Apparently, Kathleen tripped over a frayed carpet edge at the top of the stairs and fell to her death. However, on inspection at the time, officers couldn't find evidence of the carpet being in need of repair."

"What did the police report say about it?"

"Not much. Serena said at the time it was classified

an accident. They figured if she didn't trip, she must have lost her balance. I guess given the recent birth and the fact it was in the middle of the night, they assumed she was dizzy and disorientated."

"It sounds like this William had a lot of tragedy in his young life."

Addie recalled her own personal tragedies. She knew all too well the gut-wrenching pain that follows losing everyone you love. "It was shortly after her death that William and his parents had the falling out and he left for good."

"What happened to the baby?"

"Apparently he left it with his parents when he took off. Then five years later they both died."

"What was the ruling in the deaths of Arthur and Maeve?"

"Double suicide." Addie pressed her lips into a thin line. "Locals believe that it was the continual sightings of Kathleen's ghost that brought about their deaths. It's still rumored to this day that her ghost, and most likely theirs, too, still walk the corridors of this house."

"And what happened to the child?"

"No one knows, he disappeared the same night they died. Just vanished—they couldn't find any trace of him."

"I'm sure the police didn't believe the ghost-story rumors. Their investigation must have showed something. Some evidence pointing to what happened?"

Addie shook her head. "Remember, it was 1950, and they didn't have the benefit of current fingerprinting techniques and a DNA database. At the time, investigators could find no evidence of what happened to the child, or a murder weapon, or signs of an intruder having entered the house."

"Plus, they couldn't really admit it could have been Kathleen's ghost that caused all the events, could they?"

"No, they couldn't." Addie frowned and shot forward in her seat. "I just had a thought. Maybe that's why William never sold the house. He was hoping his son would return someday."

Simon glanced over at the fireplace.

"What are you thinking?" she asked, following his gaze.

"Maybe he did . . . or never left. He would have been about five when his grandparents died. Maybe in all the commotion he got scared and went into hiding but got trapped. That stench in the tunnel . . . it makes you wonder if one of the mysteries might be solved soon."

The library doors burst open and Addie shot to her feet. Marc's soft-brown eyes darkened as he pinned her with a look.

Chapter 24

"Well, well, why am I not surprised to find you here, Miss Greyborne?" Marc stood at the door, his arms folded across his chest. "It seems you just can't stay away from the scene of a crime, can you?"

Addie prepared a snappy comeback, but Simon placed a warning hand on her arm. "I think you'll be most interested in seeing what our Miss Greyborne has uncovered, Chief." Simon motioned toward the fire place opening.

Marc's eyes never left Addie's face. "That's not hard to believe. You always were good at finding hidden compartments, weren't you?" His lip turned up in a half smile before he moved toward the fireplace.

"I think," Simon said as he joined him, "this answers a lot of questions about how the thief got into a locked room and managed to sneak all the missing antiques out of the house. It's the perfect place to store stuff until the house is vacated for the day and take it out under the cover of night."

"That still doesn't answer the question about the

staff returning to find the doors locked with no signs of forced entry—or, in this case, forced exit. Unless"— he crouched down and peered into the small brick room.—"this leads somewhere."

"Then you might want a couple of hazmat suits." Addie stepped up beside Marc. "We also found a staircase hidden under the floorboards. If your people can find evidence that it's been recently used, then maybe it leads to another exit."

Marc's brows knitted as he frowned. "We can't find any evidence of another door or entry into the house other than the front door and the rear door off the kitchen."

"Well, it might be worth checking out anyway."

"We will." Marc stiffened. "After all, that *is* what the police do." He snapped on a pair of blue rubber gloves and ducked into the brick room. Close on his heels were Jerry and another officer who motioned for Addie and Simon to remain on the library side.

Not wanting to miss a word of what was going on, Addie crouched down so she could overhear what was being said.

"It looks like we have a bit of work to do in here. Steve, can you run out to Jerry's van and get two of those disposable hazmat suits?"

Addie looked up at Simon. A Cheshire cat grin spread across her face. Steve crawled out past them back into the library and, by the puzzled expression on his face when he stood up, Addie could see that he, too, wasn't certain what to make of the unexpected reveal. All the way to the library door, he shook his head and could be heard muttering to himself.

"Miss Greyborne, Dr. Emerson, can you join us please," Marc called.

She winked at Simon as they ducked under the mantel and joined him inside the small room.

"Show me where you discovered this hidden door covering the staircase."

Addie ran her foot over the floorboards until her toe caught on the uneven edge. She bent down, slid her fingers under the lifted corner, and pulled. The three-by-three hinged door opened up, revealing their earlier discovery. She leaned the lid against the back wall and stepped away as the putrid odor from below threatened to send her toppling in a faint down the algae-covered staircase.

Marc held his hand to his face and gasped. "What is that wretched smell?"

Jerry sneezed and turned his head away.

"It smells like a corpse to me and if a suspicion I have is right, that's exactly what you're going to find down there," Simon said, seemingly unaffected by the wafting stench.

Addie veered her face away "You must be used to this."

"One never gets used to the smell of death. It only becomes less obtrusive over the years."

Bile formed in the back of her throat. She came to the quick conclusion that Simon could keep his dead bodies and nasty-smelling job.

Steve returned, wearing a white hazmat suit and oxygen mask. Another suit was draped over his arm, and he juggled a second mask and a coil of rope with his gloved hands. Addie curled her fingers into her palms to keep them from ripping the mask off his face and covering hers.

Jerry wrestled into the other one. If the odor in the small room had not been so revolting, Addie might have laughed at the sight of the two police officers dressed in their alien space suits.

Marc gave his men instructions, unraveling the long rope that was attached by a clip on the belt of each man. Little by little, as they descended into the depths of the house, he released more of the rope. There was a sharp jerk followed by a crackling noise across the speaker of the police radio on his shoulder. The rope went slack.

Marc pulled on it. The rope bounced up in a snarled heap at his feet. "Why would they unclip themselves?"

"I guess they are farther than the two hundred feet of rope you have." Simon toed the coiled rope at the edge of the abyss.

Marc tried to reach the two officers on his police radio. No answer. "What happened? They couldn't have just disappeared." Panic edged in his voice.

"Hey, Chief," a garbled voice came over Marc's radio, "can you go into the garden by the back door?"

Marc acknowledged the request and glanced at Addie and Simon. "What the heck?"

The three sprinted out onto the back porch. Addie shielded her eyes from the blazing sun on the horizon and laughed. There, by the yard sale tent, stood the two officers, their once-white suits covered with grime and greenish-gray sludge.

Marc rammed a hand through his hair "What the—?"

Jerry stepped forward—at least Addie thought it was Jerry based on the size of the looming swamp creature. He waved his hand toward the back stonewall fence and said something none of them could make out.

"Take your mask off, Jerry," Marc barked.

Jerry raised his oxygen face mask and repeated.

"The stairs lead to a tunnel that comes out under a trapdoor buried in the overgrowth at the back of the garden."

Addie caught her lip between her teeth to keep from smiling. "I guess that answers the question of how someone got the missing property out of the house." She cut Marc a smug glance.

"Not really, Miss Greyborne." Jerry tucked the mask under his arm. "The green slime doesn't appear to have been disturbed by anything larger than critters in probably a hundred years."

"Oh." Addie winced and glanced apologetically at Marc.

"What about the decaying corpse smell?" Simon piped in.

"Rats, lots and lots of rats, and some carcasses. Looks like mostly racoons and squirrels."

"No human remains?"

"Nope."

"So much for my theory." Simon shot Addie a side glance.

"I guess we're back to my original theory." She nudged Simon's arm. "The culprits hid out in the brick room until the coast was clear and took the stolen loot out of the house after everyone left for the day."

"That still doesn't answer the question of the staff returning in the morning to find the house locked up and no signs of a break-in." Simon turned a probing eye on Marc.

"That's true," Addie said. "Blake's theory about it being a staff person might be right after all."

"It's time we ran a complete background check on his entire crew." With a head tic, Marc gestured to Jerry and Steve. "You guys get cleaned up and meet us back inside."

"You two"—Marc waved a finger at Addie and Simon—
"wait in there." He pointed to the library door as he
veered off toward the sound of Blake's voice coming
from the top of the stairway.

"Okay," Marc said to Addie and Simon a few minutes later from the library doorway, "tell me everything you found today, how, and what you touched."

When Jerry and Steve returned, looking much better after their tunnel adventures, he instructed them
to comb through the brick room and around the mantel with a fine-toothed comb.

"So," he said, eyes focused on Addie, "what made
you think of using the tip of the feather pen as a lever
to open the hidden chamber door?"

"Because the pen was on the desk the morning I discovered the body. But when I came back earlier
today—"

Marc's brows shot to his hairline.

Well, when one steps into a pile of doo-doo, there's
no wiping it off to cover it up, so she had to at least
make it look good. "I came back this morning to see
Blake, but he was busy with the police. I was concerned about the books in the library, because . . ."
She brushed some hairs from her eyes, buying time
until she remembered the reason aside from her insa-
tiable curiosity. "I saw smoke in the hallway." She was
on a roll now. "Jerry came in to check the room with
me. That's when I noticed the pen wasn't in the inkwell, and I asked him why the police took it." She
flicked a glance at Jerry and decided to not count the
bulging veins on Marc's forehead. "He said it hadn't
been taken in evidence and had no idea where it
went."

Marc shot Jerry a piercing glare. Jerry resumed dusting the mantel for prints; red blotches mottled his face.

Addie wove her fingers together then took them apart in front of her. The awkwardness of the situation didn't escape her, but she knew Marc well enough to know it was best to ignore the tension between him and Jerry, even though she'd brought it on. Her calling attention to it would only hinder not help. She shifted her weight and forged ahead with her statement. "Later, Simon and I came in to have a look, because Blake told us there had been more thefts and asked me to check the table for any more missing first editions. I found the pen lying on the floor in front of the fireplace."

Without looking up, Marc scribbled in his notebook. "What then?"

"It seemed odd that it wasn't here earlier then suddenly it was. So it made me think that the pen must mean something. I took another look at the scrollwork on the mantel edge and noticed one of the decorative holes had some fine scratch marks around it. On a hunch, I picked up the pen." She hitched her hands on her hips. "Don't go getting your boxers in a bunch. I had a glove on. Anyway, where was I?"

"Picked up the pen," Simon offered, a smile playing at the corner of his lips.

"That's right. I stabbed the pen into the center of the hole." She waved her hand toward the open hearth. "And this is what we discovered."

"Simon, can you corroborate this?"

"Yes." His eyes narrowed. "It happened exactly as she said."

"Now"—Addie didn't care that her voice possessed

an edge of defiance—"will you consider my theory that Charlotte's death and the book thefts are related?"

"How so?"

"Obviously the killer was hiding in here to wait for her to leave. Maybe he or she got tired of waiting and decided to rush things along?"

With no acknowledgment of her sharpened tone, Marc directed his focus on Simon. "Have you completed the autopsy yet?"

"No, I'm still running a few tests."

"There you go, Addie. No proof of a murder, and unless there is, all I can do is investigate a grand larceny case." His voice sounded strangled.

"All done in there, Chief." Steve emerged from the chamber. "There's nothing. No prints, no fibers. It's as clean as a whistle."

"Even on the step stool?"

"No, Chief. I'd say our thief is a pro."

"What about the wood ash dragged into the chamber opening by someone? Any usable footprints there?"

"No, there wasn't enough ash for a good mold. Only partials, nothing conclusive."

"Pack it up, then. I guess we're done. At least this is a lead on where the merchandise was likely stashed until it could be moved out. We only have to try and figure out who knew about this hidden room."

"That could be one of over twenty people." Jerry pressed the pen nib into the hole Addie had shown them earlier. The back of the hearth slid back into place.

"Can we go now, Marc?" Addie asked. "It's late, and neither of us has eaten."

Marc glanced at his watch. "You're right, and I'm late for a dinner date." He snapped his notebook closed. "That's all for now, but I may have more questions—"

"I know the drill. Don't leave town and all that, yadda, yadda, yadda." Addie swung her tote bag over her shoulder.

"By the way." Marc shoved his pad into his jacket pocket. "Just before I got your call, the DA phoned and said he was dropping the charges against you."

"And you've been here how long now and didn't say a word about that?"

Marc ignored her comment. "It seems Simon was most convincing in the evidence he produced showing that you were, in fact, asleep at the time of the robbery."

Addie puffed out her chest. "I think these other robberies also prove that I was never the guilty suspect." She spun on her heel and stopped. "Does your new *partner*"—she emphasized the word, knowing Marc never liked it when she called herself that— "know about this?" At the tic of his right eye, she grunted. "I take it she doesn't. Where is she? I've gotten used to seeing her shadow you."

"Not that it really concerns you, but she had another matter to look after today." His gaze dropped. "I'm meeting up with her soon."

"Give her my best when you tell her the news about me no longer being her number-one suspect. I'm sure she'll be *thrilled*."

Marc fixed his cheerless eyes on hers. "Addie, it was never her intent to implicate you in any of this."

"Wasn't it? Right from the beginning, she did nothing but try to prove to you that I was guilty of stealing the Holmes books."

"That's not it. It's just that she's very good at her

job, and she was following the evidence, as all good officers of the law do."

"I think she took it a bit too personally, though, don't you?"

Simon laid his hand on Addie's arm and steered her from the room. "Don't go poking the bear," he whispered. "Just count yourself lucky, and let's go." When they were in the hallway, his blue eyes were void of their usual sparkle. "Care to tell me what's going on with you two?"

"What do you mean?" She searched his face.

"All this back-and-forth snipping between the two of you." He dropped his gaze. "It's all too reminiscent of when you were chasing his ghosts last year."

The corner of her mouth twitched as he walked away.

"I *am* chasing a ghost," she called, her voice uneven.

He stopped at the door but didn't turn to look at her.

"Only it's not the one you think." She ran to him, threw her arms around his shoulders, and nestled her cheek into his back. "Don't worry, ever," she whispered. "That ghost was laid to rest. We've both moved on. It's the person he's moved on with who concerns me."

"What I don't understand is why you're letting her get under your skin if you're not still feeling something for Marc?" His blue eyes darkened and filled with the pain. "Are you jealous of her?"

"Me? No, of course not. Why would you even ask? Marc and I have been over for months. You're my person, not him."

"Are you sure about that? It's just that I can't ever go back to the way it was before: always the three of us even when you and I were alone, him lurking in the shadows of your mind."

"Stop right there." She cupped his face in her hands and placed a whisper-light kiss on his lips. "I just don't like being accused of theft. It's like a sane person trying to prove she's not crazy. The more she protests, the crazier she appears. I was starting to feel like that until you finally proved I couldn't have been there."

Simon leaned his forehead against hers. "I guess I just wasn't prepared for all this when he finally came back. It was nice when he was away. I knew I had your full attention. I guess my insecurities got the best of me. It's just that I . . ."

"You what?"

"Nothing. Forget it." He opened the door.

"Wait, we can't forget—" She eyed her lamp with the SOLD tag waiting for her by the front door. It probably wouldn't fit in his Tesla Roadster anyway. She could pick it up tomorrow. After all, it was Sunday, and her shop was closed. Besides, it would give her an excuse to come into the house while everyone was busy with the final day of the sale out back. There were still too many questions about the evening's discovery and too many puzzle pieces that weren't fitting. She glanced up at the top of the stairs, pursed her lips, and then stepped out onto the porch.

"Wait for what?"

"Me." Slipping her hand into his, she rested her head on his shoulder as they ambled down the sidewalk.

Chapter 25

Addie shoved the last piece of her burger into her mouth as Simon slurped up the last dregs of his strawberry milkshake. She tossed the wrappings into the trash can beside her back-room desk and sucked on the straw of her chocolate shake, reviewing the information on her blackboard.

Kalea, her disappearing cousin.

Blake, and the argument between he and Charlotte proving there was no love lost between them.

Then there was the altercation Blake had with Duane, Charlotte's brother, and how Blake had threatened him.

She set down her shake and wrote *Duane $?* and underlined it twice to highlight the man's desperation for money.

Robert, assistant to Charlotte who did not keep his feelings about his overly demanding employer private.

Garrett, Blake's nephew who would take over the auction business once Blake deemed him worthy, and the last person to see Kalea. She drew a line between

Garrett's name and her cousin's. *Was he the inside source, or was he the reason no one had heard from or could find any trace of Kalea?* Addie shivered, pushing aside the images that thought conjured in her mind.

She refocused on the board. *Philip Atkinson,* unscrupulous broker, and in general an all-around jerk, complete with a vendetta against her. He hadn't gotten over her shaming him with the board of directors at the British Museum when she proved his false accusations against her were just that.

"There's a lot of information on there," Simon said. "Any ideas yet how it all fits together?"

A grin spread across Addie's face. "I think it's time we put on our Sherlock Holmes caps, light our pipes, and see how all these pieces fall into place. As the Master Detective himself would probably say—there has to be one key element here."

Library door bolted from inside

Windows securely latched from inside – sash warped, unable to be opened without breaking window

No other entrance to room

Tipped over teacup

Books on floor dropped after tea spilt

Feather pen from inkwell on desk missing

Missing laptop?

Rare books and original magazine edition of debut story exchanged for cheap reproductions

Angle of the desk chair turned toward fireplace

Books on center display table, disturbed missing price/info cards

Firebox ashes smeared across hearth and floor

Faint footprint on throw carpet by desk – stepping in spilt tea?

My fingerprints on window ledge and pry bar and broken acrylic nail found outside of window!

Simon wiped his fingers on a paper napkin, plucked the piece of chalk from Addie's fingers, and added *reappeared* beside *Feather pen from inkwell on desk missing.* Then he wrote *hidden chamber* beside *No other entrance to room,* then drew a line from it to *Door bolted from inside* and an arrow to *Windows securely latched from inside.* "I think with our discovery of the chamber we solved that one."

"Except," she said, glancing at him, "that's not an entrance. It's just a possible hiding place."

"You're forgetting about the tunnel that leads out to the edge of the back gardens."

"You heard Jerry. He said it doesn't look like anyone's been inside there for over a hundred years."

"True, but it would only take once or twice for someone else to make that trek. It's dark down there and smelly. Jerry and Steve were probably a little disturbed by the rats and dead racoons they stumbled over. My guess is that their investigation was a fairly quick one. They might have missed some small clue like a piece of disturbed moss or scraped algae on the old brick stairs."

"Look at you go, Sherlock." Addie laughed.

"Does that make you my Watson?"

"I always thought more of myself as Holmes and you Watson." She stole back her chalk and wrote *Peephole in picture above fireplace. Plastic stepladder* and *other books and collectables missing.*

"Very good, now what would Holmes say in a case like this?" Simon gestured to the board.

"He'd say, 'Not everything is as it appears; sometimes it's what we don't see by clues and evidence that's the most important.'"

"You mean a gut feeling?"

"Not really, but think about it. By all evidence we

have and the police, too, this simply looks like a poor woman suffered an untimely heart attack, and, by coincidence, some very valuable books were stolen. My gut does tell me that the two are connected, and Charlotte's death wasn't a natural event."

"Addie." Simon shook his head. "As I've said before, there's no indication that she was intentionally killed. So far, I haven't been able to find any evidence of poisoning, trauma, injection. Her blood work is normal except for an elevated adrenaline level. There is no suggestion of foul—"

"You said she had a high adrenaline level?" Addie read over the notes on the board. "The tipped-over teacup."

"Why would that have anything to do with her adrenaline level? The tea was a regular common blend, probably Earl Grey."

"No, I don't mean she was poisoned, but I've been trying to figure something out regarding the tipped-over teacup. The contents had obviously dripped down the side of the desk onto the book below it. Charlotte must have been working on that book and the other one I found on the floor when she suffered her heart attack. The chair was facing the fireplace, and the book was under the desk with the tea stain *on* the cover not *under* the book."

"She would have had to drop the books first, knocked the teacup over, spilling the tea on the book, and then turn to face the fireplace. That doesn't make sense if she were having a heart attack. Why would she—"

"Because whoever was hiding in the fireplace chamber. waiting for her to leave for the night, must have decided to make his or her move when it was going on three a.m. and she was still working."

"She heard a noise behind her . . ."

"The hidden door opening." Addie snapped her fingers.

"And jumped, dropping the books and knocking the cup over when she spun around in the chair to see what the noise was, and—"

"Boom!" Addie slapped her hands together. "Her heart gave out. My gut tells me she was murdered, and it's the perfect murder, isn't it?"

"But the autopsy—"

"I know what it shows, but think about it. When we look at all the facts there are two different versions, and both are completely plausible." Simon's brow furrowed, showing his confusion. "One is that she was actually killed by a ghost. The other is it was made to *look* like a ghost committed the murder."

"You're saying we're looking for a hundred-year-old murderer?"

"Or someone with the knowledge of what took place in this house seventy-five years ago." She tapped the chalk stick in her palm. "The problem is to prove which version is true."

"Come on, Addie, you can't be serious. There is no such thing as ghosts, so it's the latter."

"Are you sure? Strange things can and do happen. Just ask poor Paige and her run-in with a poltergeist."

"I hope you're joking. You were the one that thought Serena and Paige and half the town were mad for believing the tall tale. Now look at you."

"But it does get in your head, doesn't it? I just can't forget the look in Charlotte's eyes when I found her, and then the look on Paige's face when I found *her*." Addie hugged her arms across her chest. "I need to get back into that house tomorrow and have another look.

I *know* logically there is no such thing as ghosts. So that means someone has tried hard to make it look like there is. There has to be another clue we're missing that will prove it. Otherwise, we're back to option number one."

"Well, none of that's not going to happen tomorrow."

"Why? The yard sale is on another day. Besides, we didn't pick up my lamp on our way out. It's a perfect cover for dropping in on Blake again and getting access to the house."

He lifted her chin, a grin on his lips. "Addie, did you accidentally on purpose leave the lamp there to give you an excuse to go back tomorrow?"

"I didn't think it would fit into your car." She couldn't keep a poker face around him and surrendered to a rather cheeky grin.

"You're probably right about that, but you're forgetting one important thing: We made plans last week with Serena and Zach for tomorrow."

"I forgot. We're meeting them for lunch, then going on that tour of the new dock and information center for the cruise line."

"Exactly, and there is no way you're going to be able to convince Serena to take a walk through a house she's terrified of. I'm surprised she even went to the sale with you today."

"It did take some convincing, and I did have to promise her she wouldn't have to go in."

"There, you see? The urgency of investigating is gone now since the charges against you have been dropped. Now you're only investigating because you're like—"

"A dog with a bone, I know." Addie smiled. "Okay, it won't hurt to take a day off. I want to stop in and check on Paige before we go tomorrow, anyway."

"Good plan. I think then that I'll go into the lab for a while in the morning."

"I thought you were off all weekend."

"I am, but you got me thinking, and there's something I want to check out."

"See, it's contagious."

He blinked owlishly.

"The sleuthing bug. You can't let it go any more than I can. Someone is dead, and some valuable books and antiques have gone missing. You want as badly as I do to figure it all out."

"My reasons are a bit different than yours, though."

"How so?"

"Because now I'm afraid I've missed something in the autopsy. You're right. It's too much of a coincidence that Charlotte died and the books were stolen from the locked library at the same time."

"And what?"

"And . . . truth be told, Ryley Brookes got under my skin, too, when we were meeting with the DA. I would like nothing better than to solve this whole thing just to prove to her how far off base she's been." He rubbed the back of his neck. "Unless, of course, your suspicions are correct and she's behind this"—his head shot up—"and then we can nail her on it!"

"Simon, you shock me." She gave a shaky smile and lost herself for a moment in his sea-blue eyes. "Revenge like that should be *my* motive."

"Not when it involves the woman I love."

Did I hear him right? Did he just say he loves me? She struggled to form the words back, her tongue tied with shock and pleasure. His face fell, and she knew she was too late to utter the words back to him. The special moment was lost. He was her friend, her person, her confidant, her safety net. *But love?*

"Too soon?" An awkward smile twitched at the corners of his lips. "Anyway, getting back to the case—"

Addie clasped his shirt collar and in one, swift movement urged him closer. He pulled her into his arms. His lips sought out her mouth. Her breath quickened as he drew her nearer, his lips hard yet soft against hers. Even though they had kissed before, for Addie this moment seemed like the first time.

Chapter 26

It was a perfect summer morning made even better by the fact that Paige was being discharged later today. Her doctor prescribed a few days off work and rest, but other than that she was fit to go.

Addie prepared to make some adjustments to accommodate Paige's absence. Daily sales in the shop had skyrocketed last year, and Paige's part-time status had been increased to full-time with benefits. Perhaps it was time to hire one more person to fill in part-time and help Paige pick up the slack when Addie was off on her book-buying—or sleuthing—adventures.

Addie danced a little jig in the driver's seat of her car at the realization that her shop had been a success, especially given the bumpy ride she'd endured when she was first opened. Back then she thought she'd be closing any day and worried about how she was going to pay Paige with the meager amount of money coming through the doors. Her heart pounded, knowing how proud her father would have been. She would never forget his words of wisdom after David's death:

"I didn't raise a quitter. Take your time to mourn, and then adjust your sails and set a new course." *Well, Dad, I did it. I didn't quit. Look at me now.*

She parked on one of the side streets off Marine Drive, the road running parallel to the seawall. This was the area of town where she and Serena spent many a Sunday. Both their shops were closed for the day, and they loved to check out the unique souvenir, antique shops, and vintage clothing stores in the area, and, of course, eat lunch at one of the quaint restaurants. She headed for their favorite fish-n-chips eatery. Simon was running late and said he'd meet up with them as soon as he could get away. Serena and Zach were no doubt already there and champing at the bit to get the day started. When she checked the time on her phone, she paused. There was a missed call from a number she didn't recognize, and a voice message.

"Hi, Addie. It's Kalea."

Addie sucked in a small gasp and pressed the phone to her ear.

"I know you must be furious with me for ditching you and disappearing like I did." Her voice cracked. "I only wanted to say I'm sorry"—sniffle—"but it couldn't be helped. I was forced to leave. There was no option. I'm okay and will call back and explain later. Bye."

"What's the matter?" Simon scanned her face. She had been so intent on the message she hadn't even noticed him walk up to her.

"It's Kalea. She left a message. Listen to this."

"I think," Simon said, after listening to the message, "we can write number one beside Kalea's name on your list of suspects."

"Sounds like it. She was forced to leave? I need to find out more about her boss, the antique collector. Maybe he forced her to steal the books, or he was actually in town and did it, and then ended up killing Charlotte in the meantime."

"Would he have knowledge about the hidden chamber?"

"Who knows? Maybe he's not a stranger to Greyborne Harbor. After all, she said they lived in Cape Cod. He might know about Hill Road House."

"That's a lot of speculation." Simon placed his hand on the small of her back, ushering her through the door of the restaurant where they were greeted by Serena and Zach.

Addie pushed her half-eaten seafood salad away. It was no use. She couldn't stay focused on the spirited conversation around her. The concern for her cousin played heavily on her mind. As though reading her thoughts, Simon asked for the check, paid the bill, and hurried the little group out into the bright afternoon sunshine. His fingers laced through hers, and the four of them walked along the seawall in the direction of the new pier and information center built on the rocky outcrop where the old lighthouse stood.

It only was a week since they'd been down here. At the time, there was a hum heavy in the air with the construction crews putting the final touches on the glass visitor's center. Today, there was still a buzz, but it was interested locals flocking to the site for a peek at what the future held in store for their sleepy little town.

If the cruise line information and shore excursion itineraries were any indication, harbor residents' summers were to be nothing like they'd ever experienced before. The local festivals and annual summer sailing regatta would be dwarfed by the ships' eager tourists inundating the area every Tuesday for the next five months. Tourists who were ready and willing to see what the little town had to offer in the way of dining experiences, culture, and local history.

Greyborne Harbor locals were pulling out all the stops to remain competitive with the adventures that lay just thirty minutes up the coastal highway in Salem, a longtime favorite shore excursion for this particular shipping line's clients. Addie wondered if Art was on the right track with his idea to market Hill Road House as a major tourist destination.

Hot and tired of being jostled around by the hordes of curious onlookers in the center, Addie hunted out some peace. Through the window, she spotted an ice cream truck in the parking lot. Grabbing Simon's hand, she tugged him along behind her as she zigzagged her way through the crowd. Her heart sank at the long line up at the take-out window, but at least she was back in the fresh sea air and sunshine.

As they waited their turn, Addie's gaze checked out the parking lot that a small carnival had commandeered. Judging by the number of visitors waiting for rides and buying cotton candy, it meant the amount of people attending the Hill Road House yard sale would be few and not enough to help Blake clear out the rest of the merchandise. Her heart went out to him. Right from the start his auction had its challenges, and had not only hurt him financially, but with the thefts and Charlotte's untimely demise, his reputation was also at stake.

When they reached the front of the line, Simon

stepped up to place their orders. As she leaned in to tell him what flavor she wanted, a familiar form caught her attention. Over on the seawall overlooking the lighthouse, Philip Atkinson sat, licking the melting ice cream from around the top of his waffle cone. Addie muttered, "I'll have a double-chocolate fudge," and skirted around Simon.

She made a direct line toward the man she least wanted to talk to on an otherwise pleasant Sunday afternoon. But they had unfinished business, and she needed to find out if his uncanny awareness of the publisher's reproductions in her shop was due to his involvement in the crime or a lucky guess.

Addie plopped down on the top of the stone ledge and closed her eyes, revelling in the smell of fresh sea air and the sun on her face. If she'd been born a cat, there's no doubt she'd be purring. Not only because of the rays of sunshine beating down on her, but also because of the uncomfortable shifting of the rat seated beside her on the wall. She toyed with the idea of playing with her prey for a few minutes before striking, but Simon would be along at any moment, and she couldn't let this opportunity slip away.

"It's a glorious day, isn't it, Philip? I imagine you don't get many like this in Dublin." There was no answer from the man seated to her right as he continued to lick the drippings from his cone. "I am surprised to see you here today. I was under the impression that the VIP preinaugural docking this week embarked yesterday and left port?"

"I had a few loose ends to tie up." He went back to licking his cone.

"Not taking in the final day of the yard sale?"

"Blake wasn't serving ice cream."

"I see." She shifted on the stone ledge. "Did you take in the sale this morning, or are you one of those that show up at the end of the day to haggle for the lowest price possible?"

"There's not too much wiggle room on what I'm looking for." He pierced her with a glare.

"Whatever are you talking about?" Addie feigned innocence. "Blake is always open to any reasonable bid."

Philip jumped off the ledge and tossed the remainder of his cone into a trash bin. "Time to head back to the sale, as there are a few remaining items that my purchaser has expressed interest in acquiring."

"You do know the book sale won't be held now until next month in Boston?"

"There are many priceless items still to be found in the estate's collection."

"Really? I was under the impression that the higher-valued items went at auction and only the lesser-valued merchandise was being presented at the public yard sales."

"It does make one question the quality of the McAdams appraisals, doesn't it?" He winked and sauntered off.

"Addie, here." Simon handed her a double-chocolate-fudge cone. "And I suggest you close your mouth before you catch a fly."

"Did you just hear what Philip said?"

"Can't say as I did," Simon said, making himself comfortable on the spot that Philip had just vacated. "I was too focused on getting this across the hot pavement before I was wearing both yours and mine."

"He just implied that Charlotte's appraisals might not have been accurate."

"Well, you, as an appraiser yourself, must know that

there is no guarantee of an item's—in your case, book's—value. It's like a house. It's only worth what someone is willing to pay for it."

"I know that, but what if Charlotte was hiding the true appraisal worth of certain items?"

"For what purpose?" He licked a drip from the top of his cone.

"So that she could send in a shell bidder who would pay the lower price, and then she could turn around and sell at the actual higher-valued price."

"You think she was scamming Blake?"

"It's one theory we hadn't thought about, and I saw firsthand that there was no love lost between him and Charlotte."

"Do you think Blake knew or caught on?"

"Maybe he suspected." Her tongue lapped up a drip from the bottom of her ice cream scoop. "After all, she was very private with her catalogue and inventory lists. She wouldn't even allow Robert to work on her computer."

"Perhaps Blake did manage to see the true appraisals and discovered she was trying to cheat him?"

"He might have. He did say to me that he learned from the best, my father. It would stand to reason that over the years he had made some other contacts that he could turn to who would give him an honest appraisal of some of the more questionable items he had up for auction."

"We did see that altercation between him and Charlotte's brother. I bet Blake suspects them both of trying to scam him, and that's the real reason he's not paying the appraisal bill."

"I don't know, but as much as I hate to think it, Blake's name just moved up on the murderer list."

Simon nibbled drips of ice cream from his finger.

"Look," Addie said, "I know we planned to spend the afternoon down here enjoying the shops along Marine Drive, but—"

"You want to go back to Hill Road House and see if you can learn anything else."

Addie beamed a winning smile. "Yes. Philip was heading back there now, and I want to see if I can figure out what he's up to, and if he's involved with all this."

"Serena and Zach are in line for ice cream now. We'd better let them know our new plan."

"Thank you." She planted a chocolate kiss on his lips.

"What was that for? Not that I mind."

"For indulging me."

"I have no choice, it seems," he said, his fingers playing up her arm. "After all, I'm a doctor, and I swore an oath. I'm bound to keep you from strangling yourself on that thread you're trying to untangle."

Chapter 27

Simon pulled over to the side of the street to let Addie hop out while he found a parking spot up around the corner. Addie was surprised to see the number of cars here for the yard sale given the amount of people she'd just seen at the pier.

"I'll catch up with you around back," Simon called through the open passenger-side window as he pulled away.

Addie stepped up onto the curb and made her way to the front wrought-iron gate. No matter how many times she'd been here over the past few days, the feeling she'd had on her first visit was forever engraved in her mind. *Suck it up, buttercup. This was your idea.* Chin high, she ambled up the footpath to the front door. She knew Simon would look for her around the back of the house at the sale tables, but there was one stop she wanted to make before she went out there.

Addie opened the weathered mahogany door and stepped into the massive foyer. The house wrapped her in an eerie silence so deep Addie could hear the whoosh of her blood rushing through her ears. She wished now she had joined the throng outside, in the sunshine, where noise existed. *Where is everyone?* Blake's staff was generally running around like crazed ants.

The living room had been completely cleared of tables and auction items. The study across the hall echoed in emptiness as well. It appeared that Blake had wasted no time in emptying the house as per the order from Art and Maggie. Voices resonated down the stairwell. She stopped short at the bottom of the steps and tilted her head to catch what they were saying, but it was no use. She could only make out a hum of muted murmurs. A second voice chimed in, matching the first one's tone and intensity with one difference. Addie detected an Irish lilt to this voice. It was none other than Philip Atkinson, but who was he speaking to upstairs?

Addie hustled up the stairway. With each step she ascended, the mystery voice grew louder. By the time she reached the top the voices had trailed off and echoed as though they were coming from a tunnel or stairway. They were headed to the third floor. Addie hesitated at the top, but she knew she had one chance of discovering who Philip was arguing with. She scurried down the hall following what little of the murmurs she could make out and stopped when she came to the third-floor stairway. *One, two, three. Now.* She crept upward until the voices became clear again. The mystery man was Blake. From what she could make out, the two men were arguing about money. Addie peered over the rise of the top step, keeping low in a spread-eagle position over the steps.

The attic was huge, but unlike hers, which had a number of smaller rooms off to the sides and the one larger one across the back, this was an open space and the back wall was exactly that. There were no windows, and if not for the meager amount of light coming in from the two small windows on the front of the house and one on either side of the room, it would be a dark and dank space. After her eyes adjusted to the dim light, she could see Blake and Philip, a cardboard box between their feet.

"I told you he was a cheat. Him and his sister." Philip's unmistakable plummy voice sang out.

"Well, that's not a problem anymore, is it?"

"No, it's not. At least it shouldn't be."

"You did take care of that other little matter, didn't you?" Blake's jaw tightened.

"You mean . . . ?"

Blake nodded.

"It's all as it should be. No worries there."

"Good. This is the last of it. Take it, and be gone."

Philip handed Blake a white envelope. "This should cover it."

Blake stuffed it into his jacket pocket. "You'd better not contact me again until this is all over with. We can't take the chance of—"

"I know," Philip hissed and picked up the box, balancing it on his hip. Addie scooted backward down the stairs crab-style and ducked inside an open doorway, pressing her back up against the oak wall panelling. When Blake's and Philip's voices stopped right outside the doorway, she sucked in a deep breath and pressed back harder. "At least we won't have to worry about him showing his face around here again."

A shadowy figure hovered in the doorway. Addie's teeth gnashed together. It seemed her old family friend definitely wasn't the person she thought he was, and until she could figure out whom they were talking about and why they didn't have to worry anymore. She couldn't risk being discovered.

Making herself as small as she could against the wall, she slid toward an ancient wardrobe behind the door. If she could just get inside that, maybe she could stay hidden long enough to try and hear what they were saying.

"Where did you leave it?" Addie's ears perked up at the uneasiness in Blake's voice.

"At the place we discussed earlier."

"And you're sure no one's going to stumble across it before it can permanently disappear." By the exasperation in Blake's voice Addie could picture him raking his fingers through his hair.

"Not a chance. Even with that snoopy Addison Greyborne, asking her questions and stirring everything up."

"Do you think she knows?" There was no mistaking the concern in Blake's strangled tone.

"I think she's been too consumed with her arrest that she hasn't had time to put all the pieces together." Philip's voice changed from his usual singsong lilt to all-out full Irish brogue.

"Do you think the plan is working?"

Addie's hand shot to her mouth to stifle the gasp in her heaving chest. She pressed herself harder against the paneled wall surface, wishing she could disappear inside it. A soft click, a blast of cold air, and a five-foot drop to wooden floor planks knocked her senseless. The wall in front of her slid closed, and complete blackness enveloped her. Addie felt around her on hands and knees until she touched what she knew to be her tote bag that had fallen through the doorway with her. She fished around inside it, yanked out her phone, and hit the flashlight app.

The walls were rough brick, just as they were in the hidden chamber behind the fireplace, and the floor was constructed of smooth wide-planked boards. Her one beam didn't show a wide swath of light, but it was enough to make out a passageway of sorts. No mildew, just stale air, and judging by the strands clinging to her face from time to time, a whole lot of cobwebs. *Please don't be spiderwebs. Please don't be spiderwebs.* Her hatred for spiders had her edging herself to the center of the passageway to avoid them and their probable inhabitants. Goose bumps exploded on her arms as she stumbled along the path.

The passage twisted and turned and came to an abrupt halt at a fork. *Left or right?* She shone her light down the fork to the right and could make out the start of a staircase going down. The fork to the left revealed the same thing, only the stairs were going up. She flashed the light over the walls to figure out where she was in the house. So far, she had walked on a flat surface, so she knew she was still on the second floor. That meant the staircase to her right led to the main floor. She had a hunch. Now that she knew this tunnel existed, she could always come back later and explore the stairs leading up to the third floor. Right now, she wanted to test the theory she had literally fallen into.

Addie braced her hand against the cool, damp surface of the wall, shining the light on every step before she placed her foot. It certainly wouldn't help to step on a rat or even feel one scurry from beneath her feet. On her third step, the sidewall ended, and she felt nothing but air. She flashed the light beam into the space and discovered a small nook with a one-foot-deep ledge covered with an ornate grate on the far side of it. *Is this the air duct in the hallway at the top of the stairs?* She could clearly hear voices echoing through it from the foyer below and decided it must be. Obviously, this wasn't a heating duct, but a ventilation shaft. If her eyes weren't deceiving her, there was also white scum on the ledge below the grate and the entire area was surrounded by scratches in the dust. She snapped a picture with her phone, not sure if she would even be able to make out what she was looking at now, but thought it was worth reporting to Marc, anyway.

She inched her way down the stairs, feeling the wall for more alcoves and more empty air surprises in the dim light. When she reached the bottom, she was confused. If this was built as a ventilation shaft for the house, it should open out into the fresh air someplace not hit a dead end. Addie traced her fingers around the uneven bricks of the wall in front of her, pushing and prodding. Her fingers stumbled across a thumb-styled lever tucked in a corner. She pushed it up, nothing happened. She pressed it down. It wouldn't budge. Then she remembered the similar-looking lever inside the chamber behind the fireplace and flipped it to the side. The wall slid open with a shudder. She was in the fireplace chamber.

Addie took a steadying breath and flipped the fireplace lever in the same manner. The back wall of the hearth slid open, and she poked her head out, checking for questioning eyes. Coast clear, she exited, fished her ballpoint pen out of her purse, and pressed the tip into the center hole in the scroll work on the mantel. She scurried around the large desk, the last remaining piece of furniture in the otherwise empty room and opened the library door. Scanning left and right, she slid out into the hall and mall-walked out the back door. *Simon.* She had to find Simon. But at the bottom of the porch steps, a hand grabbed her arm and spun her around.

Chapter 28

"Addie, I didn't know you were here."

"Hi, Blake. I . . . I was just inside looking for Simon. He dropped me off and then went to find a parking space." She swiped away the strings of cobwebs dangling from her bangs. "You haven't seen him, have you?"

"Yes, I was just speaking with him. I think he's over by the far table." Blake eyed her. "Were you crawling through the bushes to get here?" His eyes darted to the back wall.

"Did Marc tell you about our discovery yesterday?"

"He mentioned it, yes." He kissed her cheek. "But I must run. I'm sure you noticed on your trip through the house that the movers came last night and packed up most of what's left to take to my warehouse in Boston. The rest of what's left out here will be packed up tonight after the sale's over."

"I know this weekend didn't go as planned, so I hope you didn't have to haul too much away."

"Not too bad. A few larger pieces of the bedroom

furniture were sold, and the buyers have made arrangements to pick it up by tomorrow. The rest of the books and collectables . . ." He shrugged with a short and humorless chuckle. "Well, it's actually a blessing."

"Why would it be a blessing? You don't get paid until it's all sold. Charlotte's brother will continue to hound you."

"Duane?" He barked a laugh. "No, he's not going to be an issue anymore." Malice laced his words.

"I take it you paid him, then. You know, when we overheard you and him arguing about it."

"Something like that, but I must run now. Lots to finish up here. I hope to see you before I leave town tomorrow afternoon. If not, then promise me you'll stop by the auction house the next time you're in Boston." He pressed her hand in his and bounded up the stairs into the house.

Addie spotted Simon at the refreshment table, pouring a coffee from a large urn. "There you are." She linked her arm through his. "I've been searching everywhere for you."

His lips turned up at the corners. "Does that include crawling around in the bushes looking for me?" He picked webs from her hair. "I think that one still had its host attached." He nudged her playfully.

"Don't be silly." She shook her head and brushed her hand through her hair. "We have to talk—now. I found something important," she added in a whisper. "I know how the thief got in and out of the library, and I have a theory on how Charlotte was killed."

"We already know about the chamber, and we know how she died. What else could you have possibly discovered?"

"You won't believe what I—"

"Addie, Simon, how lovely to see you both here."

Maggie reached between them for a paper cup and proceeded to pour a coffee.

Much to Addie's dismay, they were joined by Vera and Art at the refreshment table. Sharing her recent discovery with Simon would have to wait. Maggie, full cup of coffee in hand, pinned Addie with an amused gaze. Vera's eyes mirrored the same laughter, her gaze following the wispy tail of a cobweb floating in Addie's face.

Addie chuckled and pawed at it, but not before catching the look on Art's face. Before she could decipher whether anger or concern had ignited the darkness in his eyes, his usual jovial twinkle returned.

Addie gave one last swipe over her head to dislodge any more eight-legged hitchhikers. No doubt about it, she was washing her hair tonight. Twice. "I was speaking with Blake a few minutes ago." She handed Art a paper cup from the stack. "He seems to have made quick work of clearing out the house like you wanted for the viewing this week."

"I must say I'm amazed by it." Art nodded his appreciation as he filled the cup. "I'd asked it to be done by Thursday, but he surprised us last night when the first moving truck arrived."

"Surprised? How so?"

"We weren't expecting any movement on that part until after the weekend," Vera chirped in. "But that's good. I can start staging it by tomorrow afternoon."

"But there will be nothing left to stage." Addie offered Vera a cup.

Vera waved off her offer. "We have a few spooky ideas in mind." She winked at Art.

"Yes, Mother has been doing nothing but researching Halloween haunted houses for the past few months. It seems her new hobby is learning how to create 'spooktacular' "—Maggie's fingers hooked air quotes—"special effects."

"Yes." Art grinned at Vera, his eyes gleaming with pride. "She's come up with some wonderful ideas that I can't wait to try out, after Blake and his crew are gone."

"Given the reputation of Hill Road House," Addie said, jerking her head to the house, "added special effects sound like the perfect way to grab the attention of someone considering turning it into a tourist destination. Helps potential buyers visualize the possibilities, doesn't it?"

Addie's mind whirled, connecting each encounter with the blasts of icy air, the hazy wispy figure, and the smoke spiral in the library. Someone had beaten them to their parlor tricks. *What if they weren't tricks?* She squashed that thought. It was just too absurd.

"That's what we're hoping." Art squeezed Vera's shoulder and kissed the top of her white head.

"I, for one," Maggie spouted, "will be glad when it's sold and off our listing register. I think it might have damaged my agency's reputation."

"Why would that be?" Simon stared at Maggie. "It has nothing to do with your other listings."

"Since that woman died in the house on Wednesday, and with the rumors of thefts, clients are concerned about the safety of their own listings with us."

"That doesn't even make sense." Addie looked at her in disbelief. "This house had a reputation to begin with, and it's uninhabited. Your other clients are still living in their listed properties."

"It seems it's a question of the security of the lock boxes and the keys we have. It's no secret that there was no sign of forced entry, and those wise enough don't believe the ghost tale. However, they do believe that someone stole one of our agency's keys to gain access. This mausoleum of a house better sell fast, so I can go into damage-control mode."

Addie eyed the back porch to the ivy-covered trellises. She swallowed a squeak. Her inner sleuth salivated at the idea of another mystery and she tugged on Simon's arm. "It was nice to see you all again. Good luck with the house sale"—Addie flashed Art a smile—"but Simon and I have a thing we have to go to."

Simon glanced at her and then smiled. "Yes, that's right. I forgot we have 'a thing.'"

Addie gripped Simon's hand and dragged him away from the trio.

"Mind telling me what that was all about?"

Addie pointed to the third floor of the house. "Do you see two windows up there?"

"Yes, so?"

"Except I was just upstairs, and there are no rear windows in the attic."

"What do you mean you were upstairs?"

Addie waved off his question. "I'll explain later, I promise, but I saw with my own eyes the attic is one large, empty room. There are two front-facing windows and one on either side. But the back wall is solid."

"Maybe there was a door you just didn't notice."

"No, from my vantage point I had a good view. There were no doors. I need to get back up there. We can take that hidden staircase I found. There was another door leading up to the third level that I didn't explore. I bet it comes out behind what looks like that solid wall in the back of the attic."

"What hidden stairway, and why were you in the attic to begin with?"

As they wandered around the side of the house to the front, Addie relayed the story of her most recent adventures. A sense of smugness left its telltale mark of a sly smile. She had cracked this case. "What do you think?"

Simon scrubbed his hand through his thick black hair. "I think that Philip and Blake know more about what happened here than either of them has let on, and it seems Philip's appearance here didn't come as the surprise they allowed us to believe."

"My thoughts exactly. I think Blake was so reluctant to report the thefts to the police—"

"Because he was the one committing them, or he put Philip up to it."

"It also gives me a new theory for Charlotte's death."

"You said that before, and I don't understand. It was a heart attack. There's no other indication of anything else."

"Is it possible for a person to be literally scared to death?"

"Sure, there's no question about it."

"Really? How?"

"Well . . ." Simon scratched his head. "The autonomic nervous system uses adrenaline to send signals to different parts of the body to activate the fight-or-flight response. It's the chemical that has ensured mankind's existence over millennia."

"Can it lead to death?"

"Unfortunately, yes, adrenaline in excessive amounts is also toxic because it damages the internal organs. You know, like the heart, lungs, liver, and kidneys. Most sudden deaths are attributed to the damage of the heart, though, because when the other organs fail it doesn't cause sudden death to occur."

"What exactly happens when the heart is flooded with *too much* adrenaline?"

"Let's put it this way: If the system is overwhelmed with adrenaline, the heart can go into abnormal rhythms, probably a ventricular fibrillation, which isn't compatible with life and . . ." He raised his shoulders in a matter-of-fact shrug. "A person will drop dead."

"Are there any other medical factors that could contribute to a person actually dying from fear?"

"Of course, if there's predisposition to heart disease or the person has high levels of prolonged stress. Things like that could increase the risk of abrupt death if there was also a sudden jolt of extra adrenaline, but it happens at all ages and can happen to otherwise healthy people. We talked about her high levels of adrenaline before, and in a naturally occurring heart attack they're bound to be elevated somewhat anyway. So what are you thinking now?"

"I'm thinking that whoever was smuggling stolen property out of the house might have come through the hidden library door while Charlotte was working alone and scared her to death."

"Yeah, the shock could have overloaded her system and contributed to her heart failure."

"Robert told the police that the rumors about the house being haunted had bothered her, so she was on edge whenever they had to work late—there's your prolonged stress. That night she got agitated, increasing her stress levels higher, and sent him packing. There she is by herself in this creepy old house. Picture her, sitting at the desk. It's two or three a.m., and suddenly someone is standing behind her. She knew she was alone in the room, and the door was bolted."

Simon nodded his head slowly, seemingly following the imagery she presented.

"We already discovered the peephole into the library,

so it stands to reason that someone was watching her, knew she was nervous, probably why she bolted the door on the inside, and whoever was hiding in the hidden chamber used its existence to create the perfect murder weapon."

"If causing her death was intentional, then it *is* murder."

"Really?"

"Really. After we talked about it before, I did some research and discovered that there was a case in North Carolina a few years back where a man was charged with first-degree murder of an elderly woman. Police said he scared her to death in an attempt to escape the police after a bank robbery. He never touched the woman, but she died from heart failure triggered by the terror of discovering him hiding in her house. Under the state felony murder rule, if someone causes the death of another person while committing or fleeing from a crime, such as robbery, even if unintentional, he can be charged with murder."

"Then we have to go back up, now." She seized his hand.

"No, Addie!" he said, releasing her grip on him. "This is something we have to talk over with Marc."

"You know he won't listen until we have proof."

"If the theory is correct, then we get the proof some other way. You are not to go back in there and sneak around behind the walls. Who knows what danger we'd be putting ourselves into?"

"But Simon—"

"No buts! Do you understand me? These people, whoever they are, have already proven they are willing to kill."

"I guess you're right," she said, hanging her head.

"That's my girl. Now, let's get out of here and you can plan your next move, up here," he tapped her forehead, "and not by traipsing around this old house."

Maybe Simon was right, probably the best thing she could do now was to work on her board. That way she could visualize it all in black and white to make the pieces fit before she took it to Marc. As they walked up the street to Simon's car, she rearranged all the clues in her head and saw a big empty spot in the center of the puzzle. There was still one more piece to this that she needed. One she hoped would be illuminated tomorrow morning at 8 a.m.

Chapter 29

"**G**ood morning, Tom." Addie swept past the security guard the moment he unlocked the door to the town hall building.

"Good morning, Miss Greyborne. I don't think anyone's in the administration offices yet, if that's who you're looking for," he called out behind her.

"I'm here to see Connie in Records. Do you know if she's in?"

"Connie's always the first one to arrive. I saw her go up about a half hour ago."

"Great, thanks." Addie bounded up the stairs to the clerk's office.

At the top of the wide landing, Addie followed the sign that indicated left. The overhead arrow pointing to her right gave directions to the courtroom and the court clerk's office. Connie, one of her book-club members, actually held two jobs in the building. Since the courtroom in Greyborne Harbor was only used when the county judge traveled here from Salem for his Thursday—and, if needed, Friday—court sessions,

Connie worked the balance of the week as the town clerk.

She pushed the clerk's office door open. Relieved to find the small waiting room empty, she slid up to the reception counter. No Connie. *Strange.* Connie had always been on the spot, ready to take care of business, even if that included assisting Addie with paying a parking ticket. *Totally Simon's fault.* Today, there was no sign of her. Addie leaned across the counter. "Connie?"

Off to her right, a mop of unruly, faded brown hair appeared around the doorjamb of a back room. "Addie? I'll be right there." A bang, a muttered curse, and a flustered Connie marched to the counter, favoring her right knee.

"Are you okay?"

Connie rubbed her leg. "Someone left a file cart where it shouldn't have been, and . . . well, never mind about that. What brings you by today? Your license isn't up for renewal yet." She leaned her elbow on the counter and fixed her hazel eyes on Addie. "Or did you get another parking ticket?" She arched a sly brow that magnified the laugh lines beside her eye.

Addie scrunched up her nose. "I told you already, if I hadn't had to wait for Simon to finish his shift at the hospital, I wouldn't have gotten that darn ticket. But no, today I'm hoping you can give me some information."

Connie stood upright. "Sure, if I can. What do you need?"

"I'm looking for information about Hill Road House. It's—"

"You and half the town." Connie reached under the counter and produced a pile of application forms.

"Four private requests for that same information on 555 Hill Road over the last eight months."

"Four?"

Connie nodded.

"Who requested it?" Addie glanced at the pile as Connie flipped it over to conceal the information.

"You know I can't tell you that, but I will save you the trouble of filling one of these out and tell you what I told the last three." Connie's voice dropped to a mere whisper. "Most of the records are gone."

"How can that be?" Addie pinned her with a look of disbelief. "Isn't the town required to keep records on all the properties within their limits?"

"Yup, but all I could find was the fact the house was built by a fellow named Tobias Gallagher in about 1860. He was some sort of shipping magnate out of Ireland and spared no expense in creating what he hoped was the most magnificent home in Greyborne Harbor for his wife and children. Rumor has it," she whispered, "the house and fine furnishings were all to placate the wife while he spent his evenings frequenting some of the seedier taverns down on the waterfront. If you know what I mean."

"You don't have anything more? The plans to the house he built or deeds or anything?"

"Nope, sorry. According to the records I found on my first round of searching, all that was signed out back in 1950 by Tobias's grandson, William."

"He signed out the plans to the house then? The same year his parents died?"

"That's what the logbook shows, signature and all. Now usually when those records are signed out, a photocopy is given to the requesting party, but it was almost seventy years ago." She shrugged her round shoulders. "I guess they did things different back then."

"Thanks, Connie. Believe it or not, you've been a big help."

"I have? The others got upset because I couldn't give them anything."

Addie could still hear Connie chuckling as she closed the door and started down the stairs to the street level. What Connie had shared made her wonder if she had been premature in thinking she was getting close to cracking this case. It seemed every which way she turned a new clue popped up. But with this one, she was at a loss to figure out how this latest information fit into the book thefts and Charlotte's death, or if it even did. She needed her blackboard.

"Get what you needed, Miss Greyborne?" Tom called from his station behind the information desk in the small lobby.

"I did. Thanks, Tom. Have a good day." She waved and scurried out the door, descending the sandstone steps.

When she got to the bottom stair, she stopped short. Familiar voices wafted on the breeze from the steps of the police station next door. Even though the buildings had separate entrances and offices, the distance between their stairways wasn't more than forty feet apart on the outside. There was no mistaking the voices of Marc and Ryley. Addie cringed when Marc slipped Ryley's hand into his. Ryley leaned into his shoulder and gave him a hip check.

Addie's fingernails dug into her palms. That was *her* move. The one she used to tease him with relentlessly. In that moment, Addie was struck by the full realization that she and Marc were truly over. There was no going back. Not that she really wanted to but . . . *Water under the bridge.* She chanted that over and over as she scampered across the street to the *Greyborne Harbor Daily News* office.

The receptionist helped Addie set up in a small cubical complete with a microfilm viewer. After assuring the receptionist she knew how to use the microfilm, Addie shut the door and organized the box of film spools. She only had about twenty minutes to see if she could learn more about Hill Road House and its early inhabitants, and then she'd have to go open her shop. She flipped off the overhead light and clicked through the newspaper headlines of the spool marked 1860's— GREYBORNE HARBOR DAILY NEWS EDITIONS.

With one eye on the time, she clicked through the images. There were numerous references made to the Greybornes, Davenports, and other local prominent families that she would have loved to read in greater depth. Unfortunately, there was only the odd mention of the Gallaghers, especially when it came to lists of who attended what charity function. Nothing that set off her PI radar or confirmed the scandals surrounding Tobias Gallagher's licentious behavior that Connie mentioned earlier. The family, including their four children, despite all their wealth, appeared to have led sedate and reclusive lives.

Nothing like Emily Greyborne, whose name appeared in a multitude of news stories over the course of the five years Addie reviewed. One article in particular piqued her interest. It reported Emily Greyborne as being responsible for discovering the identity of a man the police had sought in regard to the theft of a first-edition Bible on loan to one of the local churches.

Now Emily was a woman Addie yearned to learn more about. Her adventures sounded similar to the ones Addie had read about in her great-aunt Anita's journals. She felt a connection with her ancestor. She would quit toying with the idea of having her family tree traced some day and just do it now, especially after reading this. Her ancestors couldn't learn about her, but she could learn about them. By all accounts, the sleuthing bug was genetic. When she saw Simon, she would inform him she had no choice but to stick her nose where it didn't belong. It was in her blood, and she owed it to the long line of amateur sleuths before her to keep up the tradition.

Her time up, she hovered her finger over the power button, scanning the last page. Under the obituary column at the bottom of the page was something she didn't expect to see.

Mrs. Beatrice Gallagher, 36, of 555 Hill Road, after a fatal fall down the stairway in the family home on Wednesday evening, was laid to rest in a small private service today at Harbor View Cemetery. Mrs. Gallagher is survived by her husband of eighteen years, Tobias Gallagher, and their four children, Bridget, Theresa, Fiona, and Arthur. On behalf of the family, Mr. Gallagher would like to express his sincerest appreciation to the Greyborne Harbor residents for their out-pouring of support during this most difficult time.

The fine hairs on Addie's arms prickled. *Kathleen wasn't the first to die on the Hill Road House staircase.*

Chapter 30

The revelation of Beatrice's death played on Addie's mind over the block-and-a-half drive to her shop. Perhaps she'd been too quick to dismiss the ghost stories. From what she just read it could have very well been Beatrice's ghost that caused Kathleen's deadly fall. It made Addie wonder if Arthur's and Maeve's deaths were possibly brought on by the continual appearances of apparitions. If so, was it Beatrice's or Kathleen's ghost that Addie saw at the top of the stairway? These questions and fifty more rocketed through Addie's head as she pulled up in front of Beyond the Page—and the all-out wrestling match between mother and daughter.

On the sidewalk in front of her shop, Martha and Paige were in a tug-of-war over the *Rare Books* sandwich board sign. Addie sprinted to intervene.

"Addie!" Martha screeched. "Thank heavens you're here! Maybe you can talk some sense into this daft girl." Martha threw her hands in the air.

Paige took advantage of her mother's exasperation

and snagged the board, plunking it on the sidewalk. A self-satisfied smile crept across her face, and with a victorious flip of her head, she sauntered into the bookstore.

"What's going on here?" Addie feared Martha's flushed face predicted a stroke. *Right here.* She placed her hand on Martha's shoulder. "Take a deep breath and tell me exactly what happened."

"She insisted on coming in to work today, no matter what I said. She says she feels fine and is under the impression that if you work alone, then the poltergeist will attack you, too."

"Oh dear." Addie puffed out a deep breath. "Let me talk to her. Maybe I can convince her to listen to the doctor."

"I hope so." Martha dabbed her watery eyes with the corner of her apron. "Lord knows she won't listen to me. Stubborn, just like her useless father was." She spat on the sidewalk and slammed the door to her bakery behind her.

Even through the sun-reflecting window, Addie could see Paige's narrowed eyes watching her. *Just what I needed this morning.* After this was all over, she'd drown herself in a good book and a bottle of wine. Or two. Addie prepared for battle and sent the welcome bells in a tizzy.

"Did you set her straight?" Paige's eyes fixed on Addie.

Addie anchored both hands on the counter. "No. I've come in to set *you* straight."

"What? You're taking *her* side?"

"There are no sides here. We're both concerned about your health, and the doctor told you to take it easy for a few days."

"I did." Her bottom lip stuck out in a pout.

Addie bit her tongue before she could echo a quip her granny used to say to her: *A birdy's going to poop on that.* Instead, she went with the wise adult, but boring, "It's only been one day. I don't want to see you in here until at least Wednesday."

"What about the cruise ship?"

Is it really only nine thirty? In the morning? "What does the cruise ship have to do with you defying doctor's orders—and, might I add, mine?"

"It docks tomorrow, and there's going to be nearly a hundred people descending on the harbor all at once. You can't possibly handle that amount of foot traffic by yourself."

"Oh." A weak smile touched Addie's lips. "I see. Don't worry about that. Catherine enjoyed working here so much last week, I'm pretty sure she'd be happy to help out in a pinch."

"But what if the poltergeist strikes again?"

"Paige, a mischievous spirit didn't cause your accident." Addie hoped she sounded more convincing than she felt after her morning excursion.

"Then what made the books fly off the shelves, twice? And I don't buy the police theory that it was a person, because there was no one here but me." She pinned Addie with a piercing glance.

Addie struggled to come up with an answer, and by the defiant look on Paige's face she knew she needed one, fast. "Then it was most likely a big truck passing by. These old buildings are famous for vibrating and shifting with any ground disturbances."

Paige wrapped her arms across her chest. "You weren't here. You didn't see what I saw."

"That's true, but I know what I saw *after* I found you, and that was an unconscious, very pale young woman who suffered a severe blow to the head." Addie put on her sternest manager's—with a dab of big sisterly love to take a bit of the edge off—voice. "Now get your bag. I'm taking you home."

Paige's chin jutted out, but she didn't say a word as Addie flipped the door sign to CLOSED and escorted her young charge to the car. As they pulled away, Addie noticed Martha's pudgy face, complete with a grin, pressed up against the bakery window.

"What about the sandwich board?" Paige gestured to the sign by the door.

"It'll be fine. This shouldn't take more than ten minutes." When Addie glanced in her rearview mirror, she spotted Martha, broom in hand, conducting her daily sweep of the sidewalk. "Something tells me your mother will make certain no one walks away with it."

Paige's mutinied silence evaporated in a laugh. "You know her well."

Addie followed Paige's directions and pulled up in front of Martha's white-with-green-trim Dutch Colonial. She was impressed by her old nemesis' home. The house itself and the pristine landscaping with cultivated flower beds and wide sweeping lawn didn't reflect the owner's sometimes prickly exterior. Until recently, she had envisioned Martha's house looking more like . . . well, the exterior of Hill Road House—something more in fitting with the tetchy behavior she had previously exhibited toward Addie.

Addie clicked the child locks on and made Paige swear to adhere to Addie's strict terms of returning to work, to not step foot in the store until Wednesday, to leave her daughter, Emma, at the daycare for the remainder of the day, and to send her again tomorrow. When Paige agreed to all, Addie, satisfied, unlocked the doors, releasing her captive.

When she pulled up to the corner stop sign, she was

surprised to see that the cross street was none other than Hill Road. She had no idea that Martha lived this close to it. If she turned left, it would take her right past number 555.

She glanced at the clock on her dashboard. Her foot wavered between the brake and the gas pedal. For the sake of time, she should make a U-turn here and go back down the way they'd come up. The meandering route that Hill Road took would add at least five more minutes to her trip, and she still had a business to run. She recalled what she had discovered about Beatrice Gallagher's death. Her thoughts jumped to her own sighting of an apparition at the top of the stairs. Addie shivered, and her skin prickled in memory of the uncanny cold.

Then, of course, there was the concealed chamber behind the library fireplace leading to not one but two hidden stairways. Her foot pressed down hard on the brake as images of the names on her blackboard clicked through her mind like the flashes on the microfilm she'd viewed. Blake, Philip, Robert, Kalea, Nolan, Garret. All followed by the one image Addie knew she'd never be able to un see—the haunted look in Charlotte's eyes. She tapped her fingers on the steering wheel. So far, all she'd done was dump the contents of the puzzle box on the table and turn them over to check shape and color. She still had no idea how they fit together.

A car horn beeped behind her. She glanced in the rearview mirror and waved at a man in the car behind her, angrily shaking his fist. She clicked on her signal light, stepped on the gas, and made a left turn.

A few minutes later, she slid into a parking space across the street from Hill Road House. A moving van was parked in front of the gate. *What to do, what to do?*

She should get back to her shop, but on the other hand, Blake said they'd be finished up in the house today. This might be the last opportunity she'd have to get inside to test out a few of her theories. Surely being away from the shop for a *few* more minutes couldn't hurt, could it?

She groaned and rapped her forehead on the steering wheel. She had better give Marc a call and tell him everything she'd discovered so far and what she'd overheard between Blake and Philip. He was always lecturing her about staying out of investigations and letting the police do *their* job. This time she'd do just that. She fished her phone out of her tote and started to dial his number—but stopped, toying with her phone in her hand.

If this had been before he left town in February, she would have called him. He would have told her she had no proof, that they were only guesses and suspicions. Yadda-yaddaing on about how theories can't convict anyone of a crime, only evidence could. She would have mocked him back and, when all the pieces fell into place, he would have been grateful for her contribution. But now, with Ryley here . . . *Will he even hear me out?* She tapped her phone on the steering wheel. Nope, she'd first have to find the evidence he always went on about, and then *maybe* he'd listen to her. Exactly how she was going to do that, she had no idea, but it was now or never.

Chapter 31

Addie shoved her phone into the front pocket of her cropped jeans and put one foot on the pavement, only to snatch it back and slam the door shut. If she ran into Blake, she'd need an excuse for returning today. There was something about coming right out and asking Blake if he and Philip were running an insurance scam, and if by taking care of Duane McAdams they meant they killed him and/or his sister, that didn't seem like a good plan. Her legs bounced. Her pulse raced. She had always been able to think fast on her feet. She only hoped that knack wouldn't let her down today. She jumped out and hurried across the street to Hill Road House.

All the way up the sidewalk, Addie played out different scenarios on finding the evidence proving that Charlotte had been murdered, and that her death and the timing of the book thefts weren't a coincidence. Simon had confirmed it was possible to scare someone to death. What Addie had to do now was prove what or who had brought on Charlotte's heart attack.

Addie's foot alighted on the first porch stair. Every groan of the wooden boards whispered the ghostly rumors, the horrid events in the house swirling under her feet. She swallowed. But she knew one thing now she didn't know the first time her feet touched these steps: five people may have met their untimely demise here, but today she wasn't hunting for ghosts. She was hunting for a flesh-and-blood thief and killer.

She stared blankly at the weather-worn mahogany door. She still needed an excuse to be back in the house today. *Breathe, Addie, just breathe.* Her lamp! She'd forgotten all about it. A sense of relief swept through her as she stepped into the wide foyer. The lamp was gone.

"Can I help you?" Two burly men, one redheaded, the other dark-haired, stood at the top of the staircase, an 1820s—by Addie's quick appraisal of the color and shape of it—Biedermeier dresser, suspended between them.

"I was looking for the lamp I purchased. It was supposed to be here by the door for me to pick up."

"Sorry, can't help you." The dark-haired man began a backward decent down the stairs.

This was her opening. "Did you happen to see if someone moved it up to one of the bedrooms?"

"Nope." The ginger-haired man stepped down, balancing the upper end of the dresser. "Everyone's out back. You can ask someone out there."

When the men and the dresser reached the foyer, Addie ran her hand over the smooth marble top. "This is a beautiful piece. Is it going to the auction house in Boston?"

Ginger pulled a shipping slip from under his rolled T-shirt sleeve. "Nope, some antique store in Concord. All the bedroom furniture's going there."

"And you didn't see a lamp about yea-high"—Addie

measured in the air to her chin—"heavy marble base, wine-colored, fringed lamp shade up there? Maybe you already took it out to the truck?"

"Nah, would have remembered that 'cause everything else left upstairs is big, heavy—"

"Yeah, we're going to be asking double for this job." Ginger grunted as he picked up the back end of the dresser.

The dark-haired man followed his lead. "Can ya hold the door open for us? Thanks." He nodded as they slipped past Addie and out the door.

The movers had said everyone was out back, probably busy packing up the tents and tables, and what, if anything, was left over from the weekend sale. She could ask about her lamp, or she could go searching for it herself. She sucked air between her front teeth as she grappled with the decision in her mind. There was still the matter of the hidden staircase leading up to the third floor. The one she hadn't had time to explore yesterday. If her hunch was right about it, there was more than likely the only access to the windowed room she'd seen from the backyard, because there was no evidence of an entry from the attic side.

She bit on her lip and glanced down the hall toward the kitchen, and then back up to the top of the stairs. *Oh, what the heck.* She raced up the stairs and into the bedroom with the sliding wall panel she'd stumbled on yesterday. Someone had gone to a lot of work to keep that third-floor room hidden and there had to be a reason why.

She surveyed the room, figured out exactly where she'd been hiding, and began pushing on the center panel. She measured her head height and turned with her back against it and pressed back. No luck. She edged farther down the panel to the molding where two pieces joined, gave it a shove in the center. *Click.* A rush of cool, dank air engulfed her.

Addie stepped inside the hidden corridor, tugged her phone out, and flicked the flashlight app. As her eyes adjusted to the glaring light, she took a deep breath to steady her nerves and made her way down the narrow corridor. At the crossroads of stairs, the toe of her shoe rolled over a bump she didn't recall being there yesterday. She froze. The hairs on her neck and arms prickled as visions of Indiana Jones in a booby-trapped cave flashed through her mind. Hand shaking, Addie aimed the beam of light down to her feet. An orange extension cord. Her heart hammering against her chest wall, she traced the trail across the passageway landing and down the stairs as far as the light would illuminate it. She retraced it back toward her and up the stairs to her left. Addie warily lifted her foot. Nothing happened. There was no explosion or, from what she could see, no poisoned darts flying out of the walls.

She braced her wobbly knees and ascended to the third floor. She pressed her ear against the door at the top and listened for sounds of movement. Satisfied it was unoccupied, hand trembling, Addie turned the brass doorknob and stepped up the last step into the room. She strained to see exactly what it was she'd walked into. The muted light of the morning sun through the closed curtains on the two small windows provided just enough light for her to see a makeshift switch box on the wall beside the door. She flipped it on and a bare, overhead lightbulb dangling from a hook on the wooden ceiling illuminated the room in a harsh white blaze. With a small yelp Addie's hand flew to her chest to steady her heart's erratic beat. The room wasn't large, but it was functional as a hideaway for someone, right down to the bed in the corner. The sheets were unmade but they appeared clean, so this wasn't a room that had been uninhabited for seventy years. It was clear by the hotplate and dirty dishes sitting on a table that somebody lived here. She peered into a coffee cup. Dark liquid covered the bottom of it. And lived here recently. The ring on the cup's bottom hadn't set yet.

Addie's gaze lingered, scanning the shelves along the walls filled with antiques and knickknacks. The same ones Blake had reported stolen from the estate. It was all here: the record player, the music box, everything that had been on the list he'd given to the police. She eyed the Georgian Irish decanter she'd coveted on her first visit.

Addie dialed Marc's number. The line was dead. She checked the reception bars. No service. "Crap," she muttered, digging around in her tote bag until she found her travel pack of tissues. Careful not to touch the crystal decanter, she wrapped it in tissues and placed it into her bag. Since she couldn't bring Marc to her, she'd have to take proof to him. The way things were now, he wouldn't simply take her word for it and launch an investigation based on her word alone. When she stepped back, her butt bumped the table behind her, sending a stack of books tumbling to the floor, the clatter echoing like cymbals in the small room.

What the heck? The first-edition set of the Holmes books lay butterflied open on the dusty floor. Trembling, she wrapped her last tissue around her hand and restacked them. They were all here. When she picked up *A Study in Scarlet*, a cold chill raced across her shoulders. The binding had a clean slice from the heel of the spine to the top and flapped open. She examined the cut line. Between the front and back sections of the bound cover was the corner of a yellowed piece of paper.

With the tip of her pinkie nail, she managed to get a hold of the corner and slide it out. It was a birth certificate for a child named Tobias Gallagher born in 1945. This baby must have been the great-grandson of the earlier Tobias Gallagher, the builder of this house with its many secrets. Addie searched between the binding pieces to see if a death certificate was also tucked inside, but all she could find was a small plastic bag with a lock of brown hair wrapped in a blue ribbon.

She stared at the plastic bag, her mind racing. *If he was born in 1945, that means this person would be approximately seventy-five years old now.* She ran through a mental list of the suspects on her board, figuring out which one might be the right age. Blake, Philip, Duane McAdams, Robert. No, they were all too young. Not one of them came close to being the right age. Whoever this Tobias was, living or dead. He was important enough for someone to have damaged a valuable book to get at this certificate. Not to mention continue with the charade of making the house seem haunted and even murdering someone to get his hands on this book.

Chills skittered up Addie's back. She dropped the book into her tote bag, one more piece to add to the sizable puzzle growing on her blackboard. She took one more visual sweep of the table. Her heart constricted in her chest when she caught sight of Charlotte's laptop and a piece of paper with the Greyborne Harbor town seal sticking out from underneath it. She snatched a pen from her bag and, using it as a barrier to fingerprints, released the paper from under the laptop. It was the 1950 missing documents from the town clerk's office. "Wow, here're the architect plans for the house, too." She snagged another page from under a pile of papers. There definitely was more than enough evidence here to convict whoever was behind these thefts, and if she could prove it with the hidden chamber and staircase, also Charlotte's murder.

Addie shuffled through the rest of the papers, and her breath caught. Here was the plastic-wrapped first edition of the Beeton's *A Study in Scarlet*. She puffed out a sigh of relief. This meant that her cousin hadn't helped herself to it, right? Or had she? Addie surveyed the room. Was Kalea the person living up here? Is that why she disappeared without a word? Addie closed her eyes and drew in a slow, deep breath and shook her head. No, this area obviously was inhabited by a man. There was definitely the faint, lingering scent of cedarwood and patchouli, with an undertone of cinnamon and woody amber, in the air. When she worked with Kalea, she noted a light, springtime fragrance surrounding her. This room, without doubt had recently been used as a hideout by a man. She sniffed again. Yes, she was certain. And whatever the aftershave was, it was very seductive, and . . . familiar.

She knew she had smelled it recently, but how recent, and on who? The men she had been in close contact with over the past few days paraded like a slide show through her mind. Nolan was dismissed since she had never met him. Then there was Blake—no, he was Old Spice. Philip Atkinson was always a possibility. Both he and Garrett were well-groomed and this scent definitely came from a high-end product. There was also Robert. She cringed. Not a chance. There was more of an old-gym-sock aroma about him, which also eliminated Duane—for the time being—since the only aroma coming off him the day Addie was close to him to detect a scent was the pong of soured gin.

She racked her brain, trying to remember where and who she had smelled the scent on previously. Maybe Marc or Simon would know. As soon as she could get cell reception she'd have to call Marc anyway. This room was something he'd have to see to believe. Perhaps he might even know what the brand of the aftershave was; then maybe she could figure out who in town wore it.

Addie opened the door a crack, listened for any sounds of someone returning to the room. Coast clear, she hustled to the small landing that veered off to the tunnel toward the bedroom access. She hesitated. It would be the quickest way to get cell reception but never having entered the bedroom from this side, she wasn't sure if the latch would be obvious or not. It might take longer. Better safe than sorry.

One hand on the wall for balance, she scurried down toward the chamber room behind the fireplace. When her hand felt the ventilation shaft indentation, she paused at the sound of a soft sputtering sound emanating from the alcove beside her. She flashed her beam of light into the opening. It was a cool mist humidifier with a jerry-rigged nozzle attached to disperse the vapor precisely into the upper main hallway at the top of the stairs on the other side of the ventilation grate. She scanned the entire area with her flashlight. Mounted behind the humidifier on a stone ledge was a small special-effects light projector. She flashed her beam back up the stairs and back down to the shaft opening. This was also where the extension cord ended.

"Apparition my foot. Just wait until I tell Paige and Serena their ghosts are nothing more than a few well-placed humidifiers."

She chuckled as she made her way to the bottom door, slid the wall lever to the side, and tiptoed into the stone chamber. She scanned the room with the flashlight beam, and her heart sank. It showed her what she'd forgotten. The police had taken the step-ladder into evidence and without it, there was no way she could reach the peephole to check if anyone was in the library.

Fingers crossed, like the day before no one would be in there because they were all out back, and her un-expected appearance wouldn't have the same effect a surprise visitor had on Charlotte. She whispered a little prayer and pressed the lever. When the door slid open, she knew her prayers had been ignored.

Chapter 32

"Hi," Addie squeaked.

The look in Vera's eyes reflected the same horror that had been on Charlotte's dead face. Art, on the other hand, had an entirely different expression. She couldn't read it, but she didn't miss the sarcasm of his welcome.

"Addie, how nice it is to see you."

She swallowed twice. "I suppose you're here to plan the staging of the house?" A nervous laugh did nothing to shore up her bravery. His ominous tone and eyes foretold a very un-cordial meeting. She needed to stall until she could figure out what was going on. "As you can see," she said, motioning to the hidden chamber entrance, "here's a little something you might be able to use in your creation of a haunted house experience for perspective buyers." She glanced from Vera's drawn face to Art's firm set jaw. "I can explain. You see, I was—"

"Never mind trying to come up with an excuse." Art took a step closer to the fireplace. He raised his umbrella and with a jab poked the tip into the center notch of the design on the mantel, triggering the opening to close. "I know exactly what you've been up to." His eyes glimmered with malice as he extended his umbrella and clicked a button on the ivory handle, projecting a six-inch blade pointed directly at Addie's throat.

"Very James Bondish of you." Addie swallowed in an attempt to dislodge her heart from her throat and knew then why the aftershave smelled familiar. There was no question about the lingering aroma of cedarwood and patchouli emanating from Art.

His top lip curled up at the corner. "I thought when I set it up so all the evidence pointed to you and you were arrested, that would be the end of your nosing around, but you don't take hints very well, do you?" His eyes bore into Addie's with an intensity that made the hairs on her arms quiver. "It seems even the events I staged in your shop weren't enough to sway you or that shop girl of yours." Addie flinched. "I admit she wasn't as skittish as I thought she was. When the books tumbled off the shelves, thanks to my trusty little contraption here"—he waved his dagger-ended umbrella— "I thought she would bolt and run away. I never expected her to start to turn around to see what was causing the chaos I was creating. I had to stop her before that happened and she recognized me. That's when . . . well, let's just say you saw the result." Addie swallowed hard to squelch the queasiness in the pit of her stomach. "I guess I'll have to do something about that now, won't I?" He took another step toward her.

"Artie, what are you doing?" Vera shrieked.

Art waved the knife tip in her direction. "Get over there beside Miss Greyborne. Now!"

"But, Art, I don't understand. What's going on?"

"Shut up, you silly woman. I've had enough of you and your whiny daughter. There's only so much I can put up with."

"You said you loved me." Vera's eyes filled with tears as she edged her way over to Addie.

"Love." He spat out the word. "Hardly."

"But when we met on the cruise ship last year, you came back here with me to start over, to start a new life, with me."

"Yeah, just part of the plan." He barked out a laugh and he waved the blade in their direction.

Tiny shivers raced up Addie's spine. "I'd say by what I discovered up in that secret room, you've been planning this for some time."

He set his daggerlike eyes on hers. "You have no idea how much has gone into this little venture."

There was something about the darkening expression in his eyes that looked familiar. She glanced up at the portrait of Tobias Gallagher and then back at Art. "You're Tobias."

"I knew it was only a matter of time until you'd figure it all out, the way you were nosing around here. You see, I've been watching you." He chuckled. "Through the eyes of my great-grandfather, so to speak."

"Art, please explain to me—"

"Be quiet, woman." He raked his hand through his thick silver hair. "Now I know why my grandfather pushed my mother down the stairs. He'd had enough of her incessant whining."

Addie clutched at her throat. "Your grandfather, Arthur, killed your mother?"

"That's what it said in my father's journal that I found after he died." Art's eyes narrowed—a distant look came across them. "It said she suffered from what they call today postpartum depression, after my birth.

My grandmother apparently had taken me out of my crib because I was crying, and my mother wasn't attending to me. My mother thought she was stealing me and chased after her. My grandfather tried to stop her, and they struggled. He pushed her down the stairs."

"Maybe it was an accident?"

"That's what they tried to tell my father."

"William?"

"Yeah, but he didn't buy it. They had always disliked my mother, said she wasn't good enough to marry a Gallagher. Her family was trash. My father left this house that night—left me. And didn't return for five years."

"He came back? I'd heard when he left that night in 1945, he never returned to the house again." Addie studied Art as he edged his way closer to the doorway. Was he going to bolt out of here, or bolt the doors to keep them in? She had to think fast. *Keep him talking, Addie, keep him busy.* She took a step forward, pushing Vera behind her.

"Yeah, for me, I guess—according to his journal— but my grandparents weren't going to let him take me. I was hiding around the corner at the top of the stairs, and I heard him tell my grandfather that he'd finally gotten clean. He'd been on a long bender after my mother died, and that he'd come back for me. My grandparents didn't believe him because he reeked of whiskey. They refused to let him take me. They fought, and we left. Then the next day it was in the newspapers that they were both found dead."

"But where did you go? What happened? Why couldn't the authorities locate you when they were searching for heirs to this estate?"

"Because my father was a crazy old man, and he changed my name so they couldn't track me and implicate him in their deaths. As far as anyone knew, he'd never returned here. But he never got over my mother's death. He hated me, and every time he looked at me he told me how much I looked like her, and he hated me more for it. Then, when I finally had enough of his abuse when I was sixteen, I took off and changed my name again, and never looked back."

"Did he report you as missing?"

"Yeah, and when they couldn't find me, I was presumed dead."

"How did you find out about this house and the sale for back taxes, then?"

"I had started a lucrative property investment business, of sorts, in Seattle. It was the perfect location for supplying high-end property to out-of-country buyers and flipping it for them."

"Laundering money through real estate, in other words."

"Call it what you want, it kept me in the green for a number of years. Then I heard my father's house on Bainbridge Island was coming up for sale. I did a bit of nosing around and found out he'd died leaving no heir."

"He thought you were dead, too?"

"I'd been dead to him my whole life. I never understood why he even took me from my grandparents' house—this house!" A large blue vein throbbed at his temple. "It wasn't until I read his journal and realized my mother died because of my grandfather that I knew. My father thought he was saving me, but what he did was destroy me. He never got over believing I was to blame for her death."

"But you were just a baby and had nothing to do with it."

"He never believed that."

"But he must have at some point because he came back for you." Addie's eyes pleaded for him to understand. "He must have wanted you."

"He only wanted to punish me, and he never stopped until the day I hit back and ran from his home. I never went back until I learned he'd died. As a real-estate agent, it was easy enough to get access, so I went in and took anything and everything I felt that old codger owed me for stealing my life." Tension emanated from his body, his voice raw with hatred. "I found a box of his journals, and let's just say they made for some rather eye-opening reading."

"Is that when you found out about this house?"

"Yes, and being in the industry, I could check around and discovered it was going up for auction, and I started to percolate my plan. After all, this is *my* family home, the one I was deprived of my entire life. Now it's going back into the hands of a Gallagher. A legacy my father deprived me of when I was too young to have a say." Art toyed with the umbrella in his hand. He clicked the knife attachment back up into the shaft.

Addie inched toward him. If she was going to make a run for help, this was her opening, but Vera bolted past her, an unearthly sound gurgling from her throat.

Vera's fists flew wildly in the air as she ran at Art, screaming, "I thought you loved me!"

Art wrapped the crook of the handle around her neck and yanked her ear to his lips. "Stop squirming, my dear. You'll only make it worse."

"What's going on?" she whimpered. "I still don't understand any of this."

"It's easy. You were my ticket into this town. Are you really so naive as to believe our meeting on that cruise was accidental?" His question was met with silence.

"Has it dawned on you yet that you were part of my plan from the very beginning, my dear?" He tightened his grip around her throat. "And now you're going to be my ticket out." Addie took another step toward him. "Stop right there, or I'll snap her neck like a twig."

Addie stopped, her gaze darting around the room for something, anything, to use as a weapon, but it was no use. Blake had cleared the room of everything except the large desk.

Vera squirmed under Art. Her hands flew to her throat, her fingers struggling to work their way under the ivory handle. By the discoloration on Vera's lips, Addie knew she was in trouble. She had to think fast.

"Why don't you let her go, and you can tell me what this is all about."

"There's nothing to tell. The plan has been in the works since before I met this lovely lady last year. I discovered her daughter owned a real-estate company in Greyborne Harbor, and that since the authorities thought I was dead, my family home was going to be sold for back taxes. I needed an in, and"—he stroked Vera's cheek with his free hand—"what was a better in than befriending the lonely widow of the real-estate owner who would be handling the listing? I played my cards right. It gave me access to the keys for the house, and I began squirreling away the items I knew I could sell and make a lot of money from. Then I found my grandfather's journal stashed in here and my ticket to a different future: heir apparent to the Gallagher estate."

"But you destroyed a valuable book in the process. It could have added to your wealth."

"Collateral damage, my dear, one small sacrifice to find the birth certificate my grandfather had hidden inside it. How else was I going to prove the right to my inheritance since I had been presumed dead?"

"Did you find the journal upstairs in that hidden room?"

"Yes, it seems my great-grandfather liked to entertain his lady friends up there. That's why he built it and the tunnel leading up from the garden."

"The rumors about Tobias Gallagher were true. He was a womanizer."

"He was that and much more. What's written in the journals about him would curl your toes, my dear. Let's just say that secret room and tunnel provided his family with a very affluent life. It's just too bad my great-grandmother couldn't live with what he was involved with and took her life because of it."

Addie shivered, recalling the news article she'd read. "You learned all this from your grandfather's journals?"

"It seems I'm not the first of the Gallaghers to take a walk on the dark side." His face twisted in a mock laugh. "From what I read, I knew the certificate was somewhere in this mausoleum. There were clues in his journals, too. I just had no idea at first what they meant. I only knew it was hidden inside something in this house. Then I discovered the barrister's case hidden in one of the wings in the attic. It seems your good friend, Blake, and his Irish crony were running a scheme of their own, which was foiled when a staffer discovered the case and brought it downstairs for appraisal. I had already found the books in there and the one that matched the vague clue about a scarlet thread running through the skein of life. I had ordered the replicas just in case my hunch about that book was right."

"It obviously was." Addie kept her eyes on his as she shuffled closer to the desk.

"But who knew you'd show up and start asking questions and discover the originals were gone before I could claim my inheritance?" His grip around Vera's throat tightened. "With that piece of paper and a DNA match to the lock of hair with it, I can now put a stop to the sale of the rest of my property, and I don't have to leave town with the loot I've taken like I had first planned."

"You're forgetting one important factor." Addie edged her way around the desk. "You now have two witnesses to all this who know what you've been doing."

He smirked, turning his body to match her position. "Do you really think I have any intention of letting either of you go?" Vera wheezed as his hand tightened on her neck. "This one will escort me out of town so we can celebrate our honeymoon in which she'll meet with a most unfortunate accident while we walk the path around the Grand Canyon."

"And me? What do you have planned for me?" Addie touched her cell phone in her front pocket.

"You? Well, I'm aware that you know the tunnel hasn't been used for years. When they find your body down there, it will be put down to you getting in over your head in proving your innocence. You must have gotten trapped down there and met your demise when you were attacked and eaten by a rat or a few hundred. Now give me your cell phone."

"It's in my bag. I'll have to dig through it to find it."

He dragged Vera over to Addie. "Hurry up, then, and no tricks, or I'll have to make new honeymoon plans. Perhaps with the lovely Maggie."

Vera screeched; her fingers clawed wildly at his arm.

"Stop squirming, woman," Art snapped, and smacked

the side of her head with the umbrella handle. Addie eyed the distance between her and Art. She leaned on one hip, fussing with both hands in her bag as she inched her way along the desk until she was within arm's reach of him.

"What are you doing? Hurry up and give me that damn phone!"

"Sorry, I can't seem to find it." With two hands in her bag, Addie grabbed what she hoped was the decanter and swung unseeing, clipping Art on the side of the head. He stumbled to the floor, pulling Vera with him. Addie pushed Vera out of the way, and dropped, legs straddled over his writhing body.

She dug her phone out of her jeans pocket and pushed it across the floor to Vera. "Call nine-one-one."

Addie looked at what she held in her hands. It wasn't the decanter. "How fitting." She chuckled. "You've just been taken down by the very book you saw as collateral damage."

Art shifted his body under her and raised his head. Addie whacked him again. "Do you know why Sir Arthur named the book *A Study in Scarlet*?"

Art groaned, trying to raise his shoulders.

Addie brought the book back down on his head. "Well, let me tell you the story." She dug her knees into his shoulders to still him. "There's a scene where Holmes tells a friend that he thought of his murder investigation as his study in scarlet because 'there's the scarlet thread of murder running through the colorless skein of life, and our duty is to unravel it, and isolate it, and expose every inch of it.' Rather fitting, wouldn't you say, Art?"

The library doors flew open, and Marc appeared, gun drawn. His gaze darted between Addie and the man she had pinned beneath her.

"That was fast. I think Vera just hung up."

"I was on my way here," Marc said. "Martha called when you didn't return after dropping Paige off. She said your sandwich board was still on the street, but your CLOSED sign was on the door. One of my officers spotted your car out front, and I headed over. That's when Vera's call came in. What happened?" He eyed the book Addie brandished like an ax.

"Marc, I'd like you to meet Hill Road House's resident ghost, Tobias Gallagher." Tobias lifted his head and moaned. Addie thwacked him once more with the book for good measure, but then a sound behind her caused her to jerk. She glanced over her shoulder just in time to witness the portrait over the mantel crash to the floor, the frame splintering into pieces on the stone hearth. "Or at least one of them," she said, her voice barely audible.

Chapter 33

"**P**hew," Addie puffed, flipped the deadbolt on the shop door, and turned the sign to CLOSED. "Catherine, I'm not sure I could have survived this day without you. If you ever change your mind about going back to work, even part-time, let me know. I'll hire you in a heartbeat." Addie glanced at her friend hopefully. "With this increase in foot traffic, I know I need to hire someone to help Paige out, and I would love it to be you." The corners of her mouth fought against her exhaustion as she managed a grin.

"Thanks for the offer, but I'm far too busy with my volunteer work and event planning at the hospital now to even think about taking on another commitment."

"I know, but keep it in mind. Even if it's only as long as cruise season lasts, because if today was any indication of what lies ahead, I'm going to need more help."

Catherine replaced a book she'd been paying particular attention to on the sale rack. "If the other shops in town were half as busy as we were today, I'd say the town council made the right decision to pursue the contract with the cruise line."

Addie dropped a pod in the coffeemaker. "I haven't seen Serena all day, which is unusual. I'm thinking she was as busy as we were."

"Martha, too. Everyone appeared to be carrying one of her bakery bags."

"That was a brilliant idea she had in having those reusable tote bags made up with her store logo on them."

Catherine dropped a pod in the machine after Addie took her cup. "I heard she and a few of the other shops on Main Street got together and did a bulk order."

Addie took a sip of her brew and frowned. "I wish someone would have asked me to participate. Cloth book bags are a perfect marketing tool."

"Don't worry about that. I don't think it was an intentional slight."

"I'm sure it wasn't as Martha and I have finally started to make some headway in our friendship, but still—"

"From what Mildred at the Emporium on Main told me, that's because there was more than one shop ordering in bulk. The manufacturer limited them to what design each store could order. All they could include to get the bulk rate was the name of their shop, and that was it. Now that you see what a good idea it is, you're free to order your own and can include your Beyond the Page bookstore graphic on them."

"You're right. It is silly of me to feel snubbed. I'm sure it was just an oversight." Addie took another sip of her coffee, hoping that was true and that she still wasn't feeling the effects of the townspeople having qualms about her, especially after her most recent run-in with a dead body, and her arrest. Nothing had changed, fingers crossed. She shook it off and smiled. "I could have mine made a bit larger and with longer handles so they could be carried as shoulder totes."

"That's it. Look on the bright side, they planted the seed. Now you grow it into what suits you best."

Addie gave Catherine's shoulder a light squeeze. "You always have a way of cheering me up when I start a pity party."

"Don't forget I wiped your tears and bandaged your boo-boos when you were two years old. I know my little girl and just what she needs, and when she needs it." A smile touched the corners of her lips.

Addie laid her head on Catherine's shoulder, swatted at a tear in her eye and nodded.

"Now, let's sit down and enjoy our coffee so we can perk up for the bonfire and fireworks celebration." She ushered Addie to a counter stool.

Addie groaned. "I don't think I can."

"Yes, you can. The whole town's going to be there to celebrate the inaugural docking, and we have to put on a brave face."

Addie screwed up her face. "Like this one?"

Catherine playfully slapped her arm. "Come on, I know you're exhausted after everything that happened yesterday with that horrible man, but put your best foot forward. It'll be fun."

"I need some fun. There's been too little of that lately between my arrest and then exposing a real-life ghost." Her heart dipped at the fresh memories.

A harsh knock came from the window behind them.

"Sorry, we're closed," Catherine shouted, waving the woman off.

Addie spun around on the stool. "I don't believe it!"

"You know her?"

"Yes." Addie jumped to her feet and swung the door open. "Kalea? Where have you been?"

Without answering, Kalea swept into the shop. "Mmm, that coffee smells great. Mind if I have one?" She plopped a pod in the machine without waiting for an answer.

"I take it this is your cousin?" Catherine looked questioningly at Addie.

Addie followed close behind Kalea. "Answer me. The police have been looking for you, and I've been worried sick that you were lying dead somewhere."

"Pfftt. All taken care of. And as you can see, I'm not dead."

"That's it? That's all you have to say after your little disappearing act?"

"This is a fantastic shop. I love those carved wooden pillars. I had no idea it was this big. You've done well for yourself, cuz." Coffee in hand, she flopped on the stool beside Catherine, sloshing coffee on the counter-top.

"Thanks. Now talk."

Kalea raised her hands and shrugged. "It's kind of a funny story . . ."

"Funny as in ha-ha or weird?"

Kalea took a long, slow sip. Addie tapped her finger-nails on the counter. Her patience was growing thin until she noticed a tear rolling down her cousin's cheek. "Kalea, what happened? Why did you take off like that without a word?"

Catherine stroked Kalea's back. "You can tell us. It's okay. Addie's just concerned." She flashed Addie a "behave" glance.

"Yes. As much as you scared me, I was worried."

"I know I messed up when I left like I did, but I had

no choice." She sniffled and wiped her eyes. "I went out to dinner with that guy, Garrett."

"Yes, I remember." Addie clasped her cousin's hand. "And then what happened? Did he hurt you, insult you?"

"No." Kalea shook her head. "Nothing like that. He was a perfect gentleman. I got a call from . . . from the hospital in Cape Cod. Nolan had been admitted. He had a heart attack."

"I'm so sorry. Is he okay?"

She nodded. "But . . ."

"But what?" Catherine's hand stopped their consoling strokes. Her eyes fixed on Kalea's damp face.

"He's decided to go back to his wife," she blurted. "He ordered me to move out of what was supposed to be *our* Cape Cod house because he's going to sell it and move back into their family home in Concord. Then to make it worse, he took back his gift of the car. He said the near-death experience made him realize he wasn't ready to give up on his marriage. His wife's condition to taking him back was that I would have to find another job, too." Her sniffles turned to sobs, and Catherine's hand resumed its consoling pats. "So not only am I homeless, but I have no job." Her sobs morphed into heaving wails.

Addie slid onto the vacant stool. "I'm sorry you had to go through all that," she murmured, forcing her mouth to not utter the words she really wanted to say. She'd learned from living with her cousin at college their first year that any words of wisdom or insight about becoming involved with a married man in the first place would fall on deaf ears. She sat quietly and pressed her cousin's hand into hers.

Catherine's eyes pleaded for Addie to say something to the distraught woman. Addie looked away, knowing in her heart what she should say but unable to bring herself to say it.

"Addie," Catherine said, quirking a brow, "didn't you just tell me—"

Addie shot Catherine a horror-stricken glance. Catherine snapped her mouth closed.

Addie then glanced apologetically at her old friend, but she couldn't bring herself to look at Kalea as she said, "No family member of mine will ever be homeless. You can stay with me until you get back on your feet. And if you need a job . . ." Addie gulped on the words she was about to utter. "You can work part-time for me, here in the store." Catherine gave her a slight nod, her eyes filled with pride, and Addie knew she'd done the right thing. Now she hoped this gesture wouldn't come back to haunt her.

"Are you serious?" Kalea's head shot up, her eyes filled with disbelief. "You'll let me live with you *and* give me a job?"

Addie nodded.

"Welcome to our little Greyborne Harbor family." A smile lit up Catherine's face as she wrapped her arms around Kalea.

Addie looked at the two women locked in an embrace. "Yeah, aren't families wonderful?" She was thankful she had found hers here in the Harbor, and by her cousin's reaction, her little family had just grown by one more—who, in spite of all her annoyances, truly was family to her.

Chapter 34

With Kalea in tow, Addie wove through the crowd that congregated on the beach to take in the evening festivities. She caught sight of her target.

"Simon!" she cried, and leapt into his arms snuggling into his hug.

"I was beginning to wonder if we'd have to send out another search party for you like Martha called for yesterday," he said, kissing the top of her head.

"Not today, but there has been a . . . slight complication."

He held her at arm's length. "Is everything okay? Marc hasn't gone and arrested you again, has he?"

"No." She willed herself not to laugh at the look on his face, but it was hard, and she choked out something between a laugh and a snort. "Simon, I'd like you to meet my cousin, Kalea." Addie gestured to the woman beside her, who'd stuck like a lost child to Addie's side since they left the bookstore. "Kalea, this is my good friend, Simon."

Kalea took one look into Simon's sea-blue eyes and

her whole little-lost-girl act slipped away. Her eyelashes fluttered like butterflies. She thrust out her chest and brushed strands of auburn hair behind her ear. "Simon," she cooed, extending her limp hand in greeting, "it is a pleasure to meet you."

Simon cocked his head, his lips turning up in a half smile. He draped his arm around Addie's shoulders, gave her a reassuring squeeze, and limply shook Kalea's extended fingers in reply. "It's nice to finally meet you. Addie has told me *so much* about you."

"Oh, she has, has she? I see." Kalea glanced at Simon's arm still wrapped around Addie's shoulder. Her porcelain complexion turned a rosy hue, and she averted her eyes. "What's this little celebration all about, anyway?" Kalea glanced at the crowds gathering around the large logs set out as bonfire seating areas.

"I thought I told you on our way here?" Addie eyed her cousin warily. "It's a welcome celebration for the first official docking of the cruise ship to Greyborne Harbor. We as a town thought they might enjoy a beach party of sorts and a fireworks display at the end of the eve—"

"Oh, right. Yeah, you did mention something about that." Kalea waved off the explanation. "There's Garrett over there talking to Robert." And she was off.

Addie nudged Simon and pointed to her cousin as she sashayed up to her next victim. As if on cue, Kalea shifted her weight from one curvy hip to the other and leaned in toward Garrett, whispering something into his ear. A shy grin spread across his flushed face.

Simon's husky laugh made Addie's stomach flutter. "See what I mean about her?" Addie's own laugh bubbled free, joining his.

"Good evening, Simon, Addie."

"Marc. You're here?" Addie spun around at the sound of his voice behind them.

Simon gave her a sidelong glance, confusion by her excitement to see her old flame clearly written across his face.

"I mean"—she glanced at Simon—"I didn't expect to see you tonight. You know, with the whole Art thing and the investigation and all." She wanted to kiss away the confusion from Simon's face but settled with clasping his hand in hers.

"Yeah, it wrapped up faster than I thought it would. Between your and Vera's statements, along with Maggie's added information, Art finally gave a full confession."

"Did he confess to murdering Charlotte, too?" Simon drew Addie closer to his side.

Marc's jaw tightened. "He said he never intended her to die. He was just trying to scare her."

"But I gave you a precedent case and medical—"

"I know," Marc said, "and the DA agreed. Art did confess that he had been watching and listening for months and knew Charlotte was terrified to be alone in the house. She'd bought into all the local haunted rumors. He decided to play on that fear Wednesday night when she wouldn't leave so he could get the books he was after, you know, the one you pointed out, *A Study in Scarlet* that had the birth certificate hidden inside it." Addie nodded. "Art said he'd waited long enough to get his hands on it and when she wouldn't leave that night, he knew he'd have to step up his game. He covered his face and hands with ashes from the hearth, in the hope of appearing more ghostly to scare her off. Which, as the DA said showed intent to harm."

"And it obviously worked even if death wasn't his intention." Simon rubbed his jaw.

"Yup, by everything else he said, I don't think he really cared at that point. He just wanted to get his hands on what he felt was his and stop the auction to sell his property. That's why he pulled off all the special effects he'd created over the past few months, hoping to scare everyone away from the house."

"Yeah, I told you about the humidifiers I found. He must have used them to create the cold air from the vents, and I guess he also found a way to produce just enough mist to make it appear like an entity taking form."

"He had done his research. He even manipulated Vera into helping him, all under the guise of creating a haunted experience for some fictional buyer, but his theatrics didn't stop there." Marc glanced at Addie. "He used his umbrella with the knife tip extended to be able to open the door just a crack and slid it up to push the doorbells away from the top of the frame, so he could enter your shop undetected. Then he used it extended again to make it appear that the books flew off the shelves by themselves. That's why Paige didn't see anyone. He was far enough behind her to escape detection."

"Then why did he hurt her?"

"He said he didn't want to, but when she started to turn around instead of running away in the opposite direction, he knew he'd have to knock her out before she saw him. He said he staged it all because he thought that if you were afraid the ghost from Hill Road House had materialized in your bookstore, too, then you'd take it as a warning and stop your snooping around."

Simon choked back a laugh. "He doesn't know

Addie very well, then. She only dug in her heels more and went at it with a renewed vigor."

"Dog with a bone," Marc said, words that brought them both to a chorus of husky laughter.

"Glad to see I can provide both of you with the evening's entertainment." Addie fought to suppress her own urge to laugh, which wasn't easy, but she managed it by piercing one then the other with a glare.

"Relax, Addie." Simon kissed the top of her head. "I guess we just both know you *too* well."

"Then you know I can't let this go until I know how all the pieces fit together."

Marc wiped his eyes, sniffed and looked at her. "What else do you need to know so you can bury your latest bone?" He stifled a laugh and gave Simon a sidelong glance, they both snickered.

"Gee, thanks, guys. I'm thrilled to see you find my genetic quirk to be so humorous."

"Genetic quirk," Marc choked. "It's called an obsession."

"I'll have you both know that I discovered my greatgreat-aunt Emily. Anita's mother was well known in Greyborne Harbor for her sleuthing adventures, too. Therefore, it's genetic."

Marc shook his head. "Well, that explains a lot, doesn't it?" He glanced at Simon, a smile touching the corners of his lips. "I guess this won't be the end of it, will it?"

Simon groaned.

"Come on." Addie playfully swatted at Simon and glanced at Marc, his eyes holding a twinkle of amusement. "Did you question Blake about what I told you at the station? The conversation I overheard and what Art said to me about him and Philip being involved in an insurance scam?"

"Yeah, but what they were up to wasn't illegal. Not ethical, mind you, but not illegal."

"What was it, then?"

Marc leaned toward them, his voice low. "It seems that Philip sent Blake a list of the auction items his client was after, and Blake removed them from the auction list and sold them privately to Philip for a percentage of the finder's fee."

"They were running a little side business." Addie blinked. "What about Duane McAdams, and Blake saying he wouldn't be a problem anymore?"

"Blake made a call to his father and told him what had been going on. McAdams Senior had his son committed to a rehab center."

Addie narrowed her eyes. "But what about the inventory lists that were all out of whack? They looked like someone was committing fraud."

"As a matter of fact, that's why Charlotte was working so late Wednesday. She was trying to figure out the discrepancies in the lists and that all came back to Art. He'd been accessing her laptop when it was left unattended. Remember, he'd been watching everything through that peephole. He erased the items he was stashing away upstairs so there'd be no trace of them when they showed up on the black market for sale."

Simon shook his head. "It sounds like this Art fellow really knew what he was doing when it came to planning a heist."

Marc nodded. "He was a career criminal, after all."

"Marc, there you are. I've been searching everywhere for you." Ryley planted a kiss on his cheek as she slid Addie a side glance. "Did you tell them?" Her dark eyes danced with the refection of the firelight.

Marc shook his head and his gaze darted to Addie.

"Tell us what?" Addie flinched in fear at what their big announcement was going to be.

Marc heaved in a deep breath. "Ryley is going to be staying on in Greyborne Harbor as an official detective." Marc's shoulders relaxed with the announcement.

Addie snapped her jaw closed. Not what she was afraid he was going to say, but not sure how she really felt about this news either. Simon, on the other hand, had an ear-to-ear grin as he congratulated the former FBI agent and shook Marc's hand like they were best buddies in the world. It made Addie wonder about his sudden change of attitude toward Ryley. She shrugged it off. He was most likely just happy Ryley was staying, which would solidify in his mind that Marc was really out of the picture in Addie's future.

"This deserves a toast," Simon said. "Come on, Ryley. Let's go see what we can find at the refreshment table."

When they were out of earshot Addie glanced at Marc. "What, she just up and quit the FBI?"

Marc's face glistened with perspiration. "It wasn't that cut and dry, but it's not my story to tell. You should give her a chance, though. I know you have mixed feelings, given with what happened with your arrest and whatnot—"

"Forget the *whatnot*." Addie's eyes flashed. "She actually tried to convince you that I was guilty. Was she jealous of what we used to have?"

"Stop it. No, I told you before. Like every good detective, especially an FBI agent, she was following the evidence, and the evidence at the time pointed to you."

Addie's bottom lip quivered.

"Look, Addie, I know I can't take back what happened, and I can't make excuses. But I will say she's had a rough go of it the last few years. I hope you'll give her a chance. Maybe the two of you can even come to be friends?"

Addie sputtered.

"Eventually?" Marc's brow arched.

"What was the forced leave she was on?" Marc's eyes narrowed to slits. "I heard the two of you talking as you went out the door at the Grey Gull Inn."

"Maybe I should tell you, and then you'll go easier on her."

Addie braced her shoulders, her gaze steadfast on his.

"Ryley was working on a big case down by San Diego. It was a combined task force between the DEA, FBI, and Homeland Security. They got wind that there was a mole in the ranks but couldn't figure out who it was. Ryley did some investigating and must have gotten too close for someone's comfort because she started to get death threats and had a few near misses on her life. Her field supervisor pulled her off the case for her protection and sent her to Quantico to teach for a few months while they continued to investigate who was behind the leaks to the cartel. But the threats against her didn't stop. That's when her supervisor *strongly* encouraged her to disappear for a while until they could uncover the mole. That's the forced leave you overheard."

"I'm sorry to hear that. Did they ever find out who was behind it?"

Marc hung his head, nodding. "It was her partner of over ten years."

"Wow."

"Yup, after her supervisor told her that, she decided

to leave the FBI completely. She developed a trust-issue thing, which I can understand. It's tough when you find out the person you trusted the most in life to cover you, is the one trying to shoot you in the back."

"So you snapped her up?" A soft laugh escaped her throat.

"I snapped her up." He cracked a smile. "As you say. Because she's one of the best investigators I've ever worked with, and she agreed because she decided she liked her short stint at small-town crime fighting."

"Could the real reason be because you're also a"— she squeezed her forefinger and thumb together— "teeny-tiny bit in love with her, too?"

The sparkle in his eyes vanished. "I would be . . . if I could get over you."

So that was it. Despite everything already said between them these past few days, he needed to hear the words. He needed closure. Something she'd never gotten with David's death, and it still haunted her. "It's over, Marc. We've both moved on."

"I know." He glanced at Simon by the refreshment table. "I know."

Addie studied Marc's face, and for an instant David was smiling back at her. A sense of liberating release swept through her. In the distance, she heard Simon's hearty laugh, and a soft smile touched the corners of her lips. It seemed more than one ghost was being laid to rest this week.

"Addie, Marc, good. You're together," Serena squealed, bounding toward them. "Look!" She waved her left hand in the air. A sparkling diamond shimmered in the glow of the bonfire.

Addie glanced back at Marc. David was now truly gone. She grinned and snatched Serena's hand. "What?

When did this happen?" She flung her arms around her best friend, who gave a startled laugh and hugged her back. "Congratulations, sweetie."

"Congrats, sis!" Marc cried, twirling her around in the air. "When's the big day?"

"Not until next June." Serena puffed breathlessly as he placed her back on her feet. "After Zach finishes his practicum and goes through the whole graduation thing."

"I'm so happy for you!" Addie squealed. "I know this is what you wanted."

"I gotta go and find Mom and Dad. They don't know yet." Serena squealed again and bumped into Simon, who jostled two plastic cups in his hands. She waved her hand in his face, giggled, and disappeared on the other side of the bonfire.

"What was that all about?" Ryley said, handing Marc his drink.

"It seems my baby sister's getting married."

Addie couldn't help but notice the moisture in his eyes as he glanced down at Ryley and kissed the top of her head.

"Come on," he said, his voice choked. "I want to be there when she tells our parents."

Simon tapped his cup against Addie's. "It seems there's a lot to toast tonight." He grinned over the rim of his cup at her.

"More than you know," Addie said, lowering her own. "I want you to say it."

"Say what?" He raised his cup and took a sip, his eyes not wavering from hers.

"What you said before."

He shook his head, his eyes blank.

"You know exactly what I'm talking about." She

clutched the front of his T-shirt, drew him closer, and whispered. "It's not *too soon* anymore."

A smile spread across his face, but he didn't say a word.

"You're going to make *me* say it, aren't you?"

He nodded, his smile turning into a wide-mouthed grin.

Addie stood on her tiptoes and opened her mouth to speak, but then she flinched. Her eyes filled with horror. "What's Gloria's dog, Pippi, dragging behind her?"

Simon spun around. "Good grief! It looks like a human leg bone." He started toward the small dog, its load three times the size of it, and tugged it from the dog's jaws. He began to laugh.

"What is it? Is it a leg—"

"No, it's a piece of driftwood with a large knot on the end." Simon waved it in the air. He tossed it away from the crowd, and Pippi raced to retrieve it.

"Thank goodness." Addie patted her pounding chest. "The last thing we needed was a body turning up at the celebration."

"Darn you. How is it whenever I go to kiss you, you become distracted, just like that time in the park last Christmas?" Simon said, pulling Addie into his arms. "Now, where were we?" he whispered as his lips placed feather-light kisses across her cheek.

"I have no idea what you're talking about." Addie pulled back. Her best pouty face set firmly in place— containing the urge to laugh wasn't easy for her, but she managed it—she cupped his face in her hands, fluttering her lashes and feigning innocence.

A smile tugged at the corners of Simon's lips. The fireworks overhead reflected the bursts of colors mirrored across the harbor water in his sparkling eyes. "You were just going to tell me you loved me, too," he whispered, and kissed the palm of her hand as he curled his fingers around hers, then nestled her hand against his chest.

"I was, was I?" A smile dangled at the corners of her mouth as she stood on tiptoes and softly placed her lips on his. Who knew that vanquishing ghosts both old and new would come with such delightful perks?